M

Dillon didn't want to like her.

He didn't want to enjoy Blair's company or desire her so much that he dreamed about her at night and woke up hurting all over.

Every day she glided across the barnyard like a queen, her head high, shoulders back and her hips swinging with each graceful stride. And the blasted, contrary woman worked hard, learned fast and never gave a rip how dirty she got. He was gruff, unfriendly, even downright rude. None of it fazed her.

Working with Blair was a lot like stepping into quicksand. The more he struggled to push her away, the greater his danger of drowning.

"Had enough yet, DuMaine?" he asked.

"Not yet, Walker." Blair flashed him a sassy grin and closed the space between them. "In fact, I'm really starting to like it here."

❤ ❤ ❤

HEARTS OF WYOMING:
Rugged and wild, the McBride family
has love to share...and Wyoming weddings
are on their minds!

Dear Reader,

September celebrates the onset of fall with a refreshing Special Edition lineup!

We begin this month with our THAT SPECIAL WOMAN! title. *The Secret Wife* by bestselling author Susan Mallery is book two in her TRIPLE TROUBLE miniseries and tells an uplifting tale about an estranged couple who renew their love. Look for the final installment of this engaging series in October.

Travel to the mountains of Wyoming with *Pale Rider* by Myrna Temte—a story about a lonesome cowboy who must show the ropes to a beautiful city girl, who captures his heart. Can she convince this hardened recluse that she loves him inside and out?

The sweet scent of romance catches these next heroes off guard in stories by two of our extraspecial writers! First, veteran author Carole Halston spins a delightful tale about a dad who's in the market for marriage but not love in *Mrs. Right*—book three of our FROM BUD TO BLOSSOM promotion series. And look what happens when a hard-driven city slicker slows down long enough to be charmed by a headstrong country gal in *All It Takes Is Family,* the next installment in Sharon De Vita's SILVER CREEK COUNTY series.

Finally, we round off the month with a story about the extraordinary measures a devoted dad will take for his infant son in *Bride for Hire* by *New York Times* bestselling author Patricia Hagan. And keep an eye out for *Beauty and the Groom*—a passionate reunion story by Lorraine Carroll.

I hope you enjoy each and every story to come!

Sincerely,

Tara Gavin,
Senior Editor

Please address questions and book requests to:
Silhouette Reader Service
U.S.: 3010 Walden Ave., P.O. Box 1325, Buffalo, NY 14269
Canadian: P.O. Box 609, Fort Erie, Ont. L2A 5X3

MYRNA TEMTE
PALE RIDER

Silhouette®

SPECIAL EDITION®

Published by Silhouette Books
America's Publisher of Contemporary Romance

To my fellow extras in *Dante's Peak,* Wallace, Idaho, 1996. You were all such fun! Here's hoping we all made it to the silver screen. And to Terry, Mary Pat, Kathie and Mary H.—you all know why. Thanks. My thanks as always to Debra Sims of Douglas, Wyoming, for help with information on ranching, and to the many crew members who worked on *Dante's Peak,* who took the time to answer my questions about making movies.

 SILHOUETTE BOOKS

ISBN 0-373-24124-0

PALE RIDER

Copyright © 1997 by Myrna Temte

Printed in U.S.A.

MYRNA TEMTE

grew up in Montana and attended college in Wyoming, where she met and married her husband. Marriage didn't necessarily mean settling down for the Temtes—they have lived in six different states, including Washington, where they currently reside. Moving so much is difficult, the author says, but it is also wonderful stimulation for a writer.

Though always a "readaholic," Ms. Temte never dreamed of becoming an author. But while spending time at home to care for her first child, she began to seek an outlet from the never-ending duties of housekeeping and child-rearing. She started reading romances and soon became hooked, both as a reader and a writer. Now Myrna Temte appreciates the best of all possible worlds—a loving family and a challenging career that lets her set her own hours and turn her imagination loose.

McBride Family Tree

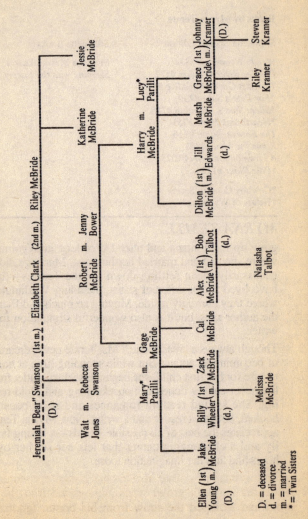

Jeremiah "Bear" Swanson (1st m.) ---- Elizabeth Clark ---- (2nd m.) Riley McBride

Rebecca Swanson (D.)

Walt Jones m. Rebecca Swanson

Robert McBride m. Jenny Bower

Katherine McBride

Jessie McBride

Mary* Parilli m. Gage McBride

Harry McBride m. Lucy* Parilli

Ellen (1st) Young m. Jake McBride (D.)

Billy (1st) Wheeler m. Zack McBride (d.)

Cal McBride

Alex (1st) McBride m. Bob Talbot (d.)

Dillon (1st) McBride m. Jill Edwards (d.)

Marsh McBride

Grace (1st) McBride m. Johnny Kramer (D.)

Melissa McBride

Natasha Talbot

Riley Kramer

Steven Kramer

D. = deceased
d. = divorce
m. = married
* = Twin Sisters

Chapter One

"Aw, nuts," Dillon McBride muttered when he spotted the snow-covered sedan parked behind the house. He'd been out delivering calves all night. He was exhausted, frozen and wet, and the last thing he wanted was to have to cope with company. Well, at least now he knew why his cousin Jake hadn't shown up to help him this morning.

Shooting the car an irritated glance, Dillon rode his palomino gelding, Sunny, straight up to the back steps, dismounted and flexed his aching right hand. Damn thing always gave him trouble in the winter. It was March now, though, so the cold weather couldn't last much longer. He hoped. He tipped his Stetson back on his head, then pulled the newborn calf draped behind the saddle horn into his arms. The animal didn't even try to struggle.

"Hang on, little fella," Dillon murmured. "You'll be warm in no time."

The aromas of coffee and freshly baked cinnamon rolls made his stomach growl when he stepped into the mudroom and stomped the snow from his boots. Ignoring the circle of surprised faces gathered around the kitchen table, he strode to the fireplace, went down on one knee and laid the calf on the hearth.

"I need some old towels, Grace," he said to his sister. "Hurry."

Damn. The little critter was so cold and still, there wasn't a second to lose. Stripping off his soggy gloves, Dillon rubbed the calf's flanks and legs as briskly as his stiff fingers would allow. He heard chair legs scrape the tile floor, and more than one set of footsteps. Then a sultry feminine voice he didn't recognize spoke from somewhere over his left shoulder.

"Is there anything I can do to help?"

Maintaining his rhythm, Dillon looked up and darn near swallowed his tongue. *Pretty* wouldn't begin to describe the woman leaning over him. *Beautiful* didn't come much closer. No, for this woman, you needed a whole phrase. *Drop-dead gorgeous* might do.

The weird thing was, he'd seen her somewhere before, but he knew he'd never met her; a man would have to be legally blind to forget meeting this woman. While Dillon had more than his share of physical defects, bad eyesight wasn't one of them.

Her thick, tawny hair curled around her shoulders, framing a face with dainty, well-formed features and a peaches-and-cream complexion. Her eyes were a rich, deep blue, and they widened ever so slightly when they met his.

His mouth dried out. A shudder snaked down his spine. Lord, it felt like she was looking into the murky depths of his soul.

Her eyebrows drew together, creating a delicate frown that expressed the same confusion, the same odd sense of recognition he was feeling. She cleared her throat and, with what appeared to be an effort, directed her attention toward the calf.

"It's just a baby," she said. "Do you have to be so rough?"

Her low, husky voice set up such lusty vibrations along

his nerve endings, it took a second or two for her words to sink in. When they did, Dillon wrenched his head back around, looked at his small patient and felt his heart take a nosedive. The calf's eyes were closed; its breathing was labored. If it got any weaker...

"Where the hell are those towels, Grace?" he shouted.

"Here, Dillon," his sister shouted back. "Catch! I'll mix some formula."

He reached up and snagged the towels out of the air with his right hand. The quiet, appalled gasp from behind him sent an embarrassed wave of heat up the back of his neck. Why he was disappointed with the woman's reaction to his missing thumb, he couldn't say. After nineteen years of receiving similar reactions from strangers—especially women—he should be used to it. She'd probably pass out when she got a good look at the left side of his face.

Well, tough, he thought, rubbing the calf with even more vigor. He didn't know or care who she was, and he had more important things to worry about than offending her sensibilities. If she didn't like looking at him, she could damn well go somewhere else.

The calf's breathing sounded better now. Dillon flipped him over to dry the other side. The woman knelt beside him, picked up a towel and gently wiped the calf's head.

"Is it a boy or a girl?" she asked.

"A bull."

"Where is his mother?"

"Dead."

A rumble of laughter came from the table. Intentionally keeping his left cheek turned away from her, Dillon looked over and spotted Jake drinking coffee with Dillon's brother Marsh, who lived in Los Angeles, and two other guys he'd never seen before.

What the heck was Marsh doing in Wyoming at this time of the year? And why was Jake sitting there jawing like he had all day, when they had cows dropping calves in snow-drifts, for God's sake? Marsh wasn't much of a cattleman, but it wasn't like Jake to ignore a distressed calf.

"Hey, Jake," Dillon called. "This is one of Samson's get. How about finding a box and some blankets for him? And a hot water bottle while you're at it?"

Jake said something Dillon couldn't quite catch and left the kitchen. Grace carried a pop bottle with a rubber nipple attached across the room and handed it to Dillon. "I'll get the hot-water bottle," she said. "Jake'll never find it."

Dillon shrugged out of his heavy coat and lifted the calf onto his lap. The animal had finally warmed up enough to struggle a little. Holding his left hand on the back of its neck, Dillon clamped the first and second fingers of his right hand around the bottle of formula.

"Easy there, bud," he said. "Nobody's gonna hurt you."

He brushed the tip of the nipple over the calf's mouth, but the dumb critter twisted his head away.

"Come on, boy. I know this ain't your mama, but you need some nutrition. Open up."

The calf wasn't having any of it. He let out a pathetic bawl and strained away every time Dillon brought the bottle back to his mouth.

"I can hold the bottle for you," the woman said softly.

Dillon glanced up at her and felt his heart clench. Damn, but she was a gorgeous thing. Especially with that girlish, eager expression in her eyes, as if she really wanted to help. It wasn't her fault he had a mutilated hand and a nightmare face. Was she Marsh's latest Hollywood honey? Or did she belong to one of those other guys? Aw, what did he care, anyway? Regular women found him repulsive enough. A woman like her...

Irritated, he shook his head and answered more gruffly than he'd intended. "Better not. You'll get dirty."

"I don't mind," she said.

Eyeing her elegant powder blue slacks and sweater, he shook his head again. "This little guy doesn't know how to suck or swallow. When I get this stuff into his mouth, he's gonna cough and choke and sneeze all over the place. Grace can help me."

The woman pursed her lips, lifted her chin and, to Dillon's surprise, snatched the bottle out of his hand. He glared at her for a moment, then shrugged and grabbed the calf's muzzle, applying pressure to the sides of its mouth. When the calf bawled in protest, the woman popped the nipple into his mouth.

As predicted, the animal gagged and spewed formula every which way, his eyes rolling with fright. Dillon stroked the underside of its neck, hoping it would get the idea and swallow. The woman grasped the little varmint's muzzle the way Dillon had earlier and poked the nipple back into his mouth.

"Come on, baby," she cooed. "Take the bottle, sweetheart. It's so good for you. Oh, be a good boy. Do it for me, sugar. That's right. Do it for Blair."

Her voice was lighter and softer now, as if she were talking to a human infant instead of a Hereford. Even so, there was a smoky, husky undertone to it that commanded attention. The calf's eyes focused on her face, and he stopped fighting. She petted his head, coaxing and smiling, practically seducing the little critter.

Dillon found himself feeling seduced, as well. The backs of his ears tingled, as if she were stroking them instead of the calf's. The temperature in the room shot up at least twenty degrees. If she didn't stop soon, he wouldn't be able to let the calf get off his lap without embarrassing himself something fierce. The stupid critter was staring at her like a lovesick fool, drooling formula out the sides of his mouth.

Dillon didn't blame him. If she ever turned that sultry voice and those big blue eyes on him that way, he'd probably roll over on his back like a dog begging to have his belly scratched. Forcing his gaze back to the job at hand, Dillon massaged the calf's throat. "Come on, fella. You'll like this stuff."

The calf rolled his eyes at the sound of Dillon's voice, then went back to staring at the woman and drooling. Dillon sighed with impatience. "Raise the bottle a little," he ordered. "And hold on tight. Once he figures it out, he'll suck like a vacuum cleaner."

When she complied, he tipped the animal's chin up, forcing the liquid to the back of its throat. The calf gagged again and tried to thrash his head, but Dillon restrained him until he swallowed in self-defense. It didn't take long after that for the calf to understand what he needed to do.

"Oh, he's so hungry," the woman said, laughing with delight. "And he's so cute. Does he have a name yet?"

Dillon shook his head. "We don't name cattle."

"Then who is Samson?" she asked, giving him a puzzled frown. "From what you said to Jake, I thought he was a bull."

"He is, but we usually keep them around a long time. But you don't make pets out of animals that'll wind up on a dinner table someday."

A stricken expression crossed her face. She glanced at the calf, then looked at Dillon, as if he'd just announced he was a serial killer. "Is that what's going to happen to him?"

"Unless we decide to use him for breeding, which isn't likely. Far as I know, that's about all Herefords are good for."

Frowning, she gazed at the calf for a long moment, reached down, scratched his ears and fluffed the little white whorls of hair on his head. It twirled around her fingers. Then she gave her head a decisive shake and looked at Dillon. "I'll buy him from you. And I'll call him...Curly."

While Dillon admired her sense of compassion, he couldn't repress a snort of laughter. "Right. Where you plannin' to keep Curly? In your backyard? Next to the pool?"

"I'll think of something."

"Lady, get serious. He's a cute little guy right now, but he's gonna weigh over a ton when he's full-grown."

Before she could reply, Jake returned with a big box and a couple of old blankets under his arm. Grace followed close behind him. Jake squatted on one heel and spread the blankets out. Dillon lifted the calf into the makeshift bed, tucked him in with the hot-water bottle and stood. The woman patted the calf's head one last time, then accepted Jake's offered hand and scrambled to her feet.

"Hey, Dillon," Marsh called from the table. "Come on over here and meet these guys."

Dillon turned his head to answer, heard another soft gasp from the woman and knew she'd finally seen the left side of his face. Unable to stop himself, he looked straight at her, challenging her to say something. She didn't, of course. Nobody with any manners ever knew what to say to a guy who looked like Dr. Frankenstein had used him for sewing practice. But hey, who needed words when silent revulsion said it all?

Nuts. He wished he'd taken the calf to the barn. Wished his stomach didn't tie itself in knots every time this happened. Wished like hell he could have his old face back so he didn't shock folks speechless.

Ignoring the formula and calf slobber on his hands, he leaned down, grabbed his coat and put it back on. Grace touched his arm. Knowing he couldn't stand the sympathy he'd see in her eyes, Dillon patted her fingers and headed for the doorway without looking at her.

Jake folded his arms across his chest and stepped into Dillon's path. "Stay and talk for a minute," he said quietly. "Marsh has a proposition you need to hear. It's important."

Dillon considered shoving his cousin out of the way, but the hard expression in Jake's eyes told him it would cost him plenty. "You handle it. I've got work to do."

Grace came up beside him and put her hand on his arm again. "Dillon, please. It really is important, and we need you to be in on the decision."

Though he might get a certain amount of satisfaction from going one-on-one with Jake, Dillon had never been able to refuse his baby sister much of anything. Especially after the accident. Dammit, what could be important enough to put that pleading look in her eyes? Well, the worst was already over. From here on out, everyone would pretend he looked perfectly normal.

"All right," he said, sighing with resignation. "Let me wash my hands and grab some coffee."

"I'll get it for you," she said.

By the time he'd washed up and taken a chair between Grace and Jake at the table, Dillon had his emotions back under control. "Okay, Marsh, make it quick. Sunny's probably freezing to death by now."

"I put him in the barn for you when I went out to find the box," Jake said.

Marsh chuckled and shook his head. "Gee, it's nice to see you again, too, bro."

Dillon shrugged in response. "I haven't got time for chit-chat. In case you didn't notice, it's calving season."

"All right, all right. Let me introduce you to these folks, and I think you'll have an idea of what's going on. This is Patrick Quillen," Marsh said, gesturing toward the man on his left. Quillen was short and bald, and he had bushy gray eyebrows that stuck out like butterfly wings over his pale blue eyes.

"He's a movie director," Marsh added. "Next to him is Ian Finch. He's a producer at our production company." Finch appeared to be about as tall as Marsh, who stood six-foot-two in his bare feet. He wore his black, shiny hair slicked back in a scruffy ponytail. "And this, gentlemen," Marsh said, gesturing across the table, "is my irascible big brother, Dillon."

Dillon shot Marsh a dirty look, then nodded at both men. "Nice meetin' you fellas."

"You've already met Blair, haven't you?" Marsh asked, inclining his head toward the woman sitting on his right.

"Not formally." With a tentative smile, she offered her hand to Dillon. "Hello, Mr. McBride. I'm Blair DuMaine."

Dillon gulped. Blair DuMaine. Of course. No wonder she'd seemed familiar to him. He'd watched a couple of her movies and had seen her picture splattered all over the tabloids at the grocery store for the past five years. Good

Lord, the woman's whole family was Hollywood royalty. And he'd be damned if he'd stick his mangled paw out there for her to shake.

Using his left hand, he tipped his hat to her. "Thanks for helpin' with the calf, ma'am."

"It was my pleasure, Mr. McBride."

Marsh winked at her. "We've got five Mr. McBrides in the family. Seven if you count Grace's boys. You'd better call him Dillon, or you'll confuse all of us, honey."

Honey, huh? Well, that figured, Dillon thought. Marsh was a good-lookin' son of a gun, and he'd always oozed plenty of charm for the ladies. Shifting impatiently on his chair, Dillon told himself their relationship was none of his business. All he wanted was to get the heck out of here, away from these strangers and their curious eyes.

"Get on with it, Marsh," he said. "What's this proposition Jake wants me to hear?"

Marsh's dark eyes glowed with enthusiasm. "Remember that screenplay I told you about at Christmas? The one based on Great-grandma Elizabeth's romance with Riley McBride?"

"Yeah," Dillon said, though his memory of the conversation was vague at best. He tended to tune out a lot of Marsh's Hollywood talk. "So?"

Ian Finch leaned forward and braced his elbows on the table. "Blair and I have bought Marsh's screenplay. Blair will play Elizabeth and Keith Stanton has agreed to play Riley. We're going to film it early this summer."

"And they want to do it here," Jake added.

Dillon's heart sank and his stomach clenched. Aw, nuts. He could hardly stand to have three strangers staring at his face. The thought of a whole production company hanging around made him want to head for the high country. "In Sunshine Gap?" he asked, referring to the little town eight miles away.

"No, on the Flying M," Marsh said. "Since this is where it all happened, don't you think it's a great idea to film it here?"

"No. It's a lousy idea," Dillon replied. "This is a *workin'* ranch, Marsh. The last thing we need is a bunch of city folks wanderin' all over the place."

"We'll pay for the use of your property. You'll all make a lot of money from this," Blair said, leaning forward with such an earnest expression, Dillon almost forgot about her shocked gasps when she'd seen his hand and face. Almost, but not quite.

"We won't even be here that long," Marsh added. "We'll probably be done in ten weeks. Twelve weeks tops. Besides helping the ranch, making the movie here will bring in more jobs and money than Sunshine Gap's seen since the last oil boom."

Dillon shook his head. "We don't need it. Sure, it'll pump some bucks into the county for a while, but it'll bring a lot of problems, too."

"Such as?" Marsh demanded.

"Too many people who won't go home when it's over. Haven't you heard about all the movie stars buyin' land around Jackson and up in Montana? They call it Hollywood North, for God's sake. And now they're spreadin' out all over the place, and they're killin' the ranches. I don't want to see that happen here."

"I'm afraid I don't understand," Blair said. "You have an awful lot of empty space in Wyoming. How can a few people buying land harm anyone?"

"If they'd live like the rest of us, it wouldn't," Dillon said. "But they don't. They throw their money around, so the land prices skyrocket and everybody's taxes go up. They won't let anybody hunt or fish on their property. They bring in their drugs, and they want all the same conveniences they had in California. The next thing you know, you've got a bunch of stores and restaurants poppin' up, the local folks can't even afford to patronize."

"Oh, come on, Dillon," Marsh said. "You don't know if any of that will happen. Besides, a dose of progress wouldn't hurt Sunshine Gap or the other little burgs around here one bit."

Dillon snorted in disgust. "You call espresso bars progress? You can have it, Marsh. Sunshine Gap's just fine the way it is, and so is the ranch. I don't want any part of this."

With that, he pushed back his chair, retrieved his coat and hat from the counter and headed outside. Halfway to the barn, he stopped walking and took three deep breaths. The cold March air cleared his head, but it didn't do a thing to ease the tightness in his chest.

The Flying M sat at the foot of the Carter Mountains, on the west side of the Big Horn Basin. From this vantage point, Dillon could see Sunshine Gap, the Greybull River and everything to the east, stretching out to a horizon that went on forever. Due to a long, hard winter, it all looked pretty bleak right now. But by the time the movie company showed up it would be a paradise.

The sun would warm the land, melting the snow, feeding the streams and irrigation ditches and turning the grass and hay a luscious shade of green. The cattle would grow fat and sleek. The people would come out of their homes to work and play through the long summer days. Flower gardens would bloom all over town, and there'd be packs of healthy, tanned kids tearing around on bikes and taking horses out for lazy rides along the back roads.

Maybe it was hokey and old-fashioned and backward, but so what? Dillon loved it. It was home, and safe, and he didn't want any of it to change. It would, though. If those movie people came in, a lot of it would. And there wasn't a blessed thing he could do to stop it.

Oh, Jake, Grace and Marsh had done him the courtesy of consulting him, but when it came to the Flying M, he only had one vote out of seven.

Jake's brother Zack, the town marshal, might vote against the idea because he wouldn't want all those people coming into Sunshine Gap any more than Dillon did. But Jake and Grace were obviously in favor of the idea. Jake's youngest brother, Cal, owned a bar and restaurant in town, and he sure wouldn't turn away that much potential business. And since Jake's sister, Alexandra, had always wanted to be an actress, Dillon couldn't see her voting against letting the production company come in.

Shoot, Alex would probably wind up playing a part in the movie. Then she'd probably quit her steady job and head for L.A. and drag Tasha along with her, and... Cursing under his breath, Dillon rolled his tired shoulders in a backward circle.

This must be how the Indians had felt as they helplessly watched the whites invade their hunting grounds with their covered wagons and railroads and guns, Dillon thought, turning back toward the barn. When he stepped inside, Sunny raised his head and blew out a snort of welcome. Leaning one hip against the stall door, Dillon scratched the white blaze on the horse's forehead.

"How're ya doin', big guy?" he asked. "Ready to go look for more calves?"

Sunny butted his nose against Dillon's breast pocket in search of a treat. Chuckling, Dillon stroked the gelding's neck. "Sorry, pal. I was in such a hurry to get out of the house, I forgot to bring you anything."

Giving him a disgruntled sniff, Sunny lowered his head to the pan of oats Jake had left for him. Dillon sighed and turned away, then glanced back over his shoulder. Blair DuMaine's hair was almost the same dark golden color as Sunny's hide. The thought brought a vision of her flawless face to his mind, and his groin responded in a predictable manner.

Dillon cursed under his breath and went to find a dry saddle blanket, calling himself every kind of a fool. Gorgeous or not, the woman was nothing but trouble. As sure as the sun rose each morning, she was gonna wreak havoc in his life. He just knew it.

A heavy silence filled the cozy kitchen when the back door slammed shut behind Dillon. Blair scowled at Marsh. "You said your family would love having the film shot here."

Marsh shrugged, then gave her a sheepish grin. "Don't worry about Dillon. He'll come around."

Blair looked to Jake and Grace for confirmation and saw them exchange worried glances. Feeling a sinking sensation in the pit of her stomach, she turned back to Marsh. "What if he doesn't?"

"He just needs a little time to get used to the idea," Marsh assured her. "He'll change his mind once Jake and I have a talk with him."

"Maybe we should offer him a part," Patrick Quillen suggested. "Wouldn't he make a great bad guy?"

Grace glared at the director. "Because of his face? Let me tell you something, mister—"

"Now, Gracie, Patrick didn't mean it as an insult," Marsh said. "You've gotta admit, Dillon can look meaner than a two-headed rattler when he wants to."

"Well, he's not mean and he doesn't deserve to have folks making remarks about his looks," Grace said. "That's why he doesn't want the movie company to come here, you know."

"I know," Marsh replied. "And I think it would do him a world of good to have to be around more people. Maybe he'd get over being so damn sensitive about his scars."

"That's easy for you to say, Marsh," Grace snapped. "You weren't in the accident. People don't stare at you like you're some kind of a freak."

Assaulted by an attack of guilt over her own reaction to Dillon's scars, Blair winced inwardly. When he swept into the room, she'd thought he was the most striking man on the planet. Tall and brawny, his cheeks and ears flushed with the cold, the tiny calf held against his broad chest, he'd looked like the quintessential cowboy come to life.

She had felt irrationally drawn to him, almost…driven to get out of her chair and make some kind of personal contact with him. She hadn't understood her feelings at the time. She still didn't. If all she wanted was a cowboy, she should be equally attracted to Jake, who was certainly a hunk by anyone's standards. But she hadn't reacted nearly as strongly to him as she had to his cousin.

Her breath had caught in her throat, and a vision of Dillon's big strong arms carrying her as easily as they did the calf had danced through her mind. He'd seemed so confident—like a man who had his priorities straight, a man who wouldn't hesitate to do whatever was necessary to achieve his goals. She had gasped when she saw his hand, not because it repulsed her, but because it had hurt to think of the pain he must have suffered when he was injured.

She'd enjoyed helping him with the calf. Enjoyed trying to coax him into a conversation, even though everything she said seemed to amuse or exasperate him. She'd been admiring his strong profile when he suddenly turned his head and surprised another idiotic gasp out of her. There were so many plastic surgeons in L.A., you simply didn't see someone like Dillon that often, at least not in Hollywood circles.

Though the right side of his face was ruggedly handsome, a jagged, intricate network of scar tissue distorted the left half of his face from his eyebrow to his jaw. While the outer corner of his left eye drooped, the corner of his mouth twisted upward. The accident Grace had mentioned must have been violent, to have done so much damage.

However unwittingly she'd done it, Blair despised herself for letting that second gasp escape her lips. If anyone knew what it felt like to be judged on the basis of appearance, she did. People frequently stared at her, too, but they tended to fawn over her, as if her features were an accomplishment instead of a lucky accident of birth. She knew better, however, and she didn't maintain any illusions as to how many of those fawning individuals would remain her friends if she ever lost her looks or her career.

"Come on, Jake," Marsh said, pushing back his chair. "Let's go talk to him."

"All right," Jake agreed. "But let me do the talking."

"May I come along?" Blair asked. "Perhaps if I apologized—"

"No, thank you, ma'am. I think it'd be better if Marsh and I handled this," Jake said, grabbing a Stetson hanging from a peg by the door.

"And don't even think about apologizing," Marsh added. "The only thing Dillon hates worse than being stared at is pity. Especially from women."

"Pity has nothing to do with it," Blair protested. "I was unforgivably rude."

Grace gave her a sympathetic smile. "We know you didn't mean to be, Blair. It's just that seeing Dillon's face for the first time is kinda like looking at a train wreck. Most folks react worse than you did."

"But once they become acquainted with him—"

"That's the problem." Grace sadly shook her head. "Dillon doesn't hang around long enough to let folks get to know him. He backs 'em off with a glare or a snarl, and they generally leave him alone."

Marsh and Jake left the room. Grace cleared the empty plates from the table, politely but firmly refusing Blair's offer of help by saying, "Just sit down and relax."

Relax? Blair thought, barely resisting the urge to laugh hysterically. She wouldn't relax until this film was safely in the can. Despite her family name and the connections that went with it, she hadn't been offered a decent role in the past three years. Making this film with her own production company and her own money was the biggest gamble she'd ever taken.

If it turned out the way she hoped, she would finally move into the ranks of the "serious actresses." If it failed, she could kiss her acting career goodbye or resign herself to playing blond bimbos for the rest of her life. Of course, now that she was on the wrong side of thirty, even the bimbo roles were harder to get.

Gritting her teeth, she stood and paced to a window facing the snowcapped mountains on the far side of the valley. She had no idea which mountains they were, only that they were huge and astonishingly beautiful. Perhaps Dillon was right to worry about the way southern Californians would respond to this place.

Compared to L.A., it was so peaceful, so pristine, so... innocent. It called to something deep inside her that longed for a simpler, more basic existence. Darn it, she *needed* to make the film at the Flying M.

Here, she could play this part the way it should be played. For a few weeks, she would become Elizabeth McBride, the kind of woman who could carve out a place for herself in a hard, hostile world. A woman who could found a family whose members would still love and care for each other three generations later. A woman whose family could be *proud* of her.

Blair's throat tightened at that last thought. Yes, that was the real issue at stake. Everyone else in her family who'd gone into the business had won at least one Oscar. Though she'd been acting professionally for ten years, she hadn't even been nominated. When her last movie flopped, the tabloids had called her "the DuMaine without the talent."

Raising her chin, she reminded herself that she would simply have to prove them wrong with Elizabeth's incredible story. And she desperately wanted to do it *here,* at the Flying M, where Elizabeth had been and where her indomitable spirit still lived on in her descendants. If only Dillon would give his consent.

But did they even need his consent? Marsh had told her the seven McBride cousins were equal partners in the ownership of the ranch. While Jake managed the business on a daily basis, they all voted on the major decisions. Perhaps the others would outvote Dillon.

For some totally bizarre reason, that thought was as unpalatable as the thought of having to find another location. It shouldn't matter how she got permission to use the ranch, as long as she eventually got it. But Dillon McBride had obviously been hurt enough and she didn't want him to resent her. No, deep in her heart, she wanted him to...well, at least like her a little bit.

Without saying a word to Patrick or Ian, Blair whirled

around and headed for the back door, grabbing her coat on the way. This matter was far too important to leave to Jake and Marsh. She had to talk to Dillon herself.

Chapter Two

Scowling at Jake and Marsh, Dillon led Sunny out of the stall. "Give it a rest, you guys. I know you're gonna do this thing no matter what I say about it. I'll accept that, but don't expect me to like it or have anything to do with those movie people. Just keep 'em out of my way and we'll get along fine."

"Don't be such a stubborn jackass," Marsh said. "We're going to need your help."

"Hey, I already said I'd run the ranch by myself all summer. What else do you want from me? Blood?"

"It might come to that," Jake muttered.

Marsh raked his fingers through his hair, then propped his hands on his hips. "Look, Dillon, this script is the best thing I've ever written. We're talking Academy Award potential here, but it's not going to happen unless Blair turns in the performance of her life."

"Then what are you hammerin' on *me* for?" Dillon snapped. "Talk to your damn girlfriend!"

"She's not my girlfriend."

"Uh-huh. Is that why you call her honey?"

"She's a *friend,* you idiot. A pal."

"Uh-huh. I suppose you never notice her face or her body or any of that stuff?"

Marsh laughed, then punched Dillon's arm. "I wouldn't say that, exactly. She's just not interested in me that way, but that's beside the point. The thing is, Ian and Patrick want you to work with her before we start shooting."

"Work with her? What the hell are you talkin' about?"

"She needs to learn how to ride, rope, shoot guns and do ranch chores. I told them you're the best man to teach her."

Dillon thought he heard the barn door's hinges squeak, but he was too busy staring at his brother in disbelief to pay any attention. "No way, kid," he said. "Don't even think about it. Let Jake or Zack do it."

"Jake'll be tied up with the business arrangements, and Zack's too busy playing marshal. You're the only one who's going to have the time to teach her properly, Dillon. You give the word, and she'll be up here next week to get started. You'll have two, maybe three months to get her ready."

"No."

"Why the hell not?" Jake demanded. "She seems like a real nice little gal, Dillon."

Marsh continued as if neither of the others had spoken. "They'll use a stuntwoman for anything dangerous, but to understand her character, Blair really has to get inside Elizabeth's skin and do the things she did."

Dillon rolled his eyes. "Hogwash. Spare me that Hollywood drivel, will ya? What makes either of you jugheads think she's capable of learning how to do any of that stuff?"

"She didn't even flinch when that calf slobbered all over her," Jake said.

"Any fool can feed an orphan calf." Dillon retorted. "It takes years to learn how to rope worth a damn, and for all you know, she's terrified of horses."

"No, she's not," Marsh said. "She's putting almost every cent she owns into this project, Dillon, so she'll work her butt off to succeed. Besides, you'll get paid for it. You'll earn enough to finish your house and maybe even buy a new pickup."

Gritting his teeth, Dillon counted to ten, then took a deep breath. "It's not about money. I'm just not interested. Okay?"

"No, dammit, it's not okay," Jake snapped. "From where I'm standin', you're actin' like one selfish S.O.B. Maybe you don't care about the money, but the rest of us do."

"Nobody's stoppin' you—"

"Yes, you are. You're part of the deal, Dillon, and your attitude's gonna poison the whole atmosphere around here. I wouldn't blame Blair a bit for findin' another ranch after the way you acted."

"And wouldn't that just be a terrible shame?" Dillon said. "Then you won't be able to offer George Pierson another fifty thousand for his place, will you?"

"It's not just me," Jake protested. "Sure, I'd like to be able to sweeten my offer to George, but what about Grace? This'd give her a chance to put some bucks in the boys' college fund. I'll bet Alex wouldn't mind puttin' some aside for Tasha, too. Zack's had his eye on an Arabian stud for over a year. And Cal needs to put a new roof on his place."

"Please, Dillon. You don't understand how much this means to me," Marsh added. "I swear to God, I'll give you my share of the ranch if you'll do me this one little favor."

"Aw, *jeez*," Dillon grumbled, scowling from Marsh to Jake and back to Marsh again. "Are you guys sure you can't dig up any more guilt to dump on my head?"

Marsh grinned at Jake. "I think we're getting to him. Keep going."

"I would if I could, but I can't think of another thing," Jake admitted. He studied Dillon for a moment, then crossed his arms over his chest. "What I still don't understand is why you're fightin' this so hard, Dillon. It's not like you can't do the job, and it's not like it'd be any hardship to look at Blair all day. Most guys I know would kill for a chance to spend time with such a pretty woman."

Turning away, Dillon spread the saddle blanket across Sunny's back and wondered how a man as smart as Jake was about most things could be so damn dumb about this. But then, Jake, Marsh, Zack and Cal were still "those good-lookin' McBride boys." Dillon had been one of them once. In fact, a lot of folks around Sunshine Gap used to say he was the handsomest one in the bunch. Not anymore.

He hoped, for his brother's and his cousins' sakes, that none of them would ever know what it felt like to have a woman turn away in disgust at the sight of him. To have a woman shrink away from the accidental touch of a mangled hand. To have a little kid run for his mama when he saw you in the grocery store, screamin' about the "monster man."

Well, he had news for Jake and Marsh and the rest of the boys. What they were asking of him wasn't "one little favor." They'd enjoy working with Blair, all right, and why shouldn't they? Any one of them could look at her and want her, and reasonably hope she might want him back.

He didn't have that luxury. When he looked at her, he damn well wanted her as much as any other man would; his face had been destroyed in that damned accident, but his sex drive hadn't. But there was no hope she'd ever want him back. Her quiet little gasps had given him the message, loud and clear.

Seeing her day after day would make him feel like a starving man salivating over a banquet he knew he'd never be allowed to taste. Yeah, he'd be starving, all right—wanting to touch her, even in friendship, and knowing she'd probably faint if he did. It would be pure, unrelenting torture.

He wanted to strangle Jake for reminding him of Grace's and Alex's need for money. The guys could take care of themselves, but the women in his family were single mothers. They'd both been through rough times, and he couldn't bring himself to deny them a chance to earn some financial security. Jake knew that, of course. Damn his dirty hide.

"Are you afraid of Blair, Dillon?" Marsh asked.

Dillon shot him a hard look, then swung the saddle onto the gelding's back. "Of course not. I just don't want to spend the next two or three months baby-sittin' a snotty actress. Find somebody else."

"We don't want somebody else, and she's not snotty," Marsh insisted. "All you need to do is take her with you while you're working, and teach her the same way you've been teaching Riley and Steven."

"She's too soft, Marsh. Can you really see her pickin' up a hundred-pound bale? Or shovelin' horse apples out of a stall? Or fixin' a fence?"

"Why not?" Jake asked. "Grace and Alex have done all that stuff their whole lives."

Dillon reached under Sunny's belly and grabbed the rear cinch. Threading it through the D ring, he yanked it tight. "Yeah, and that's my point. Blair DuMaine probably doesn't even know how to wash dishes. I'll bet she's never put in a full day's work in her life. This is no place for a woman like her."

"Why don't you let me judge that for myself, Mr. McBride?"

At the sound of her voice coming from the shadows at the end of the row of stalls, Dillon cursed under his breath. Ignoring Jake and Marsh's chuckles, he rested his elbow on the saddle's seat and tried to assume a nonchalant expression while he waited for her to show herself. On one hand, he wished she'd hurry the heck up, have her say and leave him alone. On the other hand, he had to admire the way she strolled into the light, milking every last drop of drama out of the moment.

Head high, she moved with an easy, relaxed grace that made his chest feel tight and his loins ache. She approached Sunny without a bit of hesitation or the good sense to give his hindquarters a wide berth. Dillon leaned against the gelding's side, forcing him to shift his rear hooves away from her. Blair didn't appear to notice. Man, oh, man, they didn't come any greener.

He had to give her credit for guts, though. The top of her head barely reached his shoulder, but she gave no sign that she felt intimidated by him. Keeping her gaze focused on his face, she sashayed right up to him, her chin lifted in challenge. He caught a whiff of a light perfume, and the ache in his loins intensified.

"Why do you dislike me?" she asked.

Her blunt question startled a laugh out of him. "I don't."

"But you don't like me, either. Do you?"

"I don't even know you," Dillon said, wishing she'd look somewhere else.

"I'm glad you realize that. I was beginning to wonder if you might have a problem with prejudice."

"Prejudice! Hold on there, lady. That's a pretty ugly word."

"It certainly is. It's always ugly when people judge others by the color of their skin or what they wear or where they're from. I didn't want to think you were capable of being that narrow-minded, Mr. McBride."

Dillon winced inwardly. Boy, she had him there, and for the life of him, he couldn't think of a thing to say. His silence didn't seem to bother her. Not enough to shut her up anyway.

"Since I know you wouldn't want to be a bigot," she continued, "I wonder if you could explain why you're not willing to give me a chance to prove I can learn to do ranch work."

"Yeah, Dillon," Marsh said with a broad grin. "Explain it to her."

"Please mind your own business, Marsh," she said, glancing pointedly at the door.

Marsh shrugged, then motioned for Jake to join him and walked outside. Wanting to go with them in the worst way,

Dillon sighed and rubbed the back of his neck. "Look, it's nothing personal, ma'am."

"Excuse me, but it feels extremely personal. I'm not stupid, Mr. McBride. Nor am I lazy. As Marsh said, this project is terribly important to me. If he believes you're the best man to teach me what I need to know, then you're the man I want."

Dillon's gut twisted at her choice of words. "You don't know what you'd be gettin' yourself into. This isn't like the movies. The work's hard and dirty, and sometimes it's dangerous."

"I don't care how hard or dirty or dangerous the work might be. I don't care if I look like a fool while I'm learning. I don't even care if you despise me. The only thing I care about is making the best movie I possibly can. I'll do whatever it takes to accomplish that."

The grim determination in her eyes reminded him of Grandma Jenny McBride. She'd been a wispy-lookin' little gal, but she hadn't taken any guff from anyone. To Dillon's knowledge, nobody in the family had ever been able to deny that tough ol' bird whatever she wanted. Dillon had adored her.

Seeing that kind of spunk coming from Blair surprised and intrigued him. Aw, hell, he might as well admit he was gonna lose this battle, too, but he wasn't about to let her walk away with the idea that she had the upper hand.

"You wouldn't last a week," he said.

Blair's shoulders stiffened, her eyes narrowed, and her chin poked out with such belligerence, he almost laughed. Yeah, she was a lot like Grandma Jenny, all right. He'd better get some concessions out of her while the getting was good.

"Don't count on it, Mr. McBride," she said softly.

"I won't mollycoddle you," he warned. "Not one bit."

A spark of triumph glinted in her eyes, but she didn't smile. "Good. I don't want you to."

"I won't listen to any whinin' or bawlin' or put up with any temper tantrums."

"No whining. No bawling. No tantrums."

"I don't do small talk, so don't yak all the damn time, either. Don't ask me nosy questions and I won't ask you any."

"Understood."

"I start early in the mornin'. If you're late, I'll leave you behind."

"That won't be a problem."

"You'll do exactly what I tell you, when I tell you and how I tell you. No arguments."

She raised an eyebrow at that, but didn't voice an objection. Dillon continued. "You won't try to do anything until I say you're ready. I don't want any accidents."

"Agreed. Any other rules, Mr. McBride?"

"Just one. Marsh is right about the 'Mr. McBride' thing. Call me Dillon."

"All right, Dillon. Call me Blair. Shall we settle your fee now?"

He shrugged. "Whatever you'd pay anyone else will be fine."

"Do we have a deal, then?" she asked.

"I suppose we do."

She heaved what was obviously a sigh of relief, then cut loose with a smile that was like the sun coming up over the basin on a dark winter morning. He'd never had anyone look at him quite that way before, and he almost felt guilty about giving her such a hard time. Not giving him a lick of warning, she grabbed his right hand and shook it with all the enthusiasm of a politician.

When he realized what she was doing, he was too stunned to react. She was talking ninety miles an hour, thanking him, promising that she wouldn't be any trouble, that he wouldn't regret this. And now she was clutching his mangled hand between both of hers.

His heart pounded frantically, and a sick feeling of dread filled his belly. Oh, God, she was so excited, was she even aware of what she was touching? He should've known better than to let himself get sucked into this wacko scheme.

Any second now, she'd look down and see her fingers wrapped around his damn claw and she'd scream and fling it away from her or...

But she didn't do any of the things he'd feared. She just gave his hand a warm, firm squeeze, like she was sealing their bargain once and for all. Then she released it, as naturally as you please, stroked Sunny's neck and walked out of the barn with a cheery wave and a promise to see him next week. His scarred flesh still tingling from her touch, Dillon stared after her in consternation. *Had* she known what she was doing?

Blowing out an impatient snort, Sunny nudged Dillon's shoulder with his nose. Dillon turned to the gelding and patted his neck. "Easy, boy. No reason to get yourself all riled up."

Yeah, right, he told himself. No reason to get riled up at all. So she'd touched his bad hand without showing a flicker of disgust. Big deal. The woman was an actress, for God's sake. She was *used* to controlling her facial expressions. Under the skin, she probably wasn't a bit different from his ex-wife, Jill, or any other woman who'd pulled away from him like he had rabies.

He couldn't afford to forget that for a second. If he did, he might actually start to like Blair DuMaine. That would be a lot more dangerous to his peace of mind than lusting after her.

Well, he'd just have to keep his distance, which shouldn't be all that hard to do. After he worked her like a hired hand for a day or two, she probably wouldn't speak to him. If he was really tough on her, she might even demand a new teacher.

Sighing, he grabbed Sunny's reins, led him out of the barn and swung himself into the saddle. He took one last look at the house, trying to ignore the voice of his conscience, which kept insisting that what he was planning for Blair wasn't at all nice.

"Conscience be damned," he muttered, riding away from the barn. "A man's got a right to protect himself."

Chapter Three

Three weeks later, Dillon was back in the barn, giving Sunny a rubdown. After doctoring calves all day in pastures that were still soggy from the melting snow, he was tired, hungry and filthy. The last thing he wanted to do was spend the evening socializing. Unfortunately, he didn't have much choice, if he wanted to eat; the whole dang family was getting together for supper to officially welcome Blair Du-Maine to the Flying M.

The woman hadn't even arrived yet, and she'd already irritated him no end. He'd hoped she would turn down his family's inevitable invitation to live at the ranch until the filming was finished. The little house his grandpa had built for his grandma back in the thirties served just fine for putting up friends and relatives, but he'd thought a woman like Blair would rather stay in a motel.

No such luck. Blair had jumped at the invitation. As a result, the McBrides had been in an uproar for the past three weeks, spiffing up the place.

And that was another thing. She was over two weeks late coming back to the Flying M because of preproduction problems. Or so she'd claimed—she'd been gone so long, he'd started to wonder if she'd developed a case of cold feet at the prospect of working with him. Considering everything she supposedly needed to learn, they hadn't had all that much time to start out with. How the heck did she plan to make up for two lost weeks?

On top of all of that, ever since the word spread about a movie being filmed at the ranch, it seemed like his whole family, the whole town—shoot, the whole blasted county— had gone loco. The phone rang constantly. Everybody wanted to know about the stars, when they'd arrive and could they please meet them and get autographs?

Reporters from all over the state had come out to take pictures and wrangle permission to cover the filming. And there were all kinds of weird folks from the production company running around, finding out about getting permits and scouting possible locations for each scene in the movie. If it was this bad already, Dillon didn't want to think about how bad it was gonna get when the rest of the cast and crew showed up.

Hearing a car pull into the driveway, he gave Sunny a reassuring pat, then went over to the window to see who it was. His heart thumped when he saw a sporty red compact roll into a space beside Zack's dusty black pickup. The driver's door opened. A small, slender woman wearing jeans and a denim jacket stepped onto the gravel and raised her arms over her head like she was stretching kinks out of her back and shoulders. Then she propped her hands on her hips, shook out her long, tawny hair and gazed toward the valley.

So. Blair had returned. The back door of the house banged open and Grace hurried down the steps. Blair turned around and smiled, and Dillon suddenly found it difficult to breathe. Aw, nuts. He'd been telling himself she wasn't all *that* gorgeous. That he'd only imagined feeling so attracted to her. That he didn't give a rat's rear end whether or not he ever saw her again.

What a pack of lies.

The truth was, the sight of her put a funny little ache in the center of his chest. Even from this distance, and looking through a dirty window, he could tell she was every bit as beautiful as he'd remembered. His attraction to her was too real for comfort, and the emotion filling his chest was too close to relief that he hadn't scared her off for him to call it anything else.

The rest of the family trooped down the steps to greet her. She looked tiny standing in front of Jake, Cal and Zack. And man, oh, man, those big dumb galoots were duded up fit to kill, and grinning like they hadn't seen a woman in years. Good Lord, would you look at them puffing out their chests? Any second now, they'd start strutting like a bunch of roosters. The three of them probably had on enough aftershave to bring on an air-pollution alert.

Shaking his head in disgust, Dillon turned away from the window and went back to grooming Sunny. "If they wanna make fools outa themselves over that woman, let 'em," he grumbled. Grabbing the currycomb, he went to work on Sunny's tangled mane. "It's no skin off my behind, but somebody oughta remind Cal he's engaged."

The gelding bobbed his head and snorted. Dillon took that for agreement and went on grumbling. "Honest to Pete, the way everyone's been actin' around here, you'd think she was the queen of England or something. Well, she's not. She puts her panty hose on one leg at a time, just like any other gal."

The thought of Blair putting on panty hose brought on such a hot rush of lust, Dillon accidentally jerked out a clump of Sunny's mane. The gelding whipped his head around, laid his ears back and bared his teeth, threatening to take a chunk out of Dillon's arm if he didn't let up.

"Sorry, boy," he said, stroking Sunny's glossy neck. "I didn't mean to do that. It's just... Aw, hell, Sunny. She makes me want things I've got no business wantin'. I don't like to feel that stuff anymore, ya know?''

Sunny gave him a baleful stare, as if he wanted to say, "So what are you gonna do about it, McBride?"

Dillon let out a disgruntled laugh and shook his head. "Damned if I know. But I'll tell ya one thing, I'm not gonna fall all over myself tryin' to please her like the rest of those fools. No, sir, not me. That woman is nothing but trouble with a capital *T* and I'm keeping my distance.''

The gelding snorted—whether from boredom with his rambling monologue or blatant disbelief, Dillon didn't know. Not that it mattered either way. He went to the window again, just in time to see the orphaned calf trot across the yard and butt his head against Blair's hip.

She jumped and whirled around, then laughed, went down on her knees and threw her arms around Curly's neck like he was just a big dog. Then she fluffed his forelock and Dillon could tell she was cooing at the stupid critter. And there stood Dillon's whole family, grinning at her like she'd discovered the cure for cancer or something.

Shaking his head again, Dillon went back to Sunny. He'd been killing time out here in the barn for just about as long as he could without bringing Grace's wrath down on his head. If he got moving right now, he could grab a shower before supper, which wouldn't be a bad idea, since he probably smelled ranker than a polecat.

He led Sunny out to the pasture and watched him trot off to join his pals. Then he turned toward his own house, his spirits sinking with every step. Halfway there, he paused and took a deep breath. Dammit all, he really didn't want to go to that dang dinner, and it wasn't like him to let himself get railroaded into doing things he didn't want to do.

So why was he putting up with it this time? Oh, all right, he *did* want to see Blair again. See her smile again. Hear her laugh again. It didn't have to be a big deal. A man could enjoy watching a fire without getting close enough to get burned. The same thing should be true about a beautiful woman.

Yeah, he thought as he resumed his walk, he was worrying too much about things that didn't have to be important unless he allowed them to. Nobody ever paid much attention to him when the family got together. He'd just hang back like he always did, and Blair would never know if he was looking at her or not. And starting tomorrow, he was gonna work her cute little tush until she begged for a new teacher.

Marsh must be crazy, Blair thought as she studied the people gathered around the dinner table that night. He'd often talked about his home in Wyoming, but she hadn't understood why it was so important to him until now. If she lived to be five hundred, she would never understand how he could have left such a wonderful family to live in Los Angeles.

There were actually two McBride families from the Flying M. Harry and Lucy McBride were the parents of Dillon, Marsh and Grace, while Jake, Zack, Alex and Cal were the children of Gage and Mary McBride. Harry and Gage were brothers, and Lucy and Mary were sisters, which according to Marsh made their seven offspring double-first cousins.

In practice, they all treated each other like siblings. Blair wished she would have a chance to meet their parents. Unfortunately, the four elder McBrides were out of the country, traveling together on an extended world tour.

Blair didn't know much about any of the McBrides as individuals yet, but she was beginning to sort them out. Marsh had given her a score card to help her keep everyone straight. She had memorized it during the long layover in Salt Lake City that morning. Starting at the far end of the table, she casually studied each person, mentally matching them up with the brief descriptions.

First there was Marsh's cousin, Zack. "Bushy black

beard," Marsh had written. "Town marshal. Raises Arabians. Very close to Jake."

Next came Jake and Zack's sister, Alexandra, whom everyone called Alex. "Short curly hair. Funky clothes and jewelry. Family rebel—will say anything. Has done some acting, mostly summer stock."

Alex's thirteen-year-old daughter, Tasha, was next. She was a beautiful girl, but since Marsh hadn't said much about her, Blair moved on.

Dillon sat on Tasha's right. "Brooding, withdrawn, tends to be cranky." Marsh's description was so apt at the moment, Blair had to bite her lip to repress a chuckle. Marsh had also written, "Has a great sense of humor and a soft heart." Blair hadn't yet seen any evidence to support that statement, but she fervently hoped it was true.

Two boys, Riley and Steven, if Blair remembered their names correctly, shared a piano bench at the near end of the table. Their mother, Grace, sat on Blair's immediate left. Grace wore her long hair pulled back in a ponytail. Marsh had called her "a mother-hen type. Baby of the family, but takes care of everybody and keeps us all in line."

On Blair's immediate right was Jake's youngest brother, Cal. What had Marsh said about him? Oh, yes. "Has a fat mustache he's always stroking. Owns a bar and grill. Friendly as a pup. Everybody knows he's a soft touch."

And finally, on Cal's right, was Jake. "Oldest. Acting head of the family. Manages business affairs. Heart, soul and brains of the Flying M. If you need help, ask Jake."

Whoever had coined the phrase *tall, dark and handsome* might well have had this family in mind, Blair thought. Every single one of them had thick, shiny black hair and dark brown eyes. The men were all over six feet tall, broad-shouldered and narrow-hipped. Though Riley and Steven were only twelve and ten, they were already showing signs of developing the same builds, the same ruggedly handsome features and devilishly attractive smiles, their older male relatives sported.

Grace, Alex and Tasha were all two or three inches taller than Blair's five-foot-six-inch height. Though slender, the women had lush feminine curves and more delicate features than their male counterparts, but the family resemblance was unmistakable. As Marsh had said, "If you've seen one McBride, you've pretty much seen us all."

The McBrides had other traits that were even more fascinating than their distinctive looks, however. They were a dynamic, voluble bunch, given to good-natured teasing, bickering and laughter. With the exception of her cousin Hope, Blair had never felt half as close to another soul as these people obviously felt toward each other.

She had dined in the world's most elegant restaurants, conversed with the most sophisticated jet-setters, attended the most exclusive parties. It seemed odd, even to her, that she would actually enjoy eating a simple dinner of meat and potatoes while sitting in a big, homey kitchen. But she had never enjoyed a meal more than she was enjoying this one.

She had to conclude that it was the people who made the difference. They were all so...unpretentious, or maybe *generous* was the word she really wanted. They were friendly, but they didn't gush. They expressed an interest in her, but they didn't probe for juicy tidbits of gossip about her personal life. They included her in their conversation, but they didn't expect her to entertain them or to be "on."

From the moment she arrived, she had felt accepted, in a way she'd never been accepted before. In L.A. she was never allowed to forget that she was a *DuMaine,* heir to a Hollywood dynasty. Here, she was simply...Blair. One of the gang. An equal. Only Dillon made her feel uneasy.

He hadn't said a word to her beyond a curt greeting when he entered the dining room. Since he hadn't said much to anyone else, either, Blair chose not to take offense at his behavior. She had thought of him often over the past weeks, and she sincerely hoped to find a way to win his friendship.

As the evening progressed, however, she began to despair of accomplishing that objective. Though none of the others appeared to notice, she was continually aware that when he wasn't shoveling food into his mouth, Dillon was watching her—as if he expected her to abscond with the family heirlooms or murder one of his relatives.

Refusing to let him see that his scrutiny disturbed her, she focused her attention on the others at the table. But even in a room full of talking, laughing people, she found it impossible to ignore him completely. She felt his silent, unrelenting gaze as if it carried a physical touch, and it made her feel exposed. Darn him, he was ruining her appetite, and everything else.

She finally lost all patience with whatever game he thought he was playing and stared right back at him. His eyes widened and his nostrils flared for a fraction of a second, but he didn't look away. To her surprise and chagrin, Blair discovered that she *couldn't* look away.

His eyes were so dark, their expression so intense, that her irritation faded, then turned into anxiety as a familiar, sexual warmth invaded the pit of her stomach.

Oh, not now! a voice inside her head shouted. *And not Dillon! If you have to be attracted to a McBride, don't go for the most complicated one. Choose one of the other guys.*

It doesn't work that way, Blair silently told that little voice. You don't consciously decide you're going to be attracted to someone. It just happens.

But Dillon doesn't even like you. Why him?

I don't know, Blair answered. Maybe it's because he seems so isolated. And lonely. His eyes almost talk to me—

The voice interrupted her. *You can't save people from themselves, Blair. Didn't you learn anything from Ted?*

The reminder of her most devastating mistake released Blair from the involuntary staredown with Dillon. Dropping her gaze, she noted that her hands were trembling. She quickly tucked them into her lap and inhaled a shaky breath. By the time she felt collected enough to look up again, Dillon had pushed back his chair and stood behind it, his expression decidedly grim.

"I'll meet you at the corral tomorrow morning," he said. "Six o'clock. Don't be late."

Before Blair could even nod, he turned and stalked out of the room.

"What the heck's eatin' him?" Zack asked.

"Who knows?" Cal replied with a shrug. "Dillon's so dang moody, it doesn't take much to set him off."

Alex rolled her eyes, then shook her head. "Are you guys blind, or just incredibly dense?"

Zack scowled at his sister. "Neither. What are you gettin' at, Alex?"

"Didn't you see the way Dillon was looking at our guest of honor?" she asked, shooting a mischievous smile across the table at Blair. "He's got the hots for her."

"For heaven's sake, Alex," Grace scolded. "There are children at this table."

Perfectly mimicking her scandalized tone, Alex said, "For heaven's sake, Grace, they can see it as well as I can."

Ten-year-old Steven grinned wickedly at his aunt Alex, as if they were often coconspirators in bugging his mother. "Yeah, Mom. And we know all about *sex*."

Grace's cheeks flushed a bright pink. "You don't know half as much as you think you do, young man. Now, drop the subject. Honestly, Blair will think none of us have any manners."

Alex propped her elbows on the table, leaned forward and smiled at Blair again. "I didn't mean to embarrass you, but if you're going to hang around this bunch, you'd better get used to blunt talk. None of us are any good at being subtle."

"I don't mind," Blair answered, returning the smile. "But I believe you're wrong about Dillon."

Alex raised a skeptical eyebrow. "We all grew up together in this house, so I know my cousins as well as I do my brothers, Blair. Trust me, Dillon's interested in you.''

"What he's interested in is finding a way to convince me to go back to California," Blair said. "He's made it absolutely clear he doesn't want to teach me anything. I think he's trying to scare me into quitting before we get started.''

Alex straightened up with an indignant huff. "You're not going to let him get away with that, are you?''

"Not in this or any other lifetime," Blair replied with conviction. "This picture means too much to me.''

"Want me to talk to him again for you?" Jake asked.

Blair smiled at the concern in his voice. "No. Thank you for offering, but this is something I need to work out with Dillon myself.''

Zack gave her an approving wink. "That's exactly right. First thing you've gotta do is earn his respect.''

Everyone nodded in agreement, but Blair saw enough sympathetic expressions around the table to make her seriously question her ability to do so. "How can I do that?''

Stroking his mustache, Cal sat back and studied her for a moment. Then, giving her a devilish grin, he said, "Shouldn't be too hard, Blair. Just don't let him make you lose your temper, and never let him see you sweat.''

Dressed in the western clothes Marsh had helped her select the previous week, Blair presented herself at the corral promptly at six the next morning—and found Dillon counting off the seconds on his watch.

Oh, boy, she thought, he was not going to make this easy. Remembering Cal's advice, she forced a pleasant note into her voice. "Where are the horses?''

The wretched man looked her up and down, gave her a condescending smile and drawled, "Where do you think they are?''

Though his attitude was galling, she replied with admirable patience. "I wouldn't know, Dillon. But I believe you're supposed to be teaching me how to ride one."

"We'll get to that. Eventually."

"All right. Where do you suggest we start?"

"You've gotta be able to catch a horse before you can ride one," he said.

Although the urge to respond to his boy-are-you-ever-dumb tone of voice in kind was fierce, she plastered a bright smile on her face. "Then let's get to it, shall we?"

His eyes lit up with taunting laughter, as if he knew exactly how irritated she felt. "By all means, Ms. Du-Maine. Follow me."

He opened a wooden gate in the corral fence with a theatrical flourish and took off with such long strides, she didn't have any choice but to follow him. Her new cowboy boots felt awkward, and the heavy starch in the jeans Marsh had convinced her to buy made it difficult to hurry. She gave it her best, but by the time she caught up with him at the steel gate leading into the horse pasture, Dillon was tapping one foot in the dust.

He shot a pointed look behind her toward the opposite side of the corral. "Rule number one. Always close any gate you open."

Blair glanced over her shoulder, grimaced and dutifully retraced her steps. She shut the wooden gate, then hastened to rejoin him, silently repeating Cal's advice as if it were a mantra. Without waiting for her to get there, he shoved open the steel gate and strolled into the pasture. Blair paused to obey rule number one before she followed him again.

While she was still trying to figure out how the latching mechanism worked, he yelled, "Not *that* one!"

"But you said—"

Dillon waved an arm toward the horses at the far end of the field. "You have to drive 'em *into* the corral *before* you close the gate."

Gritting her teeth, Blair pushed the gate wide open and

marched after him. When Dillon started shouting and flapping his arms, the ten grazing horses broke into a trot, heading in Blair's direction. Wanting to do her part, she shouted and flapped her arms, too. The horses turned around and ran back toward Dillon.

Though she'd heard a wide variety of foul language on movie sets, the stream of epithets that spewed from Dillon's mouth amazed her. It wasn't what he said, so much as the creative combinations he put together and the way he said them, that made her cringe inwardly. If all cowboys cursed the way he did, no wonder Wyoming's sky was so blue!

"Are you quite finished?" she asked as he approached, raising her chin to show him she was unimpressed by his display of temper.

"Lady, I'm hardly even warmed up yet. Why the hell did you do that?"

"I was trying to help."

"Help? Ha! Now you've got 'em all so spooked, we'll be lucky to get 'em into the corral by noon. Of all the stupid—"

"Misguided," she said, poking her index finger at the center of his chest, "but not stupid. I will cheerfully admit I know nothing about horses, Mr. McBride. If you will spend less time trying to spotlight my ignorance and more time explaining what I'm supposed to do, perhaps I won't make so many mistakes in the future."

Looming over her with his superior height, he glared at her, his chest heaving with harsh breaths, as if he were barely restraining himself from strangling her. She had never felt more threatened, but she met his gaze without flinching. While she badly wanted his help, she wouldn't tolerate abuse, from him or anyone else.

He finally stepped back and looked off toward the mountains to the west. The rigid tension in his neck and shoulders relaxed ever so slightly, and she heard a soft sigh. Quietly releasing her own pent breath, Blair watched him, sensing some kind of an inner struggle going on that seemed out of all proportion to the situation.

When Dillon looked at her again, she thought there might be a grudging touch of respect in his dark eyes. Again she bravely met his piercing gaze, wondering what he found so objectional about her as the silence stretched on and on. Then he inclined his head toward the horses, who had all gone back to grazing at the other end of the pasture.

"Let's go," he said.

Blair nodded and walked along beside him, listening intently to his instructions. His voice was gruff, but not as curt. At least Blair told herself it wasn't quite as curt. Before long, she had neither the time nor the energy to worry about it.

The horses were as difficult as Dillon had predicted. Following his orders as best she could, Blair dashed back and forth across the spongy grass for the next hour, shooing the skittish animals toward the corral. By the time the last horse finally trotted into the enclosure, her hair was straggling around her face, her chambray work shirt was soaked with perspiration and her new boots had rubbed blisters on both of her heels.

She shut the heavy gate, then leaned back against it, wondering why it was so hard to catch her breath. Though she jogged five miles every weekday morning with her personal trainer, she was puffing and panting like a couch potato. Perhaps it was the elevation.

"The easy part's over, Ms. DuMaine," Dillon called from a door at the side of the barn. "Come on, it's time to get to work."

The *easy* part? Blair thought incredulously. He folded his arms over his broad chest, propped his shoulder against the doorjamb and crossed one foot in front of the other. The brim of his cowboy hat shadowed his face, but she didn't need to see his eyes to know he was watching her intently, probably expecting her to admit defeat. He should be so lucky.

Biting her lower lip to stifle a groan, Blair pushed herself upright. She raised her chin, flashed him a sassy grin and, using her entire store of acting skills, strolled across the dusty corral as if her legs didn't know the meaning of the word *fatigue* and her heels didn't burn with every step. Turning away without saying a word, Dillon walked into the barn.

Blair allowed herself a grim smile and kept moving. Elizabeth McBride had lost a child and a husband in order to start and keep this ranch for her heirs. If it would help her to adequately portray that magnificent woman, Blair DuMaine would gladly tolerate whatever petty discomforts working with Dillon inflicted on her. The big jerk simply didn't know what kind of woman he was dealing with.

Perhaps she wasn't as tough and resourceful as Elizabeth had been, but somehow, she would survive today, tomorrow and the next day. She would tolerate Dillon's scornful attitude and learn to ride one of those wretched horses. Failure was not an option. She would learn to shoot a gun and rope a cow or she would die trying. And nobody, including Dillon McBride, was going to stand in her way.

Chapter Four

During the next two weeks, Dillon found that working with Blair was a lot like stepping into a pool of quicksand. The more he struggled to push her away from him, the greater his danger of drowning by inches became. His instinct for self-preservation demanded that he struggle anyway, and struggle he did.

He made her clean stalls, wrestle calves out of mud holes and toss hay bales off the back of the pickup in the rain. He was gruff, unfriendly and sometimes even downright rude. None of it fazed her. Seemed like the meaner he acted, the sweeter she acted, and he felt as guilty as if he'd used a puppy for a football. Dang woman didn't have the sense God gave a chicken.

Neither did he.

If he had one brain cell left, he wouldn't stand here every day and watch her walk across the barnyard. She moved kinda like a queen, with her head high, her shoulders back and her hips swinging with each graceful stride. The rest of her just sort of glided along, pretty and sexy as all get-out.

Made him hard every blessed morning. But did he ever learn from it? Did he ever go into the barn and find something useful to do? Hell, no. When six o'clock came, here he was, holding up the corral fence, feasting his eyes on her like he hadn't seen a woman in years. Grace had a whole penful of chickens with more sense than he had.

"Haven't you had enough yet, DuMaine?" he asked.

"Not yet, McBride. In fact, I'm really starting to like it here." Tucking her leather work gloves into her back pocket, Blair flashed him a sassy grin and closed the space between them. "What do you want me to do this morning, boss?"

She'd slap his face if he told her the truth. Maybe he should do it anyhow. God knew he'd tried everything else he could think of to make her quit. But there was a limit to what his own conscience would allow, and he couldn't bring himself to be that...crude around her.

As usual, the orphaned calf was tagging at her heels. Dumb thing was turning into a terrible pest, but she didn't seem to mind. Shoot, she'd probably take Curly inside with her every night if she could find a way to housebreak him.

"You can stop treatin' that calf like a pet," Dillon said.

She gently but firmly shooed Curly away. "He only follows me because sometimes I feed him his bottle."

"Yeah, well, don't fall in love with him. Think of him as burgers on the hoof."

"That's a horrible thing to say. Can we please get to work now?"

"Bring in the horses," he said. "Then you can saddle up and do some more ridin'."

She studied him for a moment, then walked away without another word. Of course, he turned right around and watched her, knowing full well her backside was every bit as appealing as the front of her. If not more so. Man, did she ever fill out a pair of jeans.

He figured he could handle living in a state of perpetual arousal if she would at least act like the snotty actress she was supposed to be, so that he could honestly dislike her. But would she? Not hardly.

She'd fit herself into his family's life-style like she'd been born to it. If the truth were told, when she developed a few more ranching skills, she'd fit in at the Flying M better than he did. His family sure liked her. And why shouldn't they?

Blasted, contrary woman worked hard, learned fast and never pretended to know something she didn't. She never gave a rip how dirty she got, and she cracked jokes when she shoveled manure. She didn't take any guff off him, but she didn't go out of her way to challenge him, either. And she never once whined, complained or refused to follow orders.

Aw, nuts. He didn't want to like her. Didn't want to enjoy her company. Didn't want to desire her so much that he dreamed about her at night and woke up hurting all over. And damned if he wasn't doing all three.

She herded the horses into the corral and saddled the first one she came to, an old, rough-gaited roan gelding named Ralph. When she called Dillon over to check her work, he tugged at the saddle blanket, inspected all the straps and hardware, yanked on the horn. She'd done a good job. He could've done better, of course. But not much.

"Well?" She bounced from one foot to the other, looking more like an eager youngster than a famous actress. "What do you think?"

Dillon let her sweat for a couple of seconds, then gave her a grudging nod. "It'll do, but don't get cocky. You've still got a lot to learn."

Trying to ignore the flash of disappointment in her eyes, he retreated to the corral fence and started her riding lesson. But he couldn't escape a deep stab of guilt in his heart. The first time Grace's boys, Riley and Steven, saddled a horse that well, he'd spread on the praise thicker than butter on a fresh ear of corn on the cob.

He should have praised Blair, too. And he would have, if he hadn't felt the quicksand of liking her swallowing another inch of him. The admission did nothing to improve his mood.

"Sit up straight," he ordered. "Heels down. Tuck those elbows in. No need to flap 'em around like a pair of chicken wings."

Eyes flashing with anger, Blair opened her mouth, and for a second, Dillon thought he finally had her. Then she shot him a killing look, closed her mouth and rode off on another loop around the corral. Aw, nuts. He'd done his level best to provoke her, but he had to admit she was a champ at controlling her temper.

So far.

She was getting a little ragged around the edges now, though. Her last glare had been hot enough to fry meat, and her tongue had to be sore as hell from all the times she'd bitten it. Sooner or later, he'd say just the right thing and she'd blow her stack like Old Faithful. Then he'd quit this stinking job or she'd fire him, and he could go back to his normal life with a clear conscience.

Lord, he couldn't wait.

Not that his normal life was all that great. He was enough of an introvert to enjoy working alone on the ranch, but he wasn't really a hermit. Sometimes he even got lonely, especially during the winter. His siblings, cousins, niece and nephews provided welcome company, but it wasn't the same as having his own wife and a houseful of kids.

He'd always figured he'd have all of that someday, when he retired from the rodeo circuit. He'd even built the house with some of his winnings, before the accident drove Jill out of his life. He still kept a few home-improvement projects going, and built furniture for something to do when he couldn't sleep, but he'd deep-sixed the idea of getting married again. He wasn't just being stubborn and melo-dramatic, as a few of his relatives had implied, either.

Lots of folks said beauty was only skin-deep, and some of them probably even believed it. When push came to shove, though, there was only so much ugly most people could stomach on a daily basis. He probably could've got-ten by if he'd only hurt his face or his hand, but it was too much to expect any woman to tolerate both over the long haul.

Well, he couldn't afford to sit around feeling sorry for himself and wishing things were different. The best he could hope for now was to be left alone and to learn to accept reality. Which wasn't going to happen as long as he had to spend every day teaching Blair DuMaine how to be a cowgirl. Teaching her was even more miserable than he'd feared it would be. And yet...

He forced himself to look at the mountains, the barn, anywhere but at Blair. No, dammit, there was no "and yet." He'd already learned more than he'd ever wanted to know about rejection. But if she weren't quite so beautiful, maybe....

Disgusted at his own stubbornly tangled thoughts, he watched her complete another circuit around the corral, then beckoned her over to the fence.

"Yes, Dillon?" she asked.

Oh, brother. Now she'd gone into her robot act, the one where she didn't show any emotion at all. She did that sometimes when the atmosphere got too tense. It seemed to work for her as a defense mechanism, but he really hated it. He suspected she knew that, too. Dang woman.

Before he could tell her what he wanted her to do next, the screen door on the back porch banged shut. Jake hurried across the barnyard to the corral.

"Hey, Blair," he called, "you've got a phone call from California. You can take it in the barn."

"Thank you, Jake." Blair gave him such a sweet smile,

he blushed. Then she dismounted, wrapped Ralph's reins around a fence rail and strode into the barn.

Grumbling under his breath, Dillon loosened Ralph's cinch, crossed the corral and settled in a shady patch beside the barn to wait for Blair's return. Sometimes these calls lasted twenty minutes or more, if the caller was her co-producer, Ian Finch. In the morning quiet, he could hear Blair's side of the conversation.

"What? Ian, you've got to be kidding."

Dillon raised one knee and rested his forearm on it.

"When did she call you? Who else is available? No, he's not acceptable. You know why not. He's been through rehab twice, and I don't trust him. I will not allow any drugs on this set, Ian. Find someone else."

Though he approved of her position, Dillon rolled his eyes at her autocratic tone. The woman shifted from one role to the next so easily; no wonder she was an actress. Made him wonder which Blair DuMaine was the real one. Dammit, he wished she'd hurry up.

"I know the advance crew needs to get started," she said. "I'll do what I can to help them find accommodations, but I can't do everything, Ian. There isn't a lot to work with. Find another location manager, and get him out here."

Dillon scrambled to his feet when he heard her slam the phone's handset onto the cradle. By the time she stepped back into the corral, he had Ralph ready to continue the lesson. Giving Dillon a tight smile, she swung herself into the saddle and looked at him as if the interruption had never happened.

He patted the gelding's shoulder. "You need to be able to get on and off by yourself. Circle the corral once clockwise. Then turn Ralph around, dismount and walk him counterclockwise for a lap. Then remount, turn him around and start all over again. Got the idea?"

"Yes, I think so."

Dillon leaned back against the fence, resting his elbows

on the top rail. Blair perfectly executed every move he'd ordered, until she tried to remount. When she lifted her left foot into the stirrup, ol' Ralph took a couple of bouncy steps, forcing Blair to hop along sideways.

"Show him who's boss," Dillon called. "Tighten the reins."

Blair pulled the reins up short and raised her foot to the stirrup again. Ralph swung his neck toward her and his hindquarters away, dragging her forward when she didn't hop fast enough to keep up.

Dillon couldn't make out what she muttered, but from the expression on her face, he figured it must have been a pretty rude word. She was getting that part of being a cowboy down just fine. "What was that, DuMaine?"

She flashed him a smile, showing more teeth than the shark in *Jaws*. "Oh, nothing, Dillon."

"Loosen those reins a little and try it again."

She shot him a doubtful look, squared her shoulders and turned back to the gelding. To her credit, she did loosen the reins some. Just not enough.

When she stuck her foot in the stirrup again, Ralph reacted in exactly the same way. This time Blair was ready, though, and managed to lift herself halfway up the gelding's barrel. Ralph didn't like having so much weight just hanging there, and started crow-hopping around in a tight circle.

Blair let out a shriek, which only made Ralph hop higher and faster. Any second, he'd go into a full-fledged buck. Chuckling under his breath, Dillon hustled across the corral.

He wanted Blair to quit, but he really didn't want to see her get hurt. Grabbing Ralph's bridle, he spoke in a low, soft voice, soothing him to a standstill. Blair stuck right where she was, half on and half off the horse.

"You can get down," Dillon said.

She gulped, then shook her head. "No, I can't."

"Sure ya can. Ralph's not goin' anywhere. Just step onto the ground."

"I can't." She shot him a desperate look. "My hands won't let go."

He glanced down. Those weren't fingers wrapped around the saddle horn in a death grip; they were claws, with white, knobby joints. Poor little gal must be scared spitless. Oh, *jeez.* This was exactly the kind of thing he'd been trying to avoid, but he couldn't leave her clinging to the side of the saddle like a big ol' burr.

He was gonna have to touch her.

Not that it would be any hardship. Truth was, he'd been itching to touch her from the second he laid eyes on her. And that, of course, was the problem—the fear that once he started touching her, he wouldn't want to stop. It was always easier to avoid temptation like that in the first place. And that was what the dang woman was—temptation on the hoof.

With a stern word to Ralph, Dillon stepped behind Blair and slid his right arm around her middle to support her. She didn't seem to notice his bad hand clamped around the indentation of her waist when he pulled her close. Her firm, delightfully curved little rump snugged up tight against his abdomen.

He'd almost forgotten how wonderful it felt to hold a woman, whatever the reason. What he wouldn't give to move his hand a little higher and cup the warm, soft, roundness of her breast... Aw, nuts, he had it bad.

He coughed. Shook his head. Told himself to act like a gentleman, even if he couldn't think like one. Used his left hand to pry her fingers off the saddle horn and bridle.

Lord, but she smelled good. Through layers of dust and sweat, horse and leather, he could still make out a floral fragrance on her skin and a hint of citrus in her hair. And if he turned her around and kissed her, she'd probably taste like...

Damn. He had it bad, all right. Before he embarrassed

both of them with his baser instincts, he swung Blair away
from the horse and set her on her feet with more force than
necessary. She shook out her hands, flexing and straightening her fingers as if forcing some blood back into them.

"Thank you," she said.

Pretending not to see the perplexed look she shot over
her shoulder at him, he abruptly turned back to Ralph and
muttered, "You're welcome."

Silence oozed between them, heavy and thick as mud,
growing and expanding until it threatened to choke him.
He sensed it made her as uncomfortable as it did him, and
maybe even hurt her feelings. She was obviously used to
being liked, and she really hadn't deserved most of what
he'd been dishing out. But no matter how gruff and abrupt
he'd acted, she hadn't given up trying to learn. He respected her for that.

"What did I do wrong this time?" she asked.

He picked up the dangling reins and looped them around
Ralph's neck. "This is about how long you want 'em to
be," he said. "See, they'll pull back if he sticks his neck
out to go forward, but they're not tight enough to bring his
head around toward you and get him goin' in a circle."

"What if he goes in a circle, anyway?" Blair asked. "He
seems to like doing that."

"Then you crowd him up against the fence, so his rear
end can't go anywhere." Dillon matched his actions to his
words, showing her how to do it, as well as telling her. He
led Ralph away from the fence, dropped the reins and
stepped back. "He's all yours. Try it again."

Blair looked up at Ralph with such reluctance, Dillon
wanted to laugh. Maybe she'd finally had enough. Maybe
she'd throw up her hands and refuse to go anywhere near
Ralph. And maybe ol' Ralph would grow tap shoes on all
four hooves and dance off to Montana. The little gal had
grit to spare.

Sure enough, the muscles along her jaw bunched up as
if she was grinding her back teeth together in determina-

tion. She raised her chin and studied the gelding through narrowed eyelids. Then she squared her shoulders and marched up to Ralph like a general getting ready to reprimand his troops.

Ralph jerked his head up and away. Blair grabbed the nearest rein and hauled his head right back down to her eye level. Nostrils flaring, horse and woman stared at each other in a battle of wills every serious rider faced sooner or later.

Maintaining eye contact, Blair slowly lifted her free hand and gently stroked the gelding's neck. "It's all right, boy," she said when Ralph tried to jerk away again. "Take it easy. I won't hurt you."

Not that voice, Dillon thought, biting back a groan. Ralph might be a gelding, but *he* sure as heck wasn't. And that sweet, sexy voice could seduce any male alive, with or without testosterone.

Ralph blew out a soft snort and butted his nose against Blair's shoulder. Chuckling, she patted his cheek. Then, calm as you please, she led him over to the fence, adjusted the reins to the perfect length and swung herself into the saddle. Ralph never moved so much as an eyelash.

Dillon glared at the traitor. *Thanks a lot, pal.* If Blair kept having victories like that one, she'd never quit. And if she didn't go away soon, the quicksand would get him for sure.

Dang woman.

The next day, Blair saddled and mounted a little black mare named Molly, then followed Dillon and Sunny through the west pasture at a slow walk. Well, finally, she thought, bidding the corral farewell with silent glee. Wide-open spaces. Fresh air. Sunshine. This was more like it.

She glanced at Dillon's stern expression and had to work hard to stifle a murmur of protest. Whatever it would take to drag a single word of approval out of him was obviously beyond her paltry abilities. If she ever had him at her mercy, she would kill him.

No, killing was far too good for him. Why not torture him instead? She would make him listen to loud rap music for days on end. Feed him pasta, dainty salads and espresso instead of his beloved beef and potatoes. Force him to wear a suit, a tie and wing tips.

And then... Well then, she would really get nasty. She glanced at him again and allowed herself a grim smile. She would take his beloved Stetson and drown it in a stock tank. Make him laugh until his dour face cracked. Let her cousin Hope interview him, pester and badger him—for hours.

By the time she was through with him, he would beg for the release death would bring. Heh, heh, heh.

"What's so funny?"

She blinked, realized she must have chuckled out loud and gave him an ingenuous smile. "Oh, nothing, Dillon."

He stared at her for a moment, then turned away as if dismissing her from his mind. Ha! Two could dance that tango. Looking toward the west, she felt the familiar tug at her emotions when she saw the mountains looming on the horizon. It wasn't difficult to understand why Elizabeth had fought long and hard to keep this land for her family.

It was beautiful here. Wild. Unspoiled.

Blair heaved a soft sigh. She'd hired the best cinematographer in the business. But even if Bert Grayson did his usual magic, how could he possibly convey all of this grandeur to a movie audience? Did she honestly want him to? She would hate to see Dillon's fears about her production company's intrusion ruining the area become reality.

Oh, surely it wouldn't. Sunshine Gap was much more isolated than Jackson Hole. Much more primitive. Much too small to attract any sustained interest from her acquaintances.

Dillon's horse trotted off to the right. Molly scrambled to catch up, settling into a steady walk beside Sunny as if she couldn't bear to be parted from her dearest friend. Dillon glanced over at her. His gaze met hers, and for a moment she experienced a disconcerting attraction to him that she hadn't felt since her first night at the ranch.

The only logical explanation she could devise was that the wretched man must have potent pheromones. His surly personality certainly did nothing for her. Actually, that wasn't entirely true. In a perverse way, it was…refreshing to meet someone who didn't even like her, much less fawn over her. And Dillon wasn't always surly.

When he interacted with his family, he could be pleasant, even charming, and his protective attitude toward his sister was endearing. He tended to hang back and observe the others in action, but they were always aware of his presence and often depended on him to help solve their problems. She thought she could sincerely like Dillon, if only he would lighten up and talk to her. Just a little.

She saw a cow with five calves, started to ask him about it, reconsidered and closed her mouth again. He frowned at her. No matter what she did or didn't do, he always frowned at her. Wretched man.

"What?" he asked.

She shook her head. "Nothing."

He took a pair of aviator sunglasses from his shirt pocket and shoved them onto his face. "If you've got somethin' to say, say it."

The snarl in his voice raised her blood pressure, but she refused to relinquish her dignity by answering him in kind. "I thought you didn't do small talk."

"I don't. But that doesn't mean you can't ask questions about the ranch."

"Well, in that case, why does that cow over there have so many calves? They can't all be hers, can they?"

Dillon looked over his shoulder in the direction she'd indicated. "She's the baby-sitter. The other mamas are off somewhere, gettin' a drink or eatin'. Come out here tomorrow, and you'll find another cow takin' a turn with the kids."

"How clever of—"

Dillon's snort of laughter cut her off. "Nope, just survival instinct. Other than bein' good mothers sometimes, cows are about the dumbest critters God ever invented. Except maybe for sheep."

The horses clomped up one hill, then another and another. The saddle leather creaked in a relaxing rhythm. Slowly, almost magically, the tension between them dissipated. Dillon pointed out a cow elk and her calf on a nearby ridge, and a golden eagle coasting on the air currents. Blair asked why the tops of a stand of pines were bent over at an odd angle.

"Wind," he said. "Blows all the time in the winter, and those trees are real close to the top of that hill, so they didn't get enough shelter when they were growin'. Happens a lot in Wyoming."

"What was it like to grow up here?"

"It was okay."

She looked at him in surprise. "Just okay?"

Dillon shrugged. "Yeah. Why?"

"Marsh always makes it sound like a paradise for kids. Riding horses. Swimming in the creek. Playing in the barn."

"I think he's conveniently forgotten about stackin' bales when it's ninety in the shade and feedin' stock when it's twenty below zero."

"Oh, he mentions those things, too," Blair said. "But he makes them sound like fun."

"That's because he was always foolin' around when he was supposed to be workin'." Dillon gazed off into the distance, and his voice took on a wistful, almost sad note that made Blair wonder about the memories he must be having. "And he was always cookin' up something with Cal, Alex and Grace that was sure to get the whole bunch of us in trouble."

"But wasn't it wonderful to have so many playmates living right in your house?"

"You don't have any brothers and sisters?"

Blair shook her head. "Just my cousin Hope, but we didn't live near each other."

"Isn't she a writer?"

"Yes." Blair shot him a sidelong glance. "You've read her books?"

"Nope. I just heard Grace and Alex talkin' about her the other day. What does she write?"

"Novels. The last one was made into a movie called *All's Fair*. Perhaps you've heard of it."

Dillon stared at her. "Your cousin wrote *that?*"

Blair tipped back her head and laughed. *All's Fair* had been a box-office smash, an erotic thriller that had shocked enough people to grab major media attention before it had been released. "Don't look at me that way," she said. "*I* didn't write it."

Dillon chuckled. "Sorry. You seem so...normal sometimes, I forget all about your background."

"I'm only normal sometimes?"

He shrugged again. "Most of the time."

Blair pressed one hand to her heart, batted her eyelashes at him and put on a southern accent. "Why, Dillon, honey, that's absolutely the sweetest thing you've ever said to me."

"Yeah, well, don't let it go to your head."

"Don't worry," she said, wondering if the curmudgeon feared she would be overcome with lust and attack him if even once he was nice to her. "I wouldn't dream of it."

The trail gradually steepened, and they left the cows behind. Half an hour later, Dillon suggested they dismount and let the horses rest. Blair complied and, to her chagrin, discovered her legs had become as rubbery as a cartoon character's. Dillon grinned, but for once his grin had a sympathetic quality, rather than a mocking one.

"Takes more muscles to ride uphill than it does to ride around the corral," he said. "Walk around a little and get your circulation goin'. It'll help."

His advice worked. A discreet rub or two on her aching behind aided the process. Then she glanced through a break in the trees, did a double take and gasped with pleasure at the vista spread out far below.

A toy-size Flying M nestled in a cluster of pale green hills. Reddish brown-and-white Herefords dotted the grass, and a darker green line of trees twisted and curved across the pastures. Bathed in an ethereal shaft of sunlight, the miniature town of Sunshine Gap crouched farther down on the valley floor.

"Fantastic," Blair murmured. She twisted halfway around and, shading her eyes with one hand, traced the light's path to a notch in one of the towering granite peaks behind her. "No wonder they named it that. How dramatic."

Dillon approached on her left. "I always thought Hollywood couldn't do it any better."

"You're right." Blair turned back and smiled at him. "This is Elizabeth's spot, isn't it? Where she wrote in her diary?"

He tilted his head toward a flat boulder jutting out of the hillside, creating a sheer cliff. "Right over there."

Thrilled at the thought of standing where Elizabeth had once stood, Blair scrambled around him and made a beeline for the rock. She heard him coming behind her, but she was too excited to wait for him. Images were already forming in her mind of the indomitable woman she would soon play.

This was where a pregnant Elizabeth Swanson had watched in vain for her husband, Bear, to return from selling their yearling steers at the railhead in Montana during the fall of 1882. This was where she had first caught sight of a handsome gunslinger named Riley McBride, who had come to inform her of her husband's death and deliver the supplies Bear had bought for her in Billings. Where she'd wept for the man she had married, but never loved.

Elizabeth had described her refuge in such accurate detail, Blair felt as if she'd already been here a hundred times. Sitting on the boulder, she scooted forward until her legs hung over the ledge from the knees down. The view was so vast, it gave her a touch of vertigo, but it was worth any amount of discomfort to sit here and imagine that she could feel Elizabeth's presence.

"Careful," Dillon warned. "That's a long way down."

"No kidding." Smiling, Blair patted the spot beside her. "Come on, Dillon." She gestured toward the panorama below. "Tell me about all of that."

"All right." Settling himself a good twelve inches to her left, he leaned forward and braced his right elbow on his leg. A disgruntled sigh escaped Blair's mouth. He looked at her, one eyebrow raised in query. "Something wrong?"

She glanced pointedly at the space he'd created between them. "I don't have any contagious diseases, Mr. McBride. I brushed my teeth, and my deodorant is guaranteed for at least another eight hours. And I never, ever bite, unless I'm invited to do so."

He quickly turned his head away, but not before she saw his lips twitch. She laced her fingers together in her lap and stared at him until he looked at her again. His sunglasses hid his eyes, but she would have bet her film's entire budget they were glinting with amusement.

"What's the matter, McBride?" she said, imitating his western drawl. "You scared of me or somethin'?"

His cheeks reddened and his lips twitched again. "Why would I be scared of a scrawny little gal like you?"

"Beats the heck out of me." Bracing her palms on either side of her hips, she slid across the lichen-covered boulder until her shoulder touched his. "I'm sure you won't mind if I sit closer." Pretending she didn't hear his strangled snort of laughter, she pointed toward the meandering line of trees below. "That's a river, right?"

"Yup. The Greybull River."

"Where does it go?"

"North and east into the Big Horn. It flows into the

Yellowstone up in Montana, which flows into the Missouri, which flows into the Mississippi.''

"That water ends up in the Gulf of Mexico?"

"Uh-huh." He swung his left hand in an arc across the horizon. "All that land is part of the Big Horn Basin. It's like a huge, flat hole between the Absaroka Range behind us, and the Big Horns on the eastern side. There's oil fields all the way around the edges of the basin."

Blair smiled at Dillon. "You would have been an excellent science teacher."

"Me? A teacher?" He shuddered. "No way."

"You didn't like school?"

He raised one shoulder in a halfhearted shrug. "Some of it was okay."

"What parts did you enjoy?"

"Shop class. Football. Girls."

Blair laughed at his wicked grin. Heavens, but he was attractive when he forgot to scowl. "You dated a cheer-leader."

"Yeah." His grin faded, and his gaze veered off toward the valley. "Until she decided she liked another guy better."

Crossing his arms over his chest, he tucked his hands under his elbows. It seemed an unimportant action at first, but as a strained silence replaced the lighter mood she had begun to enjoy, Blair realized its significance.

"She dumped you when you hurt your hand?"

"You could put it that way." He shrugged. "But it was high school, you know? No big deal."

Right. No big deal. "So, how did you lose your thumb?"

"Had an accident with a rope during a roundup."

"A rope? How on earth—"

He shot her a disbelieving glance, then shook his head and uttered a soft laugh. "Okay, picture this. You're chasin' a steer, and you're twirlin' your loop overhead with your left hand."

"Why with your left hand?" Blair asked.

"'Cause you throw with your dominant hand, and I'm a southpaw, okay?"

"Okay."

"Good. Now, you've got your loop goin' with your left hand, and you're holdin' the coil with your right hand. You with me so far, DuMaine?"

"Yeah, McBride, I'm with you."

"Supposin' you catch that steer around the neck with the loop, and he's still runnin' like hell, tryin' to get away from you. What's gonna happen when your horse stops and ol' Mr. Steer hits the end of the rope?"

"You're going to hold your end of the rope really hard?"

Dillon smiled. "That steer weighs somewhere in the neighborhood of fifteen hundred pounds. If you hold the rope in your hands, you're gonna get yanked out of the saddle and give yourself a bad case of road rash."

"Then how do you stop the steer?"

"Two ways. Some guys tie the rope to the saddle horn, which gives the steer, the rope, the saddle and the horse one heck of a bad jolt. Other guys dally the rope, which means they wrap it around the horn a couple of times. That lets the rope slide a little, so you don't have that sudden stop. Only problem is, if you don't get your fingers out of the way fast enough, you get hurt."

"And that's what happened to you?"

Dillon held up his right hand to demonstrate. "The rope slipped down over the base of my thumb and just sort of sliced it off. Happens to the first two fingers sometimes, too. You see a cowboy missing one of these digits, chances are real good he dallies his rope instead of tying it."

"Were you alone when it happened?"

Dillon shook his head. "Jake was with me. He picked up my thumb and took it home, but by the time we got to the clinic, the doc figured it was too mangled and too late to reattach it."

"It hasn't slowed you down very much."

"I get by all right. It helps that I've still got my whole left hand." He fell silent. After a moment, he slid off the boulder. "Time to go back, DuMaine. We can't lollygag around here all day. We'll start your ropin' lessons this afternoon."

The return of Dillon's gruff voice didn't worry Blair. He had finally allowed her to glimpse the man behind the prickly role he played to protect himself, and she could understand his need to retreat again. Sooner or later, however, she would coax the real Dillon McBride to come out and talk with her again.

Forget all those fleeting fantasies of physical attraction between them. At this point in her life, she had neither the time nor the inclination for any sort of romantic entanglement. All she really wanted was a nice, platonic friendship to ease the stress of working with him. Surely that wouldn't be too much to ask. Would it?

All the way back to the barn, Dillon mentally kicked himself for letting down his guard with Blair. Any second now, she'd start yammering away, and either drown him in sympathy or ask him what happened to his face. Both prospects made him clench his teeth so hard his jaw ached.

When she rode along beside him without any apparent desire for conversation, he wondered what the hell she was up to. He'd caught her sneaking enough glances at him to know she'd love to find out how he'd gotten his scars. Not that he could blame her for that, exactly. Curiosity was a normal reaction to anything or anyone out of the ordinary.

That didn't mean he had to satisfy her curiosity, of course. Talking about his hand was one thing; talking about his face was something else. Especially with someone as beautiful as Blair. She just wouldn't understand. And there were secrets involved that weren't his to share.

Still, it had been...nice, sitting up there on Elizabeth's rock, telling Blair about the basin and seeing the awed wonder of it all in her eyes. Nice talking to somebody besides his relatives. Nice spending a little time alone with a pretty woman.

He hadn't realized how much he'd isolated himself until Blair arrived.

Dammit, he liked her. Liked her more than anyone he'd met in years. She'd made it plain she wasn't going to quit, no matter how mean he was to her, and he was sick and tired of acting like a jerk around her all the time. Why couldn't he just be friends with her?

He got his answer when they rode into the corral and unsaddled the horses. Grace rang the dinner bell. Blair gave him a smile that made his heart bump against his sternum.

"I really enjoyed our ride, Dillon. Thanks for taking me. I'll see you at lunch."

"Dinner," Dillon corrected. "The noon meal is called dinner here. Don't forget your roping lesson. One o'clock."

"Will it be dangerous?" she asked.

"Only for Jethro." At her questioning glance, he cocked his thumb toward Riley and Steven's wooden steer head, sticking out of a hay bale at the edge of the yard.

She rolled her eyes at him, then walked away with a soft laugh drifting on the breeze behind her. Curly came running to greet her. She petted him, then peeled off her straw cowboy hat and banged the dust out of it on the side of her leg. Her golden ponytail glinted in the sunshine and bounced in time with each swing of her hips.

His mouth went dry. His chest felt tight. His palms itched to slide over those firm, sweet curves. Damn. He liked her, all right, and it didn't have a thing to do with friendship. No way could he afford to go soft on her now.

He glanced down at the fly of his jeans and snorted in disgust. As long as Blair was around, there wasn't much danger of him going soft anywhere but between his ears. So much for being nice to her. He'd rather act like a jerk than a pathetic, lovesick fool any day.

Chapter Five

"Try it again."

Blair glared at Dillon. He gave her a bland stare, his dark eyes silently daring her to protest. Heaven knew she wanted to. Her arm and shoulder muscles burned. Sweat trickled down her sides and plastered her hair against her head beneath the hat supposedly shading her from the sun. She would have killed for a bottle of water.

Speaking of killing, she was seriously considering changing her mind about murdering Dillon. Nothing too dramatic, of course. Perhaps a bullet between the eyes the next time he—

"Come on, you're the one who wanted to learn how to do this," he said. "Hit it once, and you can quit for the day."

She gritted her teeth and dug deep for the energy to swing the blasted rope over her head one more time. Take it from the top. Find the rhythm. Get the timing. One, two, three, throw the loop at Jethro. Watch it send up a another puff of dust when it falls short of the target. Damn.

"Try it again."

Blair wiped the back of her hand across her forehead. Rolled her shoulders. Gulped at the lump in her throat. She hated it when he used that cold, impatient tone. She wanted the nice guy back, the one she'd met up on the mountain this morning.

Had it only been this morning? It felt as if she'd been standing here trying to rope this ridiculous cow head for days. Horrible, frustrating, endless days, with this big, grumpy cowboy breathing fire down her neck.

"One more time," she muttered, starting the process from the top. Again.

When she finally succeeded, Dillon grunted and walked away. Although she supposed it could have been a grunt of disgust at how long it had taken her to get it right, Blair told herself it was a sound of approval. She carefully coiled her rope and put it away in the tack room, then hobbled off to the guest house, drank a quart of water and dragged herself into the shower.

She had worked so hard to stay fit, it was a humbling experience to find herself too exhausted to do anything more than pull on a pair of panties and a T-shirt and fall facedown on her bed. The cool, crisp pillowcase felt wonderful against her cheek. The mattress cradled her aching bones. Her eyelids slammed shut. Reality vanished altogether.

As if she hadn't already suffered enough punishment for one day, a fearsome demon rode a devil horse through her dreams, effortlessly roping her doubts and insecurities, dragging them into the open for everyone to see. The demon looked exactly like Dillon McBride.

Dillon walked up to the main house for supper that evening, and automatically went to the kitchen in search of a cold beer. The room smelled of cooked rhubarb. The oven door was open, his sister Grace bent over a rack of pies.

"When's supper gonna be ready?" he asked.

Grace shoved the pies back into the oven, straightened to her full height and rubbed the small of her back. "It's almost ready now, but I'm still waiting for Alex, Tasha and Blair. Alex and Tasha should be here any second, but I tried to call Blair and she didn't answer her phone. Will you go check on her?"

Dillon would have been happy to eat a meal without Blair's disturbing presence for once, but he knew Grace wouldn't allow that to happen. Besides, Blair was going to need fuel if she intended to keep pushing herself as hard as she had today. Loads of fuel. Dang woman acted like her whole life depended on this stupid movie.

He headed out the back door and ambled across the lawn to the guest house. Blair had left the heavy inner door open. Dillon rapped on the screen, then shaded his eyes with both hands and peered into the living room. No sign of life.

He knocked louder, looked inside again, listened. There. What was that? A moan?

"Blair?" he called. "Hey, Blair, you all right?"

She didn't answer, but he thought he heard another moan. Worried about her, he jerked open the screen door and stepped into the house. "Blair? Where are you?"

The next moan came from the bedroom, and Dillon wasted no time in checking it out. Relief forced a sigh out of him when he found her sleeping in his grandparents' big old walnut bed. Lust came next, when he realized how little she was wearing. Man, oh, man, he'd thought her legs looked good in jeans, but seeing them all naked and smooth and long, and those silky little purple panties peeking out from under her T-shirt...

He shook his head hard, as if it would knock such thoughts out of his brain, then cleared his throat and stepped closer to the bed. "Supper's ready, Blair. Time to wake up."

She winced and curled into a ball, as if the sound of his voice caused her pain. Considering how gruff he'd been that afternoon, it probably did. She moaned again.

"No," she said, her voice slurred with sleep. "No, I'm really not..."

Intrigued, Dillon moved closer. "Not what, Blair?"

Her face contorted with an anxious frown, she thrashed her head and a tear slipped down her cheek. Poor little gal must be having one hell of a nightmare. God knew he'd had enough of them to recognize the signs.

"A failure," she said, sobbing. "I'm really not a failure."

"Of course you're not a failure, honey."

Her eyelids popped open like yanked window shades. Though her eyes looked unfocused, she stared at him with such horror, his heart automatically contracted with sympathy. She looked awful small and defenseless, even fragile. He reached out and gently squeezed her shoulder.

"Everything's all right, Blair. You're just dreamin'."

"No. You're— I have to—" She jerked away, cried out in pain and scrunched her eyes shut. When she opened them again, she looked more aware of her surroundings. She stared at him and inhaled a shaky breath, her eyebrows climbing halfway up her forehead. "Dillon? What are you doing here?"

Feeling his neck and ears get hot, he let go of her shoulder and held up his hands in a gesture of innocence. "Grace sent me to tell you supper's ready. When I heard you groanin', I came in to make sure you were all right."

"Oh." She raised her head and tried to prop herself up on an elbow, but gasped and fell back.

"What's wrong?" Dillon asked.

"It hurts."

"What hurts?"

"My shoulders, my arms, my back—everything." Gritting her teeth, she put both hands flat on the mattress and struggled to a sitting position.

Dillon reached out to help her, but she stopped him with a glare. He shoved both hands into his front jeans pockets. "Do you need a doctor?"

"No. It's just...sore muscles."

Grimacing with every movement, she slid to the side of the bed and draped her long, slender legs over the edge. Guilt blossomed in Dillon's chest. He should have taken better care of her. Should have made her quit practicing with the rope sooner. Should have given her the praise and approval she'd earned fair and square.

Telling himself he deserved whatever torture he had to suffer to make things right, he pulled his hands out of his pockets and sat on the bed behind Blair. The floral fragrance he'd noticed earlier, in the corral, was stronger here; it filled his nose and made him painfully aware of the warm sleepy-woman smells mixed in with it. Oh, man, he couldn't afford to think like that.

She sent him a wary look over her shoulder and opened her mouth as if she intended to protest, and his hands automatically rose to her shoulders. Her muscles were all bunched up like the sheets on the rumpled bed. He kneaded and rubbed them the same way he'd have worked the kinks out of a horse's injured leg.

"You should've told me you were gettin' so tired," he scolded, hoping to distract himself from the sheer pleasure of touching her, and Blair from the pain he had to inflict in order to give her relief.

"And let you call me a quitter?" she said.

"I wouldn't have—"

"Ha! Don't even think about going there. You would have said it and enjoyed both syllables."

She squirmed under his hands, but he tightened his grip and massaged more vigorously. "All right, maybe I would, but if that's the only reason you're puttin' yourself through all of this—"

Her head lolled back, and she groaned with relief.

"Don't flatter yourself, McBride. It has nothing to do with you."

"Then what's really goin' on here? You've made other movies. Why is this one so important?"

She turned her head and met his gaze. "It's my whole future, Dillon."

"Aw, c'mon, you're only, what? Twenty-five?"

"I *wish*," she said with a laugh. Then she looked back down at her hands while he continued to work on her neck and shoulders. "Actually, I'm thirty, and an actress's career life is short in this country. If I don't establish myself as a serious talent with this part, I'll probably never be offered another leading role."

"Would that be such a tragedy?" he asked.

She looked over her shoulder again and gave him a sad, vulnerable smile that reached down inside him and gave his heart strings one hell of a yank. "Only to me."

"And why would it be such a tragedy to you?"

"Because then I'll never be a *real* DuMaine."

"You mean they'll kick you off the family tree?"

"Well, not exactly." She sniffed, then abruptly looked away again. "But you're not born a *real* DuMaine. You have to earn it with a distinguished acting career, and that doesn't even start until your first Oscar nomination. Otherwise, you simply don't…count."

"That's rough," Dillon murmured, praying she wouldn't cry. A crying woman—any crying woman—made his guts hurt.

Blair shook her head. "Oh, I know it must sound silly to someone like you, but you'd have to know my family to understand."

"No, I understand perfectly."

"How could you?" she asked. "Your family is so wonderful, and they love you so much—"

"And they don't have a clue what it's like to wake up one day and find out you don't really belong."

"Don't be ridiculous. Of course you belong."

Dillon raised an eyebrow at her. "Do I? Somehow I don't think I'm one of 'those good-looking McBride boys' anymore."

Her cheeks turned pink, and she cleared her throat, obviously at a loss for something else to say. The warmth of her skin penetrated the thin cotton of her T-shirt, and her hair felt as silky as a kitten's fur against the tops of his hands. She still smelled good, too. Too damn good. So much for distracting himself.

To make matters worse, every protective instinct he owned reared up, urging him to wrap his arms around her, cuddle her close and comfort her, promise her everything would work out fine. Then he'd kiss her senseless and lay her back and...

His pulse lurched. Arousal roared through his system like a runaway freight train. So much for blaming everything on his protective instincts. Damn, he was losing it. He shouldn't be alone with her at all, much less sitting on a bed in which two generations of McBrides had been conceived.

Scrambling to his feet as if his drawers had caught fire, he shoved his hands back into his front jeans pockets and sidled toward the doorway. "Well, uh, I guess I'd better get outa here, so you can, uh, get dressed. Want me to, uh, send Grace down to help you?"

"I think I can manage, Dillon. Thank you."

"All right." He paused and took a deep breath. "Look, I know you're not a quitter, so stop tryin' to prove how tough you are. Take tomorrow off and give yourself a chance to heal up."

"I can't," Blair replied. "As you've said so many times, I still have a lot to learn, and my time is running short. I'll be at the corral tomorrow morning at six o'clock. Don't be late."

She looked so adorable sitting there, all rumpled and bossy and cranky, Dillon turned and fled. Dang woman. It didn't matter how hard she worked, how much he liked her or how sexy she was, he was *not* gonna let her get under his skin.

But as he hustled back to the house for supper, he imagined the quicksand closing in around his neck and a voice that sounded like his brother, Marsh, laughing his fool head off and saying, "It's too late for that, Dillon. Way too late."

Everyone else had already gathered in the kitchen by the time Blair arrived at the main house. Talk, laughter and mouthwatering aromas filled the air. As usual, Grace was directing traffic, putting final touches on the meal and delivering food to the table all at once. Alex waved at Blair and pointed to the seat beside hers. Blair nodded and made her way across the room.

"She's moving slow, but she's still moving," Alex said, grinning when Blair gingerly lowered herself into the chair.

"Hello, Alex," Blair said. "It's nice to see you again. And you, Tasha."

Tasha gave her a shy smile. "Same here, Ms. Du-Maine."

"How do you like being a cowgirl so far?" Alex asked.

The wicked twinkle in her dark eyes made Blair laugh. "It's lovely, Alex. Positively lovely."

"Uh-huh. I suppose there *is* a lot to be said for sweat, saddle sores and manure." Alex reached over, took Blair's right hand and turned it palm up. "Mmm. Nice crop of calluses you're growing there."

Pulling her hand away, Blair looked at the opposite end of the table. If Dillon had heard Alex's remarks, he didn't show it. In fact, he seemed even more withdrawn than usual.

"Hey, Alex, how's school going?" Jake asked.

"The same way it goes every spring," Alex replied with a chuckle. "The sap's rising, so half the kids are crazy and twitterpated. Nobody wants to work, because they can all smell summer vacation. The seniors are the absolute worst, of course. If it wasn't for the class play, they'd be impossible.''

"Which play did they choose?" Grace asked.

"The Glass Menagerie," Alex said.

"That's an ambitious choice," Blair said.

Alex wrinkled her nose. "True, but I've got some kids with talent. If I could just get them to loosen up and forget about the audience, they could do a good job."

"And here I thought you came all the way out here for a taste of my fried chicken and rhubarb pie," Grace muttered.

Tasha giggled. Riley and Steven glanced from their mother to Alex and back to Grace again, as if they expected an exciting argument to break out.

Alex winked at the boys, then turned a deadpan expression on Grace. "Why, Gracie, are you questioning my motives?"

"Wouldn't have to work very hard to do that," Grace replied with a sniff and a grin. "You're about as subtle as a skunk."

Halfway through a biscuit loaded with real butter and honey, Blair realized the attention had shifted from Grace and Alex and now everyone was looking at her expectantly. She hastily finished chewing, swallowed and wiped her lips with her napkin. "Excuse me? Did I miss something?"

Laughter erupted around the table, as it so often did with the McBrides. Blair had seen the phenomenon enough times to know there was nothing mean-spirited about such laughter. It was most likely directed at one of their own, not at her. She had simply been too busy shoveling food into her mouth to keep track of the conversation.

"All right, all right," Alex grumbled good-naturedly, "so I wanted to interest Blair in a little community service. It's for the kids."

"What did you have in mind?" Blair asked.

"I was hoping you might be willing to come to our first rehearsal and help me take the kids through a few acting exercises. You know, show them how you get into character and just…talk to them. Encourage them."

"When is the rehearsal?"

"Tomorrow night. Seven o'clock. At the high school."

"Okay."

"Okay?" Alex clasped one hand to her chest and shook her head, as if she weren't certain she had heard correctly. "Just like that? You really said *okay?*"

Blair chuckled at her theatrics. "Why not? It sounds like fun to me. It'll cost you, though, Alex."

"Uh, we don't really have any budget," Alex said.

Smiling, Blair shook her head. "I didn't mean money. I need someone to run through my lines with me."

Alex's big, dark eyes bulged out of their sockets. "You want *me* to help *you* with your *lines?*"

"If it's not too much trouble. My cousin Hope usually does it, but she's on a book tour, and I need to be letter-perfect before the rest of the cast arrives. I'll pay for your time, of course."

"No, it's not that." Alex jumped off her chair and paced the length of the table, words spurting from her mouth as if fired from a cannon. "I'm just so flattered, I can hardly believe it. I mean, I used to dream of going to Hollywood and meeting someone like you. To get a chance to see you at work—"

"Mom, you're babbling," Tasha said.

"Am I?" Alex halted, looked at the nodding, smiling faces surrounding the table and blushed. Then she raised both hands over her head and laughed out loud. "Well, so what? This is *way* cool. When do we start?"

Blair shot a hopeful glance at the pies sitting on the counter. "Could we wait until after dessert?"

Laughing again, Alex leaned down, hugged her and plopped back into her own chair. "Of course. But eat fast."

"Hey, Uncle Dillon," Riley said. "If Miss Blair is busy, tomorrow night, will you help me with my steer? He doesn't like that halter at all."

"Yeah, sure, bud," Dillon answered. "Just remind me so I don't forget."

The conversation turned to other topics. Blair relaxed and enjoyed her meal while the McBrides carried on with their usual laughter and teasing around her. Gradually, however, she became aware of a brooding presence at the other end of the table. It wouldn't have taken a Rhodes scholar to figure out the source of the darker mood.

Unable to stop herself, she looked in Dillon's direction and met his scowling gaze head-on. *What have I done to earn your disapproval now?* she wondered. A shiver snaked down her spine.

Whatever it was, she undoubtedly would hear about it tomorrow.

Chapter Six

"This has got to stop," Dillon said the next afternoon, glaring at Blair, when she stepped out of the barn.

She marched back to the corral and propped her fists on her hips. "I couldn't agree more. What *is* your problem?"

"*My* problem?" He tossed his rope on the ground. "I don't have a problem."

"Oh? Well, I suppose you've been sulking all day because you like it?"

"I don't sulk."

"And bees don't buzz," Blair retorted. "If I behaved the way you have, people would say I was temperamental, or that I had PMS. What's your excuse?"

He tipped back his hat, stuck the tips of his fingers in his hip pockets and gazed at a point somewhere in the distance behind her. "I don't know what the hell *you're* talkin' about, DuMaine, but *I'm* talkin' about all these phone calls from Hollywood. We don't have time for so many interruptions. Can't your partner make any decisions by himself?''

''I just told him to save all of his questions for the end of the day, Dillon. And you were grumpy long before that phone call interrupted my roping lesson. In fact, you were angry with me last night, so now is your big chance to get whatever it is off your chest. What's bothering you?''

''I'm just…worried.''

''About?''

''Alex. Leave her alone, Blair.''

''Excuse me?'' Blair picked up the rope and shook out the loop. ''I'm not taking advantage of her, Dillon. You heard me offer to pay for her time.''

He shook his head. ''It's not about money.''

''Then what is it about?'' Blair asked. ''She appeared to enjoy working with me last night.''

''She was thrilled to work with you.''

''Then I don't understand what I did wrong.''

He studied the ground for a moment, then looked back at her again. ''You didn't do anything wrong, exactly. I just don't want you fillin' her head with a lot of nonsense.''

Blair gritted her teeth and silently counted to ten. ''Define 'nonsense.'''

''You know what I mean.'' His voice roughened with impatience. ''Goin' to Hollywood. Ridin' around in limousines. Bein' a movie star.''

''You don't think she has the talent? I really can't agree with you. In fact, she's quite—''

''It doesn't matter whether Alex has any talent or not. She has responsibilities right here. And I don't want you messin' with her head.''

Blair scowled at him. ''I have no desire to mess with anyone's head, but you seem to be missing the point. Alex is a grown woman. She's perfectly capable of making her own decisions, and I don't see how this is any of your business.''

''Alex is family,'' he said, as if that explained everything. "She's always been flighty, and she's paid one hell of a price for it. So has Tasha. I don't want to see either one of 'em get hurt again."

"And you think I would hurt them? Intentionally?"

"No, that's not what I meant." Dillon pinched the bridge of his nose between his thumb and forefinger as if he had a headache. The way this conversation was going, she certainly hoped he did.

"Look, Alex finally has a good job now, and she's takin' charge of her life," he said. "It's in her best interests to stay in Sunshine Gap and teach school."

"Even if she's miserable?"

His eyebrows arched halfway up his forehead. "She said that?"

"Not in so many words, but—"

"Then don't encourage her, Blair."

Blair crossed her arms over her chest. "I repeat, Alex is a grown woman. Why not let her decide what she wants?"

"She doesn't have a great track record for stability, and even if she could make it big, Hollywood's no place for her or Tasha."

"Oh, really? How many times have you been to Hollywood?"

"I don't have to see it in person to know they're both too innocent to handle the stuff that goes on there."

"What stuff?"

"The drugs. The orgies. The violence."

Honestly, Blair thought, the big jerk probably read and believed every tabloid in print. "You think everyone in the motion-picture industry participates in all of that...stuff?"

Dillon shrugged. "Hey, I don't give a rip what kind of loose morals you people have. I only know what I want for my own family, and everything I hear about Hollywood doesn't even come close. All I'm askin' is that you leave Alex alone."

"Fine." Fiercely holding back tears of frustration and

exhaustion, Blair coiled up the rope and headed for the tack room.

"I'm not done talkin' to you yet," Dillon said.

"Tough. I'm done talking to you." Blair put one foot inside the doorway, but paused for one more shot. "I promised to attend Alex's rehearsal tonight, and I always keep my promises. After that, I will try not to contaminate her or anyone else in your family with my loose morals."

"Dammit, DuMaine," Dillon called after her, "I never said *you* had loose morals."

Clamping her mouth shut before she said something she undoubtedly would regret, Blair entered the tack room, hung the rope on the appropriate hook and exited through the second door that led into the barn's interior, half expecting Dillon to catch up with her and continue yelling at her.

Thank heaven he didn't. It was a beautiful day, and she was not going to allow that cranky cowboy to spoil any more of it. She had too many other things to worry about to allow him to drain her energy with his narrow-minded, petty faultfinding. If he still thought so little of her after working with her this long, it was time to give up trying to win his respect.

She wiped her eyes with the back of one hand and forced herself to walk faster. Curly trotted out from a shady spot in the yard. He was such a comfort to her. Blair gave him a quick petting and fluffed his little tuft of curls, then hurried on, her thoughts immediately returning to Dillon.

She didn't need the wretched man anyway, she told herself with a sniffle. She could ride and care for a horse, and she'd learned a lot about doing other ranch chores. With any luck, her stunt double could handle the roping, and anything else that was necessary.

For now, she would take a long, hot bath, put on something that wasn't made of denim for a change and drive into town to eat a salad, or perhaps some seafood, before meeting Alex. It was time she remembered her real reason for being here. To make the best damn movie she could.

"Blair!" Dillon shouted. "Come back here!"

She disappeared into the tack room, and a moment later, he heard the other door inside the barn slam. He cursed, long and loud, yanked off his hat and slammed it on the ground. The dang woman was driving him nuts. From the corral, Sunny raised his head and blew out a soft snort, as if asking Dillon what he thought he was doing.

"It's all right, Sunny boy," Dillon said. "Just a pig-headed, unreasonable woman bein' herself."

If Sunny's steady, silent regard seemed to suggest doubt about his assessment of the situation, Dillon ignored it. Sunny was a gelding, after all. What the hell did he know about women? Especially one like Blair DuMaine?

Probably more than you do, McBride, a little voice inside his head replied.

Dillon dusted off his hat, crammed it back on his head and decided to go work on the south pasture's fence. He really hadn't meant to insult Blair, but thinking back on the conversation, he could see how she might have taken exception to what he said. Well, a break from each other would probably do them both good, and they could sort out this snit after supper.

Unfortunately, Blair didn't show up for supper, and Grace said she'd decided to eat in town tonight. The only real restaurant in Sunshine Gap belonged to his cousin Cal, and the thought of Blair sitting alone in Cal's Place set Dillon's back teeth on edge. While the restaurant and lounge wasn't really a dive, it wasn't exactly high-class, either.

Everybody from U.S. senators and bankers to saddle tramps and bikers had been known to patronize the place. God only knew who Blair might run into there. Cal would look after her if the joint wasn't too busy, but he wasn't always available to keep the riffraff in line.

Some of the local cowboys could be damn persistent when they were after a pretty gal, especially if they had a snootful of liquor. And Blair was so far beyond pretty, she'd draw those randy stallions like a mare in heat. Would she have any idea how blunt she'd have to be to make those jugheads back off?

"Aw, what the hell do you care?" Dillon muttered.

"What was that, Dillon?" Jake asked from the opposite side of the table. "You want carrots?"

Dillon felt his neck and ears getting warm fast. "Uh, no thanks, Jake."

"I'll be happy to peel you some," Grace offered, automatically jumping up to wait on him.

"Sit down, sis," Dillon said. "I don't want any damn carrots."

Grace turned on him like a wet banty hen. "There are children here, Dillon McBride. Watch your damn language."

Dillon rolled his eyes in exasperation and stuffed a chunk of roast beef in his mouth. Riley and Steven snickered. Grace returned to her seat and gave them a motherly scowl. "Eat your supper, boys, before I feed it to the dogs."

An edgy silence settled over the table. Unsure whether he was causing it or just reacting to it, Dillon quickly finished eating and went out to the barn. He checked on a new litter of pups one of the cow dogs had produced in the hay loft, reorganized the veterinary supplies they kept on hand and changed the oil in the tractor.

Then he worked with Riley and his 4-H steer for an hour. When the boy went back into the house, Dillon found himself poking around in the barn again. Summer was coming on fast, and it never hurt to make sure everybody's riding gear was in good repair. With a baseball game on the radio for company, a man could spend hours in the tack room, cleaning and conditioning leather and polishing hardware.

Telling himself he wasn't really watching for Blair, Dillon puttered until ten, then gave up and admitted he was worried about her. Alex wouldn't keep a bunch of high school kids out this late on a school night. Surely the rehearsal would have ended at nine, which should have given Blair plenty of time to get home by now. So where was she?

It wasn't as if Sunshine Gap had much to offer in the way of entertainment. By eleven, he was pacing between the barn and the guest house like an overly protective father waiting for a wayward daughter who was out long past her curfew.

What if she'd had car trouble? What if she'd had a wreck? What if she'd gotten lost trying to find the ranch in the dark? Or maybe she'd met a guy at Cal's and made a late date to meet him after the rehearsal. Blair didn't seem like a woman who'd drink and drive or pick up a stranger in a bar, but what did he really know about her?

Adding his own guilt to the mix of other emotions swirling around inside him made Dillon even more anxious to see her safe and sound than he would have been otherwise. By midnight, his imagination had taken him beyond worry and guilt, to anger that she could be inconsiderate and irresponsible enough to stay out half the night, when she knew she had to get up early for work.

When she finally rolled in at twelve-thirty, parked her little red car in front of the guest house and climbed out, he was livid. He crossed the barnyard in long, fast strides.

"DuMaine, I want to talk to you."

She shut her car door, walked around the front end and met him on the passenger side, purse tucked under one arm, her expression neutral. "Hello, Dillon."

"Where the hell have you been?"

"In town."

"Doing what?"

She studied him for a moment before flashing a grim smile. "Enjoying my loose morals, McBride. What did you expect?"

"Dammit, you know I didn't mean to say that about you."

"Do I? Funny, I could have sworn I was included in that sweeping generalization you made. After all, I *am* one of those sleazy Hollywood types, you know."

The yard light washed all the color out of her hair and face, but it picked up the sheen of tears in her eyes. The hurt and bitterness in her voice clawed at his gut and wrenched his heart. "Stop it, Blair."

"Why should I? You had already charged, tried and convicted me before I ever came back to your precious ranch, Dillon. But, hey, at least you're honest about how you really feel."

"No, I'm not," he muttered.

"Excuse me? I'm sure I didn't hear what you said."

"I said, no, I'm not."

"You're not what?"

"I'm not...honest about how I really feel."

"What are you saying?"

He looked at the toes of his boots, crossed his arms over his chest and swallowed hard before he met her gaze again. "I've been waitin' around here for hours so I could apologize for what I said this afternoon. And I was worried about you tonight."

Surprise flitted over her face. "Worried about me? Why?"

"This is rough country," Dillon said. "A lot of things can happen to a woman alone out here at night."

Blair shrugged. "I can take care of myself."

"Maybe you can. I've been told I tend to be a mite...protective toward women."

"But you dislike me so much, why would you care about what happens to me?"

He swallowed hard again. Studied the scuffed toes of his boots. Shoved his hands into his front jeans pockets. "I don't dislike you, DuMaine."

"Oh, right!"

"I don't." He rounded up the courage to look at her again, and sighed when he saw the disbelief in her expression. He'd always believed a real man owned up to his mistakes and at least tried to repair the damage when he hurt someone else. He'd been so busy protecting himself, he hadn't realized just how tenderhearted Blair was.

She sniffed, then turned away, swallowing audibly. "Uh-huh. Tell me another one."

Dillon stepped closer. "All right, I will. If you can forgive me, I want to start over and be friends with you."

"To be friends, people have to like and respect each other."

"I respect you." Dillon stepped closer again, stopping when she stiffened and shot him another disbelieving look over her shoulder. "I *do*," he insisted. "You've done real well here. Way better than I ever expected you would."

"Thank you for that much," she said, her voice soft and husky with emotion. "But you still don't like me. And I don't know why. I've tried to be…pleasant."

Lord, her chin was quivering. If she really broke down and cried, his guts would never stop hurting. He moved closer again, tried to smile at her and felt the familiar tug of the scar tissue at the left side of his mouth. Well, hell, it wasn't as if she hadn't already seen it a hundred times before.

"You have been. And I like you fine. In fact, I, uh…like you a lot."

She turned back to face him, her forehead wrinkled up in a frown of confusion. "Then why do you always act as if you can't bear the sight of me?"

Aw, *jeez*, the stubborn dang woman was going to drag every last bit of this out of him. It was no more than he deserved, of course, but that didn't make it any easier to say. "Because the truth is, I, uh…like you too much."

Her frown deepened. "Too much? I don't understand."

"Nobody ever does." Dillon muttered. He cleared his throat and raised his right hand into the light, intentionally exposing his missing thumb. "I'm ugly as sin, Blair, but I'm still a man. And you are one hell of a woman."

Her mouth fell open in such a shocked expression, it would have been funny if it hadn't hurt so much. "You've acted like an insufferable ass all this time because you're...*attracted* to me?"

"Yeah." He shrugged, as if that puny little word could even begin to describe how much he'd come to want her. "But don't worry about it. I won't try anything."

"Why not?" She stepped closer, tilting her head to one side in a classic posture of curiosity that infuriated him. Surely she couldn't be that dumb.

"You have to ask?" He touched his damaged hand to the ruined side of his face. "Hell, I know exactly how I look—"

"Wait a minute. You're *that* self-conscious about your scars?"

"You thought they were repulsive enough the first time you saw 'em," he reminded her.

She huffed. "There's a big difference between being surprised and being repulsed. Besides, do you think you're the only one in the world who has scars?"

"Well, I sure don't see any on you, lady."

"Some scars don't show on the outside, but that doesn't mean they're not there. They don't have to matter—"

"That's easy for you to say, when you're so damn beautiful—"

She propped her fists on her hips. Even in the dark, he couldn't miss seeing an impressive temper blazing from her eyes.

"Is that all you see when you look at me? That I'm *beautiful?*" she demanded, in such a scathing tone it almost made him laugh.

He was not a complete fool, however, and since this clearly was real important to her, he restrained himself. He'd already hurt her feelings more than enough.

"It's pretty hard to miss," he said softly. "What did you expect?"

"I suppose I was being unreasonable." Her lips compressed into a tight, disappointed smile. "Silly me, I had hoped that you, of all people, would understand how unimportant looks are in judging a person's worth. You are more than your face, Dillon McBride, and I am more than mine."

She stepped closer to him again, went up on her tiptoes and kissed his left cheek. The scar tissue kept him from feeling the full impact of her lips touching him, leaving a hopscotch pattern of heat across his cheek. Dillon gulped, battling the urge to wrap both arms around her and kiss all the disappointment and the sadness right out of her. He would have won the battle, too, if she hadn't used that soft, sultry voice of hers on him.

"When you smile at me, I don't even see your scars, Dillon."

"Aw, Blair," he muttered, knowing even as he protested, that the quicksand was up to his chin and he'd run clean out of will to fight it. It was a mistake, and he knew it, but if he didn't get to kiss her at least once, here and now, he was going to die anyway. He might as well die happy.

He settled both hands at the sides of her waist and slowly lowered his head, giving her plenty of time to pull back if she wanted. But she didn't pull back. Instead, the dang, contrary little woman raised her face and met him partway. The soft, sweet sigh of pleasure she made when their lips finally touched humbled him. She slid her hands up over his chest and shoulders, linking them behind his neck as if she half expected him to try to get away from her.

Fat chance. She'd be lucky to run him off with a shotgun after this. Kissing her was like learning to walk again after the wreck—familiar and wonderful and exciting, and terrifying as hell, all at the same time.

He didn't feel fear *of* her now, but fear *for* her. Fear he'd miscalculate his own strength and hurt her. Fear he'd lose control and scare her. Fear he'd forgotten everything he'd ever known about kissing a woman and she'd never want to kiss him again.

The hardest part was getting past the terror to find the good stuff. And there *was* good stuff. Song writers talked about sweet kisses, but Blair's were spicy. In fact, they were sort of like a great bowl of chili—hot enough to singe a man's tongue and blow the top of his head off, but so damn delicious, he kept coming back for more. Long before that first kiss ended, Dillon desperately wanted another one.

To his relief and amazement, Blair seemed to feel the same way. She nibbled at his lips with unabashed eagerness, strained to get closer until her breasts rested firmly against his chest, pushed her fingers into his hair and clung to it the way she'd clung to the saddle horn when ol' Ralph acted up on her.

Dillon wrapped his arms around her waist and deepened the kiss even more. Lord, it had been so long…way too long since he'd enjoyed a woman's smell and softness, her touch and taste. This was so much more than he'd ever hoped to experience again. So much less than what he really wanted.

But he wouldn't think about that right now. He would focus on the kisses and only the kisses. No sense letting greedy desires shadow the pleasures he already had.

And finally, much too soon for his liking, Blair pulled back and looked up at him. He didn't know how much of him she could see, but the yard light illuminated her features enough to show him a myriad of emotions crossing her face. Wariness, confusion and the same heart-pounding arousal he was feeling gradually gave way to a teasing smile.

"Not bad for a first kiss," she said. "Not bad at all."

Then she turned and walked toward the guest house. Dillon stood there and watched her, his heart trying to beat a hole through the wall of his chest and his head swimming with too many thoughts and feelings he didn't dare examine just yet. When she reached the front door, however, he couldn't resist calling one last question to her.

"You want to be friends with me or not, DuMaine?"

Pausing, she looked back, propped her hands on her hips and put a sassy little drawl into her voice. "That's as good a place to start as any, McBride."

He couldn't move, hardly dared to breathe until the quiet snap of the front door closing behind her released him. What did she mean? That she was actually thinking about going *beyond* friendship with him? Becoming lovers? Well, probably not, but she'd been flirting with him there—

Oh, for God's sake, who was he trying to kid? Even if his scars didn't disgust her, Blair was a rich, famous actress. What would she want with a nobody cowboy like him? Hell, she'd probably only kissed him because she felt sorry for him. The thought made his skin crawl.

Cursing under his breath, he whirled around and stomped across the barnyard toward his house.

"A kiss," he muttered to himself. "That's all it was. Just a damn kiss."

It had been great, but so what? You couldn't build anything lasting on great kisses, or even great sex. They might enjoy a roll in the hay or two, but in the things that really counted, he had nothing in common with Blair. And as soon as the filming was over, she would go back to Hollywood.

For him, it would have to be enough to know that, however briefly, she had wanted him—really wanted him—scars, missing thumb and all.

Still, he couldn't help wondering what kind of scars she had that didn't show, and how she had gotten them. Sooner or later, he was going to find out. Until then, he'd better avoid any more of those kisses.

A man could get dangerously addicted to them. And to the woman who gave them to him. And then that quicksand would go ahead and swallow the rest of him.

Chapter Seven

"Dillon, about last ni—"

"Blair, we've gotta ta—"

Both of them fell silent, each casting the other a chagrined glance across the top rail of the corral fence, then looking away. Honestly, Blair thought with an inward grimace, this "morning after" couldn't have been more awkward if they'd actually gone to bed together. She forced herself to meet his gaze again.

"Excuse me," she said. "What did you want to talk about?"

He rolled his shoulders back one at a time, giving the impression his shirt felt too tight, and slid his fingers into his back pockets. "I interrupted you first. What were you gonna say?"

Worrying her bottom lip with her front teeth, she studied him. The expression in his dark eyes told her she might as well continue. There should be a picture of him in the dictionary, beside the word *stubborn*.

"All right," she said softly. "I've thought a lot about what happened between us, and I, um, well...I enjoyed kissing you very much, Dillon." He inclined his head toward her, but gave no hint of any emotions. She took a deep breath and raced through the rest of the speech she'd practiced over and over during the endless hours of the night.

"However, I'm certain I must have implied that I wanted to pursue a more...well...romantic relationship with you. You're a fascinating man, and under any other circumstances, I would be extremely tempted to do that. Unfortunately, at the moment, I'm facing the biggest challenge of my professional life, and I can't afford any distractions. I'm sorry, Dillon."

"It's okay."

"No, it's not. Honestly, I'm not in the habit of leading men on." She wrapped her arms around herself to ward off a momentary chill. "Unfortunately, set romances rarely work out, even when both parties are in the business. You and I come from very different backgrounds, and I'll be leaving as soon as we wrap here. I simply don't see how we could ever make a romance work."

"You're absolutely right."

"I am?" Surprise at his response popped the question out of her mouth. Even more surprising was the swift stab of disappointment she'd felt when he agreed with such obvious sincerity and relief. Which, of course, made absolutely no sense at all.

He nodded. "I'd say we're about as mismatched as a bird and a bear."

"Perhaps not quite *that* bad," she protested, feeling a bit insulted now. "At least we're from the same species. I think."

The tension eased from his shoulders. His eyes crinkled at the outer corners, and a deep, rich chuckle rumbled out of his chest. "Oh, yeah. We've got all the right hormones, but we don't have a blessed thing in common."

"Do you suppose that's why we feel this attraction?" she asked. "Because we're so different?"

"Could be."

There was so much she wanted to say to him and to ask him, but his smile was already fading. He squinted at the sun, pulled his fingers out of his pockets and turned toward the pasture. "Well, come on, we're burnin' daylight."

"Wait, Dillon. Please."

He frowned over his shoulder at her, then slowly turned back around to face her. She stepped closer to him, twining her fingers together at her waist. He looked so big, so impatient and solemn, that she hesitated a moment, gathering her courage to finish.

"Well, um, if you really do like me, and since we've agreed we don't want a romantic relationship," she said, "couldn't we still be friends? I'm extremely tired of feeling so much tension when we're working together."

"Yeah, me, too." His voice came out husky. The undamaged side of his mouth curved into a rueful grin. "I'll lighten up if you will. Deal?"

She reached out, grabbed his right hand and shook it. "Deal. Now, what do you want me to do today, boss?"

Dillon gazed down at their joined hands. "It really doesn't bother you to touch...that?"

"No, it really doesn't." She squeezed his fingers and gently stroked her thumb over the layer of scar tissue where once his thumb had been. "It's...different, but it's simply a part of my new friend, Dillon McBride. Why should it bother me?"

His grin stretched into a full-fledged smile, and a dimple appeared beside his mouth on the right side of his face. Feeling as if she'd swallowed a sunbeam, Blair smiled back at him. She could see in his eyes that he wanted to kiss her, and she wanted it, too. So much. So very very much.

We're friends, she reminded herself. Just good friends. Somewhere in the back of her mind, a little voice said, *Oh, right, Blair. As if that's really going to work.*

* * *

Surprisingly enough, it *did* work. With the tension eased between them, Dillon was a more patient, more helpful teacher. He gradually became more talkative and occasionally displayed a delightfully warped sense of humor. She no longer dreaded seeing him every morning; instead, she looked forward to whatever time she could spend with him.

One evening two weeks later, Blair stood at the edge of the yard with Riley and Steven, practicing rope throws on Jethro, the wooden steer head stuck into a bale of hay. Dillon lounged against the hood of his old blue pickup, dishing out advice and smart remarks, along with an occasional word of praise. If Blair didn't like the boys so much, it would have been humiliating to miss time after time, when they were hitting the target three shots out of five.

"Good try, Miss Blair," Steven called when she managed to loop one of Jethro's ears.

"Yeah, you're doin' lots better," Riley said. "Throw it just a shade harder next time."

Hearing a muffled snort of laughter coming from the direction of the pickup, Blair shot Dillon a reproving glare. "Knock it off, McBride."

"Sorry, DuMaine."

He gave her a devilish grin that made her want to laugh. Instead, she raised a reproving eyebrow at him and adopted a prim, ultraladylike manner designed to encourage him to continue his teasing, which she had begun to enjoy immensely. Not that Dillon had needed any encouragement since they became friends. He was so good at it, she believed he must have absolutely plagued his siblings and cousins during their childhood.

"You should be," she scolded. "What I lack in skill, I make up for in enthusiasm. Besides, these guys have been doing this far longer than I have."

"Yeah, keep tellin' yourself that," Dillon replied.

Before she could formulate a suitable retort, he looked

off toward the long drive leading from the county's gravel road. Following the general direction of his gaze, she spotted a cloud of dust moving rapidly toward them. A brown van emerged from the cloud and came to an abrupt halt beside the back porch of the main house.

The doors opened and five people climbed out, four men and a woman. The ranch dogs charged out of their usual spot near the barn, barking at the intruders until Dillon called them off. He straightened to his full height, widened the space between his feet and tucked his fingers into his back pockets. His new stance made his chest and shoulders look incredibly broad and gave him an aura of authority.

"Evenin', folks," he said. "What can I do for ya?"

The visitors turned toward him, gave him an automatic once-over. Five sets of eyes widened. Five mouths dropped open.

"Is he for real?" one of the men muttered.

A dark flush swept up Dillon's neck. Furiously coiling her rope, Blair stepped forward. One of the first pieces of information she would pass along to the cast and crew was that without L.A.'s incessant traffic and air pollution, sound carried farther. Then she recognized Patrick Quillen's first assistant director, Cecil Dixon. She'd known him since he was a lowly production assistant, and considered him one of a select number of real friends in the industry.

Approaching him with a big smile and her best western drawl, she said, "Well, if it's not Cecil B. Defreeze. Welcome to Wyoming."

Cecil squinted at her, shook his head and squinted again. "Blair? That can't be you, darling. You look so rough and tough, like...Annie Oakley or...someone." Clutching one hand to his chest, he wiggled his eyebrows at her. "And a rope? Oooh, kinky. Very kinky, darling."

"Oh, stop," she said with a laugh. "And be nice, Cecil. There are *young* people here." She raised her voice to make certain everyone could hear her. "Come and meet my ranching coach, Dillon McBride. He's one of the owners of the Flying M, and to answer your question, yes, he is a *real* cowboy.''

She greeted the others, including Bill, the transportation coordinator, Nancy, a casting director who would hire the extras, Randy, the new location manager and Greg, one of Randy's scouts. After guiding them all through introductions with Dillon, Riley and Steven, she pulled Cecil aside.

''I wasn't expecting you this early, and I've been so busy, I'm afraid I haven't arranged for housing yet. There isn't anything available in Sunshine Gap.''

Cecil frowned thoughtfully, then shot the other crew members a considering look. ''Well, that's not really your job, anyway, now is it? We'll drop the problem in Randy's lap and see how he handles it, shall we?''

Blair chuckled. ''It's lovely to know you haven't changed.''

''As if I would. One can't improve on perfection, darling.'' He took her arm as if to guide her back to the group, giving her an affectionate squeeze. ''What is this?''

Flexing her biceps to show off the full effect of her training, Blair grinned as he squeezed more firmly.

''Good heavens,'' he said. ''What on earth have you been doing?''

''Working with Dillon.'' Blair inclined her head in Dillon's direction. ''He didn't get that physique in a gym, darling. He earned it the old-fashioned way.''

Cecil studied her face for so long, Blair wondered what he might have seen in her eyes. Behind his breezy Hollywood affectations, Cecil Dixon was an astute observer of human emotions and motivations; it was a trait that undoubtedly would serve him well when he became a full-fledged director. ''You look wonderful, Blair.''

''Thanks. I'm glad you're here, Cecil. It's really going to happen now, isn't it?''

''Oh, yes, darling, it is.'' He clasped her face between his hands, gazed deeply into her eyes and said, his voice suddenly grave, "We're going to make a classic. And you are going to be a very *big* star."

Dillon watched Blair huddle up with the guy she'd called Cecil B. Defreeze and felt an aching sort of hollow space open up in the middle of his belly. It was sort of like watching Blair turn into someone else in the space of a heartbeat. What the hell was all of that "darling" stuff about? While he didn't detect any sexual sparks, there was obviously some kind of affection between the two of them.

Jake and Grace came to see what all the commotion was about and invited everyone inside. Though he'd just as soon have avoided any more small talk and curious stares from the newcomers, Dillon couldn't push aside enough of his own curiosity about Blair's relationships with these people to make himself leave. When they were all settled around the big kitchen table with pie and coffee, he sat back and observed the interaction.

There was a fresh glow of excitement on Blair's face. She looked relaxed, happy, and more animated than he'd ever seen her act before. Not too surprising, he guessed. These were her kind of people, who talked her kind of lingo, after all. And she'd been pretty much isolated from them for weeks. Still, it was a jarring reminder that her stay here was only temporary.

Cecil informed Randy of the housing problem. Jake and Grace batted several possible solutions back and forth, shooting Dillon questioning looks all the while. Knowing what was coming, he did his best to ignore them, but it rapidly became obvious he wasn't going to get off so easily.

It was eight miles of gravel road to Sunshine Gap, and then another fifteen miles to Cody, the closest town of any size. There just weren't all that many convenient or even workable options way out here in the boondocks. Eventually they'd have to haul in trailers or something, but it would be silly to start that now for this small group. Especially when he had a great big house that was practically empty.

Well, heck, if he really wanted to be Blair's friend, he should be willing to do whatever he could to help her succeed. Solving this one problem for her didn't seem like a whole lot to ask. But first, he wanted to make sure his idea would pass muster with these folks.

He cleared his throat, asked Blair if he could speak to her in private for a moment and led the way to the backyard. She listened intently while he explained what he had in mind. Slowly the worried little crease between her eyebrows flattened out and a smile that was prettier than a summer sunrise in the high country spread across her face.

"Oh, Dillon, you'd really do that?" she asked, her voice all soft and husky in a way that made him think of warm, lazy summer nights and rumpled sheets. "For me?"

Lord, the delight in her big blue eyes made him feel like a teenager, so eager to please his girl, he'd do dang near anything for her. He shoved his hands into his front pockets and cleared his throat again. "Well, you'd better come take a look at it before you get too excited. It's not all the way finished, and it might not suit your friends."

"But your house looks wonderful from the outside, and we don't need or expect anything fancy," she said, "especially on location. I'm sure it'll be fine."

"I'd still feel better about it if you'd take a look first." He raised his right hand and gestured toward his pickup. "Come on, DuMaine, it'll only take a few minutes."

"Whatever you say, McBride." She grinned, then hurried to the passenger side. "But if the crew takes over your house, where will you stay?"

With you. The answer was so strong, so automatic, inside his head, for a moment he was afraid he might have said the words out loud. They sounded flip and flirtatious, but they didn't feel that way. No, they felt good. Right. Inevitable. His body responded in a predictable manner.

She's a friend, he told himself. Just a friend. Way off in

the distance somewhere, he thought he could hear Marsh laughing. *Right, bro. Keep telling yourself that if it makes you feel better, but you know she's more than a friend. Way more.*

The next time his little brother came home, Dillon figured he was going to have to beat him up, at the very least. He might even have to kill him.

"I'll stay at the main house," he said. "My old room's still empty."

Bouncing along the track in Dillon's pickup, Blair glanced at him and gave her head a slight shake in confusion. It seemed that one second he was smiling and making an incredibly generous offer, and the next second he was a grim, brooding stranger. Try as she might, she couldn't think of anything she'd done to provoke such a reaction from him.

The only logical conclusion she could find to explain his mood swing was that it probably had more to do with the loss of his privacy than it did with her. Grace had told her Dillon rarely invited anyone other than family to visit him at his house. So why had he made the offer to rent it to her production company?

Should she refuse his offer? He'd given her the perfect excuse to do so. Perhaps that was what he really wanted. She glanced at him again. His jaw was so tightly clenched, it looked as if it had been carved from one of the granite outcroppings in the mountains.

Humph. Before she made a decision, she intended to get a look at the inside of his precious house. It might be the only opportunity she would ever have, and she hoped seeing his home would help her understand him. To date, nothing else had worked.

His sprawling two-story house nestled in the southern slope of a hill that was undoubtedly intended to shelter it from fierce north winds. The green stain and decorative rock work made the exterior of the house blend into its setting so well, it seemed as if it was a natural part of the environment. Big windows on each side of the entrance suggested a wish to bring as much of the outdoors inside as possible, reminding her of her own home.

Dillon drove around to the rear of the house, however, and hustled up the back steps as if he might lose his courage if he didn't hurry. Blair followed him into a combination mud room and laundry center, which seemed eminently practical, considering the type of work he did. After hanging his hat on a convenient peg, he opened another door and led her into a kitchen.

Bright and airy, it had oak cabinets, long stretches of counter space, a convenient work island and every modern appliance she had in her own kitchen but an espresso machine. A stenciled border of ivy leaves circled the room above the cabinets. Under the wall-mounted telephone, a small desk with a delicate bluebird figurine sitting on top provided a surprisingly feminine touch. Blair eyed it curiously for a moment, then concluded it probably belonged to Tasha and followed Dillon.

Next he showed her a cozy family room with a native-stone fireplace, bay windows with cushioned window seats, and built-in bookcases. Instead of books, the shelves were filled with trophies, framed photographs and big, ornately decorated silver belt buckles. Blair stepped forward for a closer look, and discovered the photographs were all of Dillon—a younger, happier, devilishly handsome Dillon—accepting one of the trophies or a belt buckle and an enthusiastic kiss from a pretty young Miss Rodeo Wherever.

Hearing him approach from behind her, Blair shot him a grin. "You must have been a pretty good bronc rider, boss."

"I did all right."

She studied the crowded shelves again, then rolled her eyes at his understatement. "Maybe it's just me, but I'm getting the impression your were better than 'all right.' Quite a lot better."

He shrugged one brawny shoulder. "I always wanted to win at the national finals, but I didn't make it that far."

"What happened?"

"This." He flicked his fingers near his scarred cheek. "After the wreck, I never had the heart to go back."

Blair would have asked more questions, but he abruptly turned and left the room. She took another long look at the photographs and prizes he'd won. Judging from the normal side of his face, she'd assumed he must have been awfully good-looking before the accident, but she'd never realized just how devastatingly attractive he'd actually been.

It would have been difficult for anyone to adjust to such a drastic change in appearance. With that face and body, Dillon would have had herds of "buckle bunnies" following him around. It must have been horrible for him when women suddenly started turning away from him.

Sadly shaking her head, Blair crossed the hall and caught up with Dillon in the formal dining room. More large windows revealed a lush meadow filled with wildflowers against a backdrop of craggy, snow-topped mountains. Oddly enough, the room had a hutch, but no table or chairs.

When Blair looked at the spot where a table and chairs should have been, Dillon said, "I never got around to replacing the stuff my ex-wife took with her, so the whole place is a little short on furniture."

"I'm surprised she didn't take this hutch." Blair moved closer for a better view of the elegant detailing and slid one hand over the smooth surface of the wood. "It has beautiful craftsmanship."

"Thanks. Jill wanted it, but the judge decided I could keep all the furniture I made."

The quiet pride in his voice drew her gaze to his face. "You *built* this?"

"And designed it." He shrugged again. "I told you I liked shop class. It's a hobby."

"Some hobby. You could make a fortune building furniture like this in L.A."

"I'd rather punch cows."

Turning abruptly, he led her through a foyer, into a traditional living room. It was pleasant and spacious, but it had a sterile, deserted aura that told her Dillon spent very little time here. After a cursory walk-through, he continued down a long hallway, past three bedrooms and a large bathroom. One of the bedrooms was obviously Dillon's, one appeared to be a guest room, and the third was filled with tools and building supplies.

"This is a beautiful house, Dillon."

"It will be if I ever get it finished."

"You mean you're building this whole house yourself, too?"

"With help from the family once in a while. My ex wanted a big house, and I had most of this floor completed when we got married. Since there's no real rush to finish the rest of it now, I just put in a piece here and there when I get the money saved up."

At the top of the stairs to the second floor were two roughed-in rooms with only bare studs to denote the perimeters. At the far end, however, was a large master suite, including a bedroom, a sitting room, double walk-in closets, a private sundeck and a luxurious bathroom. The bedroom's west wall was made of glass, providing a stunning view of the mountains. The dominant color of the furnishings was a soft lilac, with occasional dramatic accents of royal purple. The furniture provided more examples of Dillon's craftsmanship.

A thick layer of dust covered every imaginable surface, producing the same abandoned atmosphere she had noticed in the living room. This house had been designed for a family, but Dillon had created a beautiful private retreat to share with his wife, a place where they could be lovers, as well as spouses and parents. He must have loved her a great deal.

What would it be like to have a man love her so much? Not because she was a movie star with Hollywood connections and a famous family or because she was rich, but simply because she was his wife? The thought wrenched her heart. It also stirred her curiosity about Dillon's ex.

What did Jill look like? Why had their marriage failed? Was he still in love with her?

Swift and sharp as an eagle's talons, jealousy ripped through Blair, making her wince at the intensity of the emotion. Dillon shot her a questioning look.

"You all right, DuMaine?"

His low, husky voice scraped over her nerve endings. The sincere concern in his eyes made her own eyes mist. She forced a smile.

"Yeah, McBride, I'm fine," she said, telling herself it wasn't really a lie. No one had ever died from a twinge of jealousy, and that was all this was. She'd be over it in a moment or two. Well, perhaps an hour or two. Surely in a day or two. After all, they were only friends.

Underneath all of her self-reassurance, however, that nagging, mocking little voice said, *Get real, Blair. You want everything he was willing to give her for yourself. You're jealous of Jill because you're falling in love with Dillon.*

Ignoring that little voice with every ounce of determination she possessed, Blair smiled at Dillon, told him she would be happy to rent his house for her production crew, and hurried back outside to the pickup. She did not have time for this. Period. End of discussion.

Chapter Eight

For days later, Dillon left the breakfast table and stomped out the back door of the main house, muttering in disgust. Honest to God, he'd never seen people so unable, or maybe it was so unwilling, to make a decision by themselves. He hadn't taught Blair a blessed thing since the advance crew came to the ranch, because every time she turned around, there stood one of those idiots, dancing from one foot to the other like he had to go to the bathroom or something, dying to ask her a question.

According to Blair, more and more of these jokers would show up when they were needed to get ready for principal photography. As near as he could figure it, that was when the whole cast would arrive and they'd finally start filming the damn movie. The prospect of trying to get anything done with all these knotheads underfoot was enough to make a patient man shudder.

Dillon had been called a lot of things in his day; *patient* wasn't on the list. By the tenth of May, he knew something had to change, or he might as well forget about teaching Blair. When she finally sashayed out of the guest house for work that morning, he intended to tell her so.

Determined not to stand there waiting for her like an eager teenager for once, he brought the horses in from the pasture, caught Sunny and bridled him.

"Good morning, Dillon."

Gooseflesh broke out on his arms at the sound of her sultry, seductive voice. Uh-oh. As if the voice weren't enough to grab his attention, she wore a sweet, inviting smile, and there was a hip-swinging vitality to her stride that was...riveting. Temptation on the hoof? That was an understatement.

Dang woman must have been sent here to torture him for his past sins. God knew he'd committed enough of them.

"Mornin'," he muttered, turning away to brush Sunny's back before going after his saddle.

"It's a gorgeous day, isn't it?"

He snuck another peek out of the corner of his eye and damn near fell over when he saw her unselfconsciously tip back her head and stretch her arms high over her head, like she was worshiping the sun or some such foolishness. She wore a modest enough white T-shirt with her jeans, but when she reached toward the sky, it rode up and exposed a strip of skin at her waist. He wanted to touch that soft, smooth skin, and kiss it, and then push her little shirt right up over her head and—

Oh, man, he was in trouble here. Deep trouble. His mouth was dry as a dust devil, and beneath his hat, his forehead was slick with sweat.

Before he could collect his thoughts enough to tell her about his decision to stop teaching her, ol' Curly came running for his daily dose of fussing. Despite Dillon's repeated warnings, Blair was turning that dang calf into a pet, and he was getting big enough to knock a person over.

Dillon had made him a collar with a bell on it to give folks fair warning.

When Curly was finally satisfied, Blair scrambled up on the corral fence and perched on the top rail. Sunny stretched his neck toward her and whickered a greeting. She held out her arms to him as if she were welcoming a lover.

"Hello, Sunny, sweetheart," she crooned, scratching behind the gelding's ears and making kissy noises, laughing when the animal moved his lips in response. "You're such a darling boy, aren't you? Yes, you are. And you love me too, don't you? Well, of course you do, you big old shnookums."

Dillon's whole body ached with a swift, almost violent arousal. Jeez, but that voice was sexy. He wished she wouldn't use it when he was around. And he really wished she wouldn't pet ol' Sunny's neck and ears like that. Dang woman made him harder than a fence post without even looking at him.

Sunny rubbed the side of his head against her chest, nearly knocking her off the rail in his eagerness to get closer. She grabbed at his neck and saved herself with a handful of mane. She laughed again as she regained her balance, then gently pushed the gelding's head back enough to maintain it.

Together they made a striking picture; a golden woman and a golden horse, bathed in golden sunshine. If only he was included in the warmth of their mutual affection...

Dillon turned away, cursing under his breath. The truth was, he'd gotten used to having Blair's attention, and he was jealous as hell because she'd been working so much with the movie crew. And now he was even jealous of an orphaned calf and his own stupid horse. He had it bad, all right. It was pathetic.

He cleared his throat, but his voice still sounded as if he'd eaten gravel for breakfast. "Quit foolin' around, Du-Maine."

She jumped down inside the corral, using both hands to

brush off the seat of her jeans while she approached him. Of course, that motion made her chest jut out, and he had to go and spot the brownish smudge Sunny had left across her breast. She appeared to be unaware of it, and hardly anybody else would even notice it, but he could barely see anything else.

Damned if his fingers didn't itch to brush at the stain. Well, all *right*, what he really *wanted* was to touch her breast. No, what he *really* wanted was to... God, he was turning into an animal, thinking such things in broad daylight.

Pausing beside him, she looked up and smiled, gazing straight into his eyes with such complete trust, he felt lower than a garden slug.

"Okay if I saddle Molly, boss?" she asked.

Hell, she could probably put a saddle on *him* and get away with it, Dillon thought with a rising sense of panic.

"Why bother?" he grumbled.

She frowned at him. "What do you mean, 'Why bother?'"

He swung his own saddle onto Sunny's back. "It's time to give up on the lessons, Blair. This isn't workin' anymore."

"Now, wait a minute, Dil—"

The back door of the main house banged open, and the transportation coordinator called across the barnyard, "Hey, Blair, I need you to take a look at these estimates."

Dillon snorted in disgust, then reached under Sunny's belly for the cinch strap. The crew had hired Grace to cook for them until the catering company arrived. They all ate breakfast in the big old kitchen with the McBrides. They stayed there most of the day, drinking coffee, fighting over the phone because their stupid cell phones wouldn't work with the mountains in the way and taking turns bugging Blair.

Blair didn't answer the guy. Instead, she stepped closer

to Dillon. "You're still supposed to teach me how to shoot."

Dillon waved one arm in the transportation guy's direction. "Well, I can't do it with all this hullabaloo goin' on all the time."

"Look, I've got other responsibili—"

"So do I, the first of which is safety. If you're gonna mess with a gun, you've gotta be able to concentrate or you're liable to shoot yourself in the foot. Why are you payin' these folks, if you're gonna do all their work for 'em?"

She opened her mouth as if she wanted to protest, shot the other guy a glance, hesitated, then mashed her lips together in a thoughtful sort of frown. "You may have a point, Dillon."

Her response eased his frustration and prodded him into softening his tone of voice. "You know I do. These interruptions have gotta stop. You're gettin' pulled in so many different directions—"

"It's my own fault." She gave him a rueful smile. "I've never been a producer before, and I'm so excited to be getting everything started, I suppose I've interfered too much. They all must think they have to consult me over every detail."

"Want a suggestion?"

"Certainly."

"You need to be less accessible. If you really want to learn to shoot, I know a place where nobody will even think to look for you. We'll have to do some ridin' to get there, but you'll get a hell of a lot more done."

The transportation guy arrived at the corral fence, waving his papers. "I've found a company that can provide as many portable toilets as we'll need, but—"

Blair grinned at Dillon and murmured, "Give me fifteen minutes to set everyone straight, and I'll be ready to go to work. Okay?"

Dillon nodded. "Ask Grace to pack us a lunch, and I'll saddle Molly for you."

She gave him a thumbs-up sign, then scrambled over the fence, slung an arm around the toilet man's shoulders and turned him back around toward the house. Glad she was halfway hugging the portly sixty-year-old guy and not the handsome thirty-something location manager, Dillon got down to business, readying the horses, selecting a shotgun and packing shells and targets in the saddle bags.

Suddenly the sky looked brighter, the air smelled sweeter, and he had an urge to whistle while he worked. Of course, it had nothing to do with Blair, or with the prospect of having her all to himself again. Right. And tomorrow, he'd start believing in elves.

The thought should worry him, but this time, he refused to let it. He wouldn't have many more days like this with Blair. He could enjoy at least one without drowning in quicksand. Couldn't he?

Blair noted an unusual air of anticipation about Dillon as he led the way up the same trail they'd taken once before, but when he refused to give her any hints as to the cause, she settled back and admired the scenery. When he didn't want to talk about something, trying to change his mind was a waste of time and energy. Besides, she needed these moments of peace.

Five minutes after they passed Elizabeth's rock, the trail divided. The right branch wound farther up the side of the mountain; the left one headed into the woods. Blair followed Dillon onto the left fork, which paralleled a rushing creek. Molly perked up her ears and stepped off the path, blowing out a protest when Blair reined her away from the water.

Patting the mare's glossy neck, Blair spoke softly to her. "Sorry, Molly, it's not up to me when you get a drink. Dillon probably won't make you wait much longer, though.

You know, he's always nicer to horses than he is to people.''

Dillon shot a scowl over his shoulder at her. "I heard that, DuMaine.''

"Hey, if the boot fits..."

He gestured toward the trail ahead. "She can have a drink in a few minutes. We're almost there.''

"Which is?''

"Somethin' you're gonna like.''

The path curved around a boulder, and Blair gasped with pleasure at the view ahead. Towering pines covered the surrounding hillsides, but in a clearing near the creek, a log cabin nestled in a stand of aspens. Though it was ramshackle and deserted, she felt an immediate tug of affection for it.

Elizabeth had described this place so vividly in her diaries, Blair could easily visualize smoke curling from the stone chimney, snow blanketing the roof, soft lantern light in the windows. In summer, flowers would bloom beside the steps and a pair of wooden rockers would occupy the porch. She rode closer and dismounted at the hitching rail.

Walking the mare back and forth to cool her off, Blair eagerly studied every detail of the rough-hewn building, from the sagging roof to the crooked shutters. Dillon fell into step beside her.

"You know what this is?" he asked.

"It's the original homestead cabin," she said softly. "Oh, Dillon, it's just as I imagined it.... It's absolutely perfect.''

He chuckled. "Yeah, it's a real dream house, all right.''

"That's what it was for your great-grandmother.'' Blair stopped pacing and gestured with her free hand toward the log building. "For a woman of her day, a little house where she could follow her own dreams, instead of her father's or her husband's, was an amazing luxury. That freedom helped Elizabeth become an incredibly strong and independent person.''

He paused beside her, studying her face with open curiosity. "Sounds like you think you know how she felt."

Uncomfortable with his scrutiny, she started walking again. "I believe I know exactly how she felt."

"How could you know anything about a gal like her?" Dillon ambled along with her. "You've always been rich, and your family's famous, and—"

She shot him an incredulous look. "And you think money and fame should make everyone happy?"

"Seems like it oughta beat the heck outa bein' a broke nobody."

Blair laughed and shook her head. "When you put it that way, I suppose it does. But rich and famous people have problems like anyone else."

"Money can't buy happiness, huh?"

"It buys comfort and convenience, but it won't buy love, friendship or respect."

He gave her a long, piercing look that felt as if it penetrated to the depths of her heart and mind. His voice took on a husky edge. "And that's what you really want?"

"Doesn't everyone? Isn't that what *you* want?"

He glanced away, cleared his throat, then thrust Sunny's reins into her hands and headed for the cabin. "Go on and water the horses. I'll get rid of any visitors inside."

"What's the matter, McBride?" Blair drawled. "You afraid to answer my question?"

"Nope. I just don't have all day to stand here and jaw."

Rolling her eyes in exasperation, Blair let the horses drink their fill in the creek. Drat the man. Sooner or later, she *was* going to convince him to talk about himself. She led the horses to the hitching rail, wrapped the reins around it and marched into the cabin.

Her eyes slowly adjusted to the gloom of the interior, bringing into focus the old platform bed, a rickety wooden table and two chairs. Down on one knee, Dillon poked a wooden broom handle into a pile of sticks and leaves on the hearth. Nothing happened. He climbed to his feet and propped the broom handle in a corner.

"Squirrel who built that nest must've taken off or died," he said.

Blair smiled at him, and felt her heart stutter a beat when he smiled back at her. If he only knew how attractive he looked... He abruptly turned away, then leaned against the wall, crossed one booted foot in front of the other and made a sweeping gesture with his left hand.

"Don't mind me. There's not much here, but look around all you want."

Taking him at his word, Blair strolled the perimeter of the room, finding the little touches Elizabeth had described as her "feeble attempts to make this place a home." The hand-carved pegs for hats still hung beside the entrance. The semicircle of smooth rocks she had hauled from the creek were embedded in the dirt floor in front of the hearth. The shelves she had built for the kitchen were gone, but marks where they had hung were still visible on the log walls.

There was an atmosphere of self-sufficiency here, of practicality and inventing whatever was needed to get the job done, whatever it might be. Elizabeth had found incredible joy from simple pleasures—planting flowers and vegetables, caring for children, tending animals. *Loving a man.*

Not just any man, of course.

Riley McBride had been a soldier, an adventurer and a gunslinger when he arrived to help her after her husband was killed. Some had thought him a hero; others had called him a cold-blooded killer. Elizabeth had known only tenderness at his hands, passion in his arms, strength and caring and a lifetime of commitment at his side.

The thought of loving such a man drew Blair's glance to Dillon. He undoubtedly had a few more layers of civilization than his great-grandfather had possessed, but given the right provocation, she believed, he could be just as dangerous as old Riley had ever been. And just as passionate.

Perhaps she should be grateful he wasn't pursuing a more intimate relationship with her. But she wasn't grateful. If she was honest, she would admit she was not the least bit grateful.

She studied him with a sideways look, and felt her stomach clench and her pulse accelerate. It had been a long time since a man elicited such an immediate sexual response from her. It wasn't only lust, either, although lust certainly was an important element of it.

Dillon was so big, so strong, so…competent, he made her feel safe. He was often gruff, but she'd also seen a gentle, patient side to his personality whenever he dealt with animals, and she'd seen Tasha, Riley and Steven argue over whose turn it was to sit beside Uncle Dillon at the supper table. Sometimes, when he thought she wasn't paying any attention to him, he looked at her with an expression of such stark hunger in his eyes, she ached inside, wanting to comfort him and make love with him.

Call her masochistic. Call her stupid. Call her insane.

She couldn't begin to explain it, but she desperately wanted to get closer to him. Much, much closer, physically and emotionally. She wanted it every bit as much as anything she had ever wanted.

Her sideways look must have turned into a blatant stare without her becoming aware of it. Suddenly, he was staring right back at her, his eyes even darker than usual, with an intense emotion she was afraid to name. Gooseflesh popped up on her arms, her mouth went dry, and her throat constricted with a hard gulp.

As if he had read her thoughts, Dillon straightened away from the wall and walked out onto the front porch. Tucking the tips of his fingers into his back pockets, he looked up at the top of the mountain. Blair watched him leave, feeling suddenly and painfully…bereft.

Oh, yes, she wanted him, almost as much as she wanted

an Oscar. However, the stubborn set to Dillon's jaw told her, as clearly as any words he might have said, that he would fight her and his own feelings every step of the way. At the moment, the wretched, elusive Oscar seemed an easier goal to reach.

Well, she simply would have to keep her priorities in order. She was here to work, not to become involved with a man.

Inhaling a deep breath, Blair squared her shoulders and followed Dillon outside. Within ten minutes, he was giving her a lecture on safety rules, the parts of the shotgun and the basics of shooting one. Given her newly discovered feelings for him, it was extremely difficult to concentrate on his instructions.

She tried. She tried very hard. It would be positively too juvenile to pretend she needed him to stand close behind her and put his arms around her, in order to adjust her hold on the gun and correct her aim. That would be little better than a groupie hitting on a tennis pro, and Blair DuMaine was above such idiocy.

It was just that this was all so new. She had used handguns in a couple of highly forgettable cop movies, but she'd never fired a rifle, much less a shotgun, before. And, unlike many of her other coaches, Dillon cared so much whether she did things the right way, he made her feel...nervous.

The masculine scent of his soap and the warmth of his breath on the back of her neck were major distractions, too. She kept thinking that if she set the gun on the ground and turned around, she would be in his arms, and—

No. Bad idea. She would not be the one to make the first move. *Yet.* She would respect his stated wishes. *For now.* She would focus on the tin can he'd balanced on the log and blast it to pieces. That was her job.

If she didn't start doing it, she would make another mediocre film. She would be humiliated all over again by the critics and at the box office. She would never be a "real" DuMaine.

She needed to stop thinking about Dillon and start thinking about her role as Elizabeth Swanson McBride. There must be something she could do to make her character more real, more immediate. She looked back at the cabin. Yes, there was. If she—

"Dammit, DuMaine, where the hell are you?" Dillon demanded, his voice sharp enough to cut wood. "You're not concentrating."

Blair started, then cast a glance over her shoulder. The stern expression on his face immediately made her feel as sheepish as if she'd just blown a take for the tenth time. Sighing, she took off the protective earmuffs he'd provided.

"I'm sorry, Dillon. I just had this really great idea."

He took the shotgun out of her hands and clamped it in his left arm, pointing the muzzle at the sky. "Okay. What is it?"

"Well, um..." She turned to face him. "I think it would help me to understand Elizabeth even more if I...well, lived the way she did. Since I have until the first of June before everyone else arrives, why couldn't I stay up here in the cabin for a week or two?"

His mouth dropped open. Then he closed it and automatically shook his head at her. "There's no running water."

"I can carry it from the creek."

"It's not pure enough to drink anymore."

"I'll boil it."

"There's no stove and no heat."

"I'll use the fireplace."

"There's no bathroom, and the outhouse blew down twenty years ago."

"Well, what do campers do?"

He laughed. "You don't want to know."

She glared at him. "Yes, I *do*. I need to know exactly what she went through after Bear Swanson went off to Montana to sell the cattle and—"

"Aw, come on, Blair, you can't stay up here all alone for days on end—"

"But you could come back and teach me every morning and bring me food and anything else I really needed. At least let me try it, Dillon. Please?"

He propped his right hand on his hip, cleared his throat and, with eyes narrowed, looked off into the distance for a moment. She could almost hear the thoughts racing through his mind. When the side of his mouth curved upward and he slowly nodded, she sighed with relief.

"All right, DuMaine." He raised his index finger, staving off her exuberant thanks. "But I'm only agreeing to this for one night, until we see how you get along, and you have to use some modern camping equipment so you don't get sick or freeze. Deal?"

"Deal. When can I start?"

"Tomorrow soon enough? We'll bring some gear and cleaning supplies and get you set up before dark." She nodded eagerly, and when she'd finished, he handed her the shotgun and said, "All right, back to work."

Blair raised the gun to her shoulder, lined up the front bead with the tin can and gently squeezed the trigger. The can exploded, and the shotgun's recoil knocked her back against Dillon's chest. Even with the protective earmuffs on, she could hear his delighted laugh.

Straightening away from him, she pumped another shell into the chamber, took aim and blasted a second can. Then she tipped the shotgun's bore skyward for safety and sent him a smile over her shoulder.

Just you wait, Dillon McBride. I can be as tough and resilient as your great-grandmother was. And I'll prove it.

Chapter Nine

"Temporary insanity," Dillon muttered thirty-six hours later. Then he heaved a disgusted sigh and added, "Temporary, my foot—it's permanent by now."

Sunny snorted and flicked his ears. Dillon shot him a quelling look and shifted irritably on the old tree stump he was using for a chair. Only time would tell if it was temporary or permanent, but he'd definitely slipped a gear to allow Blair to talk him into letting her stay in the cabin by herself.

At the time, it hadn't seemed like such a bad idea. Of course, when Blair looked at him like a sweet, eager kid, nothing she wanted to do seemed like a bad idea. Besides, Marsh had done plenty of stranger things than that in the name of research for his writing.

Creative folks weren't always real practical, but once they got a wacky idea stuck in their brains, you might as well forget trying to change their course. The more you tried to argue with them, the deeper they dug in their heels.

Far be it from Dillon McBride to tell one of these artsy-fartsy types how to do their business.

Which was why he was sitting in the woods on this damn hard tree stump, eating a supper of cold pork and beans straight out of the can and covertly watching Blair to make sure she was okay. The minute he saw that determined set to her jaw, he'd known there was no use trying to talk her out of... How had she put it? Oh yeah, "living the way Elizabeth did."

Oh, brother. One long, miserable night ought to be enough to convince Blair the "good old days" weren't half as romantic as Elizabeth's diaries had led her to believe.

If she lasted a whole night.

Not that she wouldn't give it a decent shot. Dillon would be the first to admit she'd done well so far. She'd taken good care of her horse and tack, hauled in plenty of water, built a fire and cooked herself a meal—a better one than he was eating, if the smell of it was anything to go by.

Chances were good he could leave her alone up here all night and she'd be just fine. She sure wouldn't thank him for invading her privacy if she knew he was out here. But, hell, the sun had slid behind the mountains only an hour ago.

It was easy enough to be brave in the daylight; the forest became a whole different place in the dark. When you weren't used to them, the sounds nocturnal animals made could be pretty spooky. If Blair did happen to get scared or hurt, he wouldn't put it past her to try to ride down the mountain in search of help and really get herself into a bind.

Molly could probably get her to the ranch in one piece, but the bears were wandering out of their dens this time of year, and most of the sows had cubs to protect. He'd seen cougar and bobcat signs lately, too. Even a raccoon or a coyote could be dangerous if it had rabies, which was always a possibility in the wilds.

Okay, so maybe he was reaching—just a little—for excuses to stay close to Blair, but privacy be damned. Her safety was too important to risk on an artistic whim. She'd never know he'd ever been around unless there was a disaster, in which case, she would be so glad to see him she wouldn't care that he'd been out here in the bushes behind the cabin, keeping an eye on her.

She passed in front of the windows he'd scrubbed that afternoon, waving one arm in the air, her mouth going full speed, her face making all kinds of expressions. Lord, but she was cute. Near as he could tell, either she was practicing her lines, she had an imaginary friend, or she really got into talking to herself in a big way.

His spoon scraped the bottom of the can. He got up, silently made his way over to the creek and rinsed both the spoon and the can. When he got back to his camp, he packed them in his saddlebags. Then he spread a small tarp on the ground, unrolled his sleeping bag on top of it and pulled his saddle over to use as a backrest. If she managed to stick it out for more than a night or two, he'd bring up a tent, but it wouldn't hurt him to sleep rough tonight.

He settled back and continued to observe her, only vaguely aware of time passing. Stars gradually emerged in the inky backdrop overhead. A skinny toenail-clipping moon climbed over the towering pines. And still she worked, talking away and pacing a trench in the hard-packed dirt floor.

Suddenly, she stopped in midstride, put her hands on her hips and shut her eyes for a moment. Then she rolled her head from side to side and raised one hand to massage the back of her neck. Poor little gal was making herself all tense again.

Crossing her arms over her chest, she wrapped her fingers around the opposite elbows and came over to gaze out the window. Though he knew she couldn't see him, Dillon held his breath and felt his heart take up a heavy, throbbing beat. She seemed so small and alone, her shoulders hunched as if she felt chilled.

He thought she looked fragile and scared or maybe she was just worried. She was carrying such a heavy burden with this film, he wanted to go in there and tell her to get some rest. To keep her company and find out what had put that troubled expression on her face. To chase away her fears and massage the knots out of her neck and shoulders.

A lump grew in his throat. He forced himself to look away from the window, hoping the ache in his gut would ease off. It didn't, of course, and he couldn't resist the pull of the picture she made standing there in the soft light from the fireplace and the kerosene lantern.

She abruptly turned away, crossed the room to the make-shift kitchen he'd set up for her and put a pot of water on the camp stove. While it was heating, she rummaged around in her saddlebags and took out a towel, a bar of soap and a wash cloth. The heavy, throbbing beat in his heart went straight south as he watched her slowly unfasten her shirt.

He ordered himself to move. To turn his head away. To act like a gentleman instead of a damned Peeping Tom.

But he couldn't.

Blair's weary, unselfconscious movements mesmerized him more thoroughly than the most practiced striptease ever could have done. He loved her straggly ponytail, her long, slender neck and her well-defined biceps, her lush breasts, tantalizingly covered by a lacy bra. He gulped.

What he wouldn't give to have the right to touch her, to trace the lines of her farmer tan around her neck and above her elbows with his fingertips. Just once. Of course, once would never be enough, and then—

Dammit, it was time he admitted the truth, at least to himself. The truth was, he wanted to do a hell of a lot more than talk to her and massage her neck and shoulders. He wanted to be a hell of a lot more than her coach or her friend. He wanted to warm her up, and not by putting another log on the damn fire for her.

She unfastened the bra, let the straps slide down her arms

and set it aside. His breath caught in his chest. Her pink-tipped breasts swayed gently as she dipped the washcloth in the pan of water and rubbed the bar of soap on it. She shut her eyes again, and smiled a soft, sensuous smile while she stroked the cloth over her neck and shoulders.

Damn. He could practically feel the warm, wet material scrubbing away the dirt and sweat from his own skin from watching the expressions of pleasure skating across her face. Fighting an urge to groan out loud when she moved on to her breasts and arms, Dillon curled his fingers into fists.

The lump in his throat expanded, and he felt choked up. The ache in his gut turned into a gaping, empty hole that somehow seemed to symbolize the lonely prison his life had become. The heat in his groin threatened to scorch away any vestiges of sanity and civilization he'd ever possessed.

And all he had to do to find ease and comfort was reach out to the sweet, sexy woman inside that musty old cabin. The woman he'd wanted like hell on fire since the first moment he laid eyes on her. He'd never known he could want anyone with such ferocious, unrelenting need.

What would she do if he walked up to the door and demanded entry right now? Would she turn him away? No, he honestly didn't believe she would. Though Blair might not want him with the same fierce intensity he felt, it wasn't false pride on his part to say she *did* want him.

So why didn't he go knock on that door? He had no doubts whatsoever that he would enjoy having a fling with Blair, no matter how brief it turned out to be. It was shockingly easy to imagine losing himself in her arms, easing his soul, as well as his body.

But what would be the point? He'd had enough flings during his rodeo career to know they only left him feeling empty when they were over. Empty and cynical and sort of…sad. He didn't want to feel that way about Blair, dammit. She'd become too special to him for that.

Cursing under his breath, he scrambled to his feet and stomped down the path to the creek. After a quick wash and a check on Sunny, he moved his saddle and turned his sleeping bag away from the cabin. Then he set his rifle within easy reach, stripped down to his shorts and slid into his hard bed.

Rolling around in a vain attempt to get comfortable, he dug under the tarp, fished a pinecone out from under his right shoulder and tossed it into the brush. Resisting the urge to take just one more look at Blair, he forced himself to lie back down. It was time to get some sleep, dammit.

He'd tortured himself enough for one night.

Blair tidied up after her sponge bath and put on the thermal underwear Grace had loaned her. It was so chilly up here in the mountains, it was hard to believe it was May. She let out a jaw-cracking yawn, then banked the fire the way Dillon had taught her, carried the kerosene lantern to the old platform bed and sat on the sleeping bag Dillon had provided.

If she felt this tired, she didn't want to know how exhausted he must be. She hadn't realized how much work it would take to make this little cabin livable, and he had done most of it for her. He'd fussed over everything until she was forced to remind him that she could hardly learn what it was like to live in Elizabeth's time if he insisted on providing her with every modern convenience she had back at the ranch.

For such a tough, gruff cowboy, he had an amazing streak of the worrywart in his psyche. Smiling at the thought, she climbed into the sleeping bag and stretched out. She reached for the lantern's fuel valve, hesitated, then forced herself to turn it off. Elizabeth never would have wasted her precious fuel, and neither would she.

After continually telling Dillon she could cope with being alone in the cabin, it was difficult to admit that perhaps she *was* a bit...uneasy about being here by herself, all night, three-quarters of the way up the side of one of the biggest mountains she had ever seen. Of course, that was only natural. It was a new experience for her, after all. It didn't mean she was, to put it in western lingo, "yellow."

Elizabeth had lived alone for months while Bear was off driving their cattle to market. She'd given birth to her first child on this very bed, with only a bachelor gunslinger to act as midwife. Surely Blair DuMaine could handle it for two weeks. Or, perhaps…one week.

In reality, she only had to handle it for one night. If she'd learned anything from working with Dillon, it was that the smaller the chunk of time, the easier it was to endure discomfort. She could stand anything—cleaning stalls or roping fake cow heads or fixing fences—if she allowed herself to think about doing it for no more than one morning, one afternoon, one day, at a time.

Now, she simply wouldn't allow herself to think about the little scurrying sounds coming from the corner of the room. Or the mournful cry of a coyote drifting up from the valley below. Or, most disturbing of all to a southern Californian, the absolute absence of sounds associated with other human beings.

No car horns. No phones. No televisions. No boom boxes. No nothing. It felt as if she were the only person left alive on the planet. Maybe in the entire universe.

Loneliness such as she had never before experienced weighed on her like a blanket lined with lead, bringing a lump to her throat and an unexpected mist of tears to her eyes. She sniffled, swiped the backs of her hands over her cheeks, curled up on her side.

She missed Dillon. If he was here, she might still be cold and uncomfortable, but she would never be afraid. Yes, dammit, right now she was lonely, and afraid, too.

"No wonder Elizabeth kept a diary," she grumbled, only slightly comforted by the sound of her own voice. "She had to talk to *some*one."

She heard a soft fluttering in the beams overhead. A

shiver skittered down her spine. The hair on the back of her neck prickled, and she tried not to remember all the cobwebs and big, hairy spiders—both the dried-up-carcass and live-dashing-for-cover varieties she'd seen today in this very room, on this very spot.

"Stop imagining things," she muttered. "There's nothing there."

The fluttering came again, louder this time.

"Oh, no, oh, no, oh, no." She gripped the top of the sleeping bag with both hands, gathering it tightly around her neck.

Straining to hear over the wild thumping of her heart, she stared up into the rafters. Silence. Oppressive, threatening, terrifying silence. But she wasn't alone. Her skin crawled with the knowledge that something was watching her.

Every horror movie she had ever seen, every ghost story her cousin Hope had ever told her when they were children, every scary novel and chilling screenplay she had ever read, came back to haunt her.

The coyote let out another wail. A second one answered with a long, yipping, heartbroken cry. Clearing her throat, Blair propped herself up on one elbow and stared at the ceiling again.

A dark shape plunged out of the rafters and flew in front of the dying embers in the fireplace, giving her a clear view of outstretched wings. She gasped, and the creature changed course in midair, swooping directly toward her.

She jerked her pillow over her head, instinctively shielding her face. Something cold and hard scraped over the backs of her fingers. The bloodcurdling volume and length of her scream surprised even her.

The flying thing came back, brushing against the side of her head. She screamed again. Swung her pillow at it. Scrambled out of the sleeping bag and jumped onto the floor, scrubbing viciously at her head while horrifying visions of filthy, rabid bats tangling in her hair pulled another scream from her throat.

It was stupid behavior. Somewhere in the back of her mind, she knew it was as ridiculous as standing on a chair and screaming at a tiny mouse. But she simply couldn't stop it. The only thing she felt grateful for at the moment was that Dillon wasn't here to see her acting like such an idiot.

At Blair's first scream, Dillon ripped open his sleeping bag without bothering to unzip it. At her second scream, he grabbed his rifle and charged out of the bushes, ignoring the pain of rocks and stickers jabbing into his bare feet and legs. Before her third scream ended, he'd kicked the rickety back door open and raced inside, rifle cocked and ready to kill the bear or mountain lion or whatever it was that had caused her to raise such a ruckus.

Adrenaline pumping and chest heaving, he skidded to a halt. A small creature darted past his head and on out the door, as if it were frantic to escape. After one look at Blair, he couldn't honestly say he blamed the poor thing. Wearing long underwear, she was hopping around in a demented grasshopper dance beside the bed, screaming and ripping at her hair with both hands with what looked like enough force to tear out whole tufts of it.

He set the rifle by the door, then cautiously approached her, speaking in a low, soothing voice, so as not to make her any more hysterical than she already was. "It's okay, Blair. It's gone now."

The grasshopper dance and hair-ruffling continued. She must not have heard him over the noise she was making. Hell, she wouldn't have heard a cannon over all that screaming.

He tapped her on the shoulder and had to duck when she slapped at him with both hands, as if fending off an attack. Grabbing her shoulders, he gave her a quick shake.

"Knock it off, DuMaine. It's just me."

Her scream broke off as suddenly as if he'd cut her vocal cords. Her arms froze in place, hands still raised in front of her face. Only her eyes moved, directing her gaze toward the sound of his voice. Recognition dawned in her eyes, and the fight-or-flight tension in her muscles slowly relaxed.

Inhaling a harsh, shuddering breath, she pulled out of his grasp, turned away and let out a soft groan.

"Are you all right, Blair?"

She nodded, but didn't speak.

"Did it bite you?"

She held both hands out to the dim light from the embers in the fireplace and examined them, then stuck them into the opposite armpits, hunched her shoulders up to her ears and slowly shook her head. "No. I, uh, don't think so. It just...startled me."

"Yeah. I guess it did."

She glanced over her shoulder at him. "What was it?"

"Don't know for sure. Probably a bat or a pygmy owl. If it's any consolation, you scared him every bit as much as he scared you."

She didn't crack so much as a whisper of a smile. "Are you going to say 'I told you so'?"

"Nah." He shrugged, hoping like hell she wasn't going to cry, but not at all certain what he could do to help her relax, beyond a little teasing. "It wouldn't be at all polite."

"Since when has that ever stopped you?"

"Since we started bein' friends, DuMaine. That was some scream you let out, though. Anybody ever tell you you've got a great set of pipes?"

She inhaled another deep breath and blew it out on a shaky laugh. Turning back around to face him, she gave him a crooked grin. Then her eyes widened, she gave him a quick, but thorough once-over, and her eyes took on a wicked glint.

"Looks like I startled you, too, McBride."

Dillon glanced down at himself and realized the only

thing standing between him and nudity was a pair of blue cotton briefs. The cabin suddenly seemed smaller. Warmer. More…intimate. Then her grin vanished. Her eyes narrowed to suspicious-looking slits.

"Hey, wait a minute. How did you get here so fast?" Propping her fists on her hip bones, she thrust her shoulders back and her chin up in a posture of righteous indignation. "You've been out there all along, spying on me. Haven't you?"

He nodded. "Yeah."

"You still think I'm incompetent."

The disappointment in her voice bothered him a lot more than her anger. He stepped closer, pried one of her fists off her hip and clasped it between his palms, refusing to let go when she tried to pull it away.

"Not true, DuMaine. You did real well, but you're not an experienced camper, and the mountains are always unpredictable. I just wanted to give you a little backup."

"Elizabeth didn't have any backup."

"Elizabeth didn't have any choice, or a movie to make in a couple of weeks. You do, honey."

The fight went out of her as quickly as it had appeared. In her eyes, a new awareness appeared, as if she'd suddenly remembered they were both standing there in their underwear. All alone in the middle of the night. Her gaze drifted down over his body, and she gulped loudly enough for him to hear it.

Dillon tried to focus on her face. Tried to forget what her naked breasts had looked like in the lantern light. Tried to will his randy body into submission.

He failed miserably. The wanting came back with a swift, hard vengeance. The blood rushed out of his head and into his groin so fast he felt dizzy.

Hesitantly she raised her free hand and painted a line of fire across his collarbones. His indrawn breath sounded harsh in his ears. Her fingertips moved on, tracing the contours of his chest, gently prodding at the muscles, twirling through the patches of wiry dark hair.

He grabbed her wayward hand and held it away from his skin before she could make him completely lose control. "Not a good idea, DuMaine."

She gazed at the front of his briefs with sincere admiration and no small trace of lust in her expression. "On the contrary, McBride, I think it's a great idea." Then she looked up into his eyes, gave him a smile that nearly melted his knees and drawled, "Don't worry, darlin', I'll be gentle with you."

He snorted at her promise. The more he thought about what she'd said and the way she'd said it, the more it tickled his funny bone. His snort became a chuckle. "Yeah, right. About as gentle as you were with that little ol' bat." He scrubbed at his hair and did a couple of steps from her grasshopper dance.

She snickered in response. His chuckle grew into a full-fledged laugh. Her snickering erupted into a chorus of giggles, which escalated his own laughter into an eye-watering, belly-clutching, foot-stomping fit. Near as he could tell, she laughed as maniacally as he did.

The next thing he knew, they'd collapsed onto the side of the old platform bed, hooting and hollering away tension and stress that must have been building up inside them both for months, if not years. Dillon couldn't remember the last time he'd laughed so long or so hard, but it sure felt good to cut loose. It felt even better to know Blair could cut loose with him, too.

He'd learned long ago, on the rodeo circuit, that shared pain could seal a friendship, but nothing sealed a friendship more quickly or completely than this kind of shared laughter.

By the time they subsided into occasional chuckles and snorts, he felt about as energetic as Blair's damp washcloth, hanging from a peg on the wall. Unfortunately, the night air was raising gooseflesh on his bare arms and legs, and

FREE BOOKS!

FREE GIFT!

PLAY THE "LUCKY 7" SLOT MACHINE GAME!

AND YOU CAN GET FREE BOOKS PLUS A FREE GIFT!

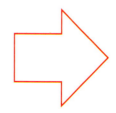

NO COST! NO OBLIGATION TO BUY!
NO PURCHASE NECESSARY!

PLAY "LUCKY 7"
AND GET FIVE FREE GIFTS!

HOW TO PLAY:

1. With a coin, carefully scratch off the silver box at the right. Then check the claim chart to see what we have for you—FREE BOOKS and a gift—ALL YOURS! ALL FREE!

2. Send back this card and you'll receive brand-new Silhouette Special Edition® novels. These books have a cover price of $3.99 each, but they are yours to keep absolutely free.

3. There's no catch. You're under no obligation to buy anything. We charge nothing—ZERO—for your first shipment. And you don't have to make any minimum number of purchases—not even one!

4. The fact is thousands of readers enjoy receiving books by mail from the Silhouette Reader Service™ months before they're available in stores. They like the convenience of home delivery and they love our discount prices!

5. We hope that after receiving your free books you'll want to remain a subscriber. But the choice is yours—to continue or cancel, anytime at all! So why not take us up on our invitation, with no risk of any kind. You'll be glad you did!

NOT ACTUAL SIZE

You'll love this exquisite necklace, set with an elegant simulated pearl pendant! It's the perfect accessory to dress up any outfit, casual or formal — and is yours ABSOLUTELY FREE when you accept our NO-RISK offer!

PLAY "LUCKY 7"

**Just scratch off the silver box with a coin.
Then check below to see the gifts you get.**

YES! I have scratched off the silver box. Please send me all the gifts for which I qualify. I understand I am under no obligation to purchase any books, as explained on the back and on the opposite page.

235 CIS CA97
(U-SIL-SE-09/97)

NAME

ADDRESS   APT.

CITY   STATE   ZIP

7 7 7   **WORTH FOUR FREE BOOKS PLUS A FREE SIMULATED PEARL HEART PENDANT**

🍒🍒🍒   **WORTH THREE FREE BOOKS**

   WORTH TWO FREE BOOKS

🔔🔔🍒   **WORTH ONE FREE BOOK**

If offer card is missing, write to: Silhouette Reader Service, 3010 Walden Ave., PO Box 1867, Buffalo, NY 14240-1867

BUSINESS REPLY MAIL

FIRST-CLASS MAIL   PERMIT NO. 717   BUFFALO, NY

POSTAGE WILL BE PAID BY ADDRESSEE

SILHOUETTE READER SERVICE
3010 WALDEN AVE
PO BOX 1867
BUFFALO NY 14240-9952

NO POSTAGE
NECESSARY
IF MAILED
IN THE
UNITED STATES

he knew that if he didn't leave soon, he would turn to Blair for warmth. And then he probably wouldn't leave at all.

Right now, it didn't seem like that would be such a horrendous mistake, but the combination of firelight, privacy and a potent sexual attraction had never been known to improve anyone's judgment. But when he started to get up, she grabbed his elbow and pulled him back down beside her.

"Please, stay with me."

Her big, vulnerable eyes and soft, sultry voice woke up every hormone in his body. Still, responsible idiot that he was, he had to try to make her see reason. Not to mention himself.

"We agreed we weren't gonna have a...romance, Blair."

"We don't have to. But I'll be scared all by myself, Dillon. Couldn't you just bring your stuff into the cabin and sleep in here?"

A marble statue with no heart at all wouldn't have been able to refuse her request. Though a certain part of his anatomy was about as hard as marble, and he knew it would be torture to be in the same room with her all night without touching her, the rest of him suddenly felt as soft and malleable as a toasted marshmallow. Dang woman had a way of doing that to him.

Giving her a quick nod, and a gruff "Yeah, okay," he headed out the back door to collect his gear. He just hoped and prayed Blair would settle down and go right to sleep. He figured he'd already demonstrated enough restraint tonight to qualify for sainthood. If she tempted him again, she was liable to find him fresh out of nobility.

Chapter Ten

Perhaps this wasn't such a good idea, Blair thought, staring across the room. Barely visible in the dim light from the banked fire, Dillon was a big, long lump on the floor. A cranky, big, long lump, judging by the negative vibes rolling off him like the waves at Malibu. Bat or owl, whatever that creature had been, it would have been a more pleasant companion than Dillon was at this moment.

She wanted the other guy back—the one who had laughed so uproariously with her. The one who had teased her, but not in a way that shamed her for being afraid. The one who had come charging to her rescue in his underwear.

The mental image that last thought produced made her want to groan with frustration. Dillon McBride was sexy enough fully clothed. In his cotton briefs, he was, to be blunt, a stud muffin.

If she had ever wanted a man this much, it had been a very, *very* long time ago. Long before she'd been disillusioned about love and learned the truth about why men pursued her. His potent sexuality aside, she supposed she found Dillon so attractive simply because he didn't want anything from her.

After all, he hadn't sought her out. He had no desire for an acting career. He didn't appear to be obsessed with money, status or notoriety, which was more than she could say for her ex-husband. If all he felt for her was lust, at least it was an honest lust.

She could respect that, even like it in a purely egotistical, sexual sort of way. What if he was the only man she would ever meet who wanted her for herself alone? Or was that a rationalization because she was feeling a bit...lusty herself at the moment?

Sighing in disgust, she rolled onto her other side, facing away from him. The sleeping bag twisted around her legs, there was a hard bump under her hip, and her pillow felt hot and lumpy. Every now and then, an imaginary—God, she hoped it was imaginary—spider crawled over her feet and ankles.

She sat up, combed her tangled hair out of her face with one hand and righted the sleeping bag with the other. Then she turned her pillow over to the cool side and punched at the more prominent lumps. Just as she was about to lie down again and try to go to sleep for the hundredth time, the lump on the floor spoke in a low, long-suffering voice.

"What the hell is wrong *now*, DuMaine?"

"I can't sleep."

"Why not?"

"I just can't." She sounded as cranky as he did, but she couldn't help it. It was his fault she felt so restless, after all. But she could hardly tell him that. "Go to sleep, Dillon."

"A dead man couldn't sleep with all that thrashin' around over there." He sat up, sighed like a man straining to hold on to his very last scrap of patience and rubbed one hand down over his face. "Talk, DuMaine. What's got you all tied up in knots?"

Glad for the cover of darkness that would hide her expression from him as much as it hid his from her, she rolled her eyes at the ceiling. "Nothing. I'm sorry I disturbed you."

"Sorry won't cut it when we have to get up and go to work in four hours."

"Message received. I'll be quiet."

"No, you won't. Once you've got something in your craw, you're about as quiet as a flock of magpies. Now, what's gravelin' your drawers?"

She choked back a laugh at his colorful—and accurate—turn of phrase. Then, to her consternation, tears suddenly filled her eyes. Furiously swiping at them with the back of her hand, she inhaled a quick, shallow breath. "I'm, uh, fine, Dillon."

There was a long pause. When he spoke again, his voice had taken on a wary edge. "You don't sound fine."

"Well, I am. Really. I was just feeling a bit...lonely."

"How can you be lonely? I've been right here for over an hour."

She had to pause and take another breath or risk letting go of a sob. She didn't want him to come closer and see her distress. She would either grab him and cling like a lost child, or jump his bones, which he obviously didn't want her to do. He wouldn't have pushed her away before, come back into the cabin fully dressed and gone to bed that way otherwise.

"Yes, I know. And please, don't think I don't appreciate it. It's just...I just..."

"Just what?"

She couldn't go on. Wasn't even sure what she would have said if she'd been able to continue. She gulped. Shook her head. Lay down again and turned her face to the wall.

After a moment of silence, his sleeping bag rustled. She squeezed her eyes tightly shut, willing the disconcerting tears away. It didn't work, of course, and then a strong but gentle hand grasped her shoulder and turned her over to face him.

Frowning, Dillon sat down beside her and traced the rivulet of tears silently sliding down her right cheek. Oh, damn. Seeing any woman cry made his guts hurt. Seeing Blair cry gave him heartburn, too.

"Hey, what's this?" he asked softly, refusing to let her push his hand away from her face.

"N-n-nothing. J-j-just l-l-leave m-me alone," she said, sobbing.

"That doesn't make sense. If you're lonesome, the last thing you need is to be left alone. What you really need is a friend, and lucky you, here I am, reporting for duty."

He'd thought all his silly yakking would at least make her stop crying, maybe even smile, if he was lucky. Instead, she sat up and glared at him through a fresh flood of tears.

"Oh, shut up, McBride." She wiped the backs of her knuckles under her eyes. "You don't understand anything."

"Well, I'm tryin' to. Why don't you explain it to me? In clear, simple terms even a guy like me can understand."

Sniffling, she drew herself up as tall as she could, then looked straight into his eyes. "Being your friend isn't enough. I want you to be my lover. There, is that clear enough?"

He gulped. His body surged in response. He gulped again. "Yeah. Clear as crystal."

She kept right on looking at him, and he couldn't look away. The room filled with tension. Expectation. Anticipation. And still she held his gaze, letting the silence stretch on and on and on, as if she intended to sit there forever, if that was what it took to get an answer out of him.

"I don't want you to have regrets and end up hatin' me," he said.

"That won't happen."

"Aw, come on, Blair. You had a whole list of reasons this would never work in the long run. Remember?"

She slowly shook her head. "All I can remember is what a wonderful kisser you are. And how safe I felt when you held me. And how much I want you to hold me and kiss me again."

"But—"

Slowly, gravely, she shook her head again. "I'm not asking for a commitment, Dillon. No promises. No regrets. I'm not convinced love lasts a lifetime anymore, but I want whatever time I can have with you."

He shut his eyes as tightly as he could, but that didn't block out the fierce leap of pleasure her words gave him. Then he opened his eyes and looked at her. What he found in her big, beautiful eyes was desire. Nothing but pure, sweet, unadulterated desire.

"Dammit, DuMaine, you don't play fair," he whispered.

"All's fair in love and war, McBride," she whispered back, reaching for him. "Let's have a mad, glorious affair."

In a dim corner of his mind, he wondered if their affair would end in love or war, but when their lips met and he felt the tip of her tongue enter his mouth, all conscious thought ended. Burying his fingers in her soft hair, he forgot about his scars, who she was and all the other reasons he shouldn't be doing this, and let instincts as old as humanity take over.

With hands faster than a calf roper's, he had her stripped and stretched out on her back beside him. He braced himself on one elbow and just feasted his eyes on her for a moment. Lord, but she was gorgeous. The weeks of hard physical labor had honed her slender figure down to long, sleek lines.

She gave him a tremulous smile and murmured, "Touch me, Dillon. Please, touch me."

He slowly traced each delightful curve and hollow, each warm, womanly part of her. Her husky moans and sighs of pleasure made his body surge again with gut-wrenching need. He gritted his teeth and forced himself to take his time.

He'd wanted this since that day back in March when she helped him with the orphaned calf. Making love to Blair was not an experience he intended to rush through, no matter how much his hormones clamored for release.

And man, oh, man, were they ever clamoring. Only problem was, Blair didn't seem to understand the sacrifice he was trying to make. She hooked one hand around the back of his neck and pulled him down for another scorching kiss.

Then her hands were all over him, stroking his hair, his ears and his neck, petting his chest and back and sides, sneaking under the waistband of his jeans and briefs until he knew he was going to lose what little control he had left.

A ferocious urge to roll her onto her back, plunge inside her and finish it hammered at him. She was as hot as he was—so hot, in fact, that he didn't think it would take much to send her over the edge with him. But there was something he had to remember, something he had to do.

Yanking his lips from hers, he inhaled a deep breath through his mouth so that her scent couldn't seduce him. The infusion of oxygen cleared his brain long enough for a scrap of sanity to return. Before it could slip away again, he lunged off the bed.

Blair reached for him. He took her hand, kissed her fingers and squeezed them, fervently promised he'd be back in a flash. Then he tore himself away and raced across the room to his gear.

It took longer to find what he needed than he'd expected. By the time he returned to the bed, Blair was up on one elbow with the sleeping bag tucked tightly around her, eyeing him with a wary expression that made him feel like a first-class jerk for destroying the mood.

"Don't look at me like that," he said softly. "I said I'd be right back, and here I am."

"What were you doing, Dillon?"

He held up the strip of foil packets that had slid to the very bottom of his saddlebags. "Tryin' to find these."

Her lower jaw dropped open in surprise for a moment. Then she closed it, and a blush climbed from her collarbones, up her neck and into her face. "How thoughtful. So tell me, Dillon, why did you really come back up here tonight? Were you expecting to get lucky?"

"Nope." He came to the bed, settled in beside her and laid his head on the other half of the pillow. "I know what you're thinkin', but you're wrong. I'll admit the idea of making love to you crossed my mind plenty of times, but I never *expected* it to happen. I just thought if it ever did, the least I could do was be responsible and protect you from gettin' pregnant."

"Really?" The corners of her mouth turned up just a tad. It was all the encouragement he needed to pull her back into his arms.

"Well, who seduced *who* tonight?" he asked. "If you hadn't started screamin' your head off at that poor little critter, you never would've known I was out there."

She blushed again, then chuckled softly. "Yeah, McBride, I see your point. I've been acting like a dope, huh?"

"A little contrary, maybe." He grinned at her. "Can't say as I blame you, though. You've had me all confused since day one. Most days I want to wring your neck one minute and kiss you senseless the next. Know what I mean?"

"Oh, yes, I'm familiar with both urges." With a wicked smile, she laid her hand flat on his chest and pushed him onto his back. "And since, as you so ungallantly pointed out, I'm the one who seduced you, I'll expect you to be quiet and cooperate."

"Yes, ma'am. Anything you s—"

To his surprise, she didn't actually say much more with words, but, Lord have mercy, did she ever communicate. This wasn't a woman who needed coaxing and wooing, not that there was anything wrong with that. But there was something mighty nice about making love with a woman who wasn't bashful about letting a man know what pleased her.

And he loved pleasing her. He loved the way her soft skin heated at his slightest touch, the little cries of pleasure that came from the back of her throat, the swift, urgent caresses she gave him, as if she couldn't touch him enough to satisfy herself. It had been so long since a woman touched him in passion.

The truth was, he just plain loved Blair, and he might as well admit it.

He rolled on top of her and nuzzled her breasts, inhaling her warm, distinctive scent so deeply into his nose and lungs that it made him dizzy. Then he strung a chain of kisses down her torso and, since she was sort of a ticklish little thing, he slung one leg over her thighs to hold her still while he worked his way from one hipbone, across her belly, to the other. He did love the way she writhed.

Before he could go any farther south, she grabbed both sides of his head and pulled him up for a hot, wet, drugging kiss. In her arms, he felt like the man he used to be. He forgot about his scars and all the people who had turned away from him in horror. He saw the man he could have been if his life hadn't taken such a sour turn, the man he probably would have been.

Turning them both onto their sides, facing each other, he twined the fingers of his right hand into her hair and deepened the kisses even more. Then he let his left hand roam, revisiting his favorite spots on her body—breasts, bottom, thighs, waist, hips—listening for those little hitches in her breathing that meant she really liked something.

For the first time in more years than he cared to remember, he felt a sense of…possibilities. Of horizons broader than Sunshine Gap. Of hope that maybe he wouldn't have to live out the rest of his life alone; if he couldn't have Blair for a lifetime, maybe, someday, somehow, somewhere out there, he would find another woman who wouldn't see his scars.

But the future would keep. Right now, the only thing that mattered was Blair. He intended to follow her lead and enjoy every blessed minute he could have with her. And if he couldn't be her last lover, he damn well intended to be the best one she ever had. Gently pulling his mouth away from hers, he headed south again.

If it was possible to die of pleasure, she was doomed, Blair thought, gazing up into Dillon's eyes. Dark bedroom eyes. Loving eyes. Hypnotic eyes, intently studying her face as if searching out her most secret, erotic fantasies.

And his hands...oh, God, his clever, clever hands. Gentle one moment, just a little rough the next. Always arousing, always strong, stroking her with the same sense of confidence he used when he worked with his animals.

No wonder the cats and dogs followed him around the ranch, vying for his attention. A little more pressure here, a hint of a squeeze there—he explored her body with a slow, deliberate thoroughness that would have made her blush if it didn't feel so wonderful. He knew just how to touch her in order to stimulate pleasure points below the surface of her skin.

And he was patient. Lord, was he patient. There were times when she found the slower pace of country life irritating beyond belief. This was not one of them.

She gasped his name when his lips closed over the tip of her breast, instinctively arching toward him, clasping his head with both hands. His thick, dark hair slid through her fingers, and she wanted to rub her cheek against it, bury her lips in it. What a crime it was for a man with such nice hair to cover it with a hat all the time, even if the hat was a Stetson.

He laughed when she told him so, the sound a low, raspy rumble that vibrated over her dampened nipples and made her shiver. He laughed again, then rolled to his back and settled her in a straddling position on top of him, as easily as he tossed around the big hay bales she could barely lift. He was an earthy, physical man, and he took such obvious delight in her body and her reactions to his loving, she found it amazingly easy to shed her inhibitions.

With his eyes glinting wickedly, he drawled bawdy suggestions to her and groaned with approval when she carried them out. Nothing was too outrageous, too daring, too inventive, for this man. Seeing him in this mood was like meeting a younger, more playful Dillon—the appealing, laughing man she'd glimpsed in the photographs stored with his trophies.

It wasn't so much a question of what went where, or who did what to whom; it was a shared sexual quest, unlike anything she had ever known. With Dillon, giving pleasure was a pleasure in and of itself, and he was not a man who did anything in moderation. Whether he was working on the ranch or making love, it appeared his motto was that nothing counted if you didn't put your whole heart and soul behind it.

And he was tireless in his efforts. The superb physical conditioning that gave him impressive strength and endurance at work served him equally well in bed. Yes, she was going to die of pleasure, but she wasn't going to die alone. Not when she could have such fun taking him with her. She started to laugh.

"What's so funny?" he asked between kisses across the backs of her knees.

"Oh, nothing, Dillon." She flashed him a smile over her shoulder. "I'm just planning new ways to torture you when I've recovered."

He raised his head and wiggled his eyebrows at her. "Kinky ways?" He started kissing his way up the back of her left thigh.

"Kinky? You dare call *me* kinky?" She yelped when he gently nipped her buttock with his teeth, then sat up, meeting him in midair for a kiss that left them both trembling. "Look who's talking about kinky."

"Hey, all I did was lick your toes a little. You're the one who yodeled loud enough to scare all the deer off the mountain."

Giggling against his smiling lips, she wrapped her arms around his neck and lay back, pulling him up beside her on the hopelessly rumpled sleeping bag. Turning into his embrace seemed natural and right, as if this were the one place in the world where she truly belonged. She nuzzled the wiry hair on his chest. He rested his chin against the top of her head and exhaled a deep sigh that somehow echoed the utter contentment she felt.

If she hadn't been in love with him before, she certainly was now. Given her track record with men, the thought should have terrified her, but it didn't. No matter what happened, she could never regret loving Dillon.

He sighed again and pulled her closer. His breathing slowed and deepened. She dozed in the comfort of his arms, rousing a few moments later when she heard him mutter something.

"What was that, Dillon?" she asked.

He muttered again, the words so slurred she still couldn't understand them. The only one that sounded even halfway clear was "quicksand," which made no sense to her at all. He was frowning, though, and knowing how much he needed rest, she wanted to soothe him if she could.

"It's all right, love," she whispered, smoothing his hair back off his forehead. "There's no quicksand here."

Chapter Eleven

At the familiar sound of Sunny's hooves trotting into the clearing, Blair swung the ax one last time, burying the blade in the chopping block. Then she straightened and rubbed the small of her back with both hands. Her heart automatically leaped into her throat at the sight of the big palomino gelding, and her mouth automatically smiled at the big man on the horse's back.

She loved the easy smile he gave her in return. And what was that in his right hand? A bouquet of wildflowers? How incredibly sweet.

The past two weeks had been nothing short of a revelation about Elizabeth and Riley, about relationships and about herself. She had never known living with a man could be so intense, or so much fun. Nor had she known she could love anyone as much as she loved Dillon.

She had used her days at the cabin well, and she no longer felt dreadfully awkward when she did the chores. After Dillon rode away every morning, she tended to her work, coped as best she could with whatever happened and enjoyed her time to think and make mistakes without an audience. She was rarely conscious of feeling lonely, but when Dillon came back at suppertime and she could talk to him, touch him and kiss him, her world suddenly felt...complete.

He rode Sunny right up to her, and with the delightful agility and strength she had come to expect from him, he swung himself to the ground, swept her into a bear hug and spun her around, kissing her until her heart thundered and her toes curled. By the time he set her back on her own feet, her head was swimming crazily, whether with dizziness or passion, she couldn't have said. Nor did she care.

"Hi," she murmured, sighing with pleasure against his lips.

He hugged her tightly, surrounding her with warmth and the smell of man, horse and leather. "Hi, yourself. Have a good day?"

"Yeah. How 'bout you?"

"Not bad." He chuckled at her. "You're startin' to sound just like one of us, DuMaine." Pulling back slightly, he handed her the bouquet. "Thought you might enjoy a little color in the cabin."

"Oh, Dillon, thank you." She buried her face in the flowers, inhaled deeply, then smiled up at him. "They're lovely."

A flush rose out of his open shirt collar, coloring his neck and ears. "Don't get all mushy on me, now. Most of 'em are just weeds."

"Don't you dare call them that." With a mock-indignant sniff, Blair carried the bouquet into the cabin. She poked through the garbage sack until she found the small pickle jar she'd emptied at lunch, rinsed it out and filled it with fresh water she'd hauled from the creek but hadn't boiled yet. Then she arranged the flowers in it, set it in the middle of the table and stepped back to admire the result.

It was difficult to believe how thoroughly unpleasant

she'd once found him; impossible to believe he was even the same man who'd been such a wretch that first morning at the corral. But she was on to him now. Beneath that gruff exterior beat the soft heart of a true romantic.

It didn't matter if he'd brought her weeds or flowers. She knew from personal experience how long and hard Dillon worked every day. To think he'd taken the time to dismount, something a cowboy never did if he could avoid it, and collect them for her—one at a time, from a hot, dusty hillside, no doubt—meant more than any outrageously expensive arrangement delivered from a professional florist's shop.

God, how she loved him.

She couldn't tell him yet. She'd promised him no regrets, and what she promised, she delivered. But perhaps someday she *would* tell him. Because he loved her, too. He appeared to, anyway.

He probably wasn't completely aware of it yet; the words had never passed his lips. But the love was there. She had seen it in his eyes, heard it in his voice, felt it in his touch, and not only when he made love to her. For a man like Dillon, those wildflowers were as good as any declaration in a church.

Swallowing at the sudden lump in her throat, she went back outside and joined him at the makeshift corral behind the cabin. Molly had come over to greet Sunny, and Blair petted both horses while Dillon unfastened the panniers lashed to the back of his saddle. Curious to see what he'd brought, she reached for one of the canvas bags, but he grabbed it before she could pick it up and set it behind him.

"No peeking. I'm cookin' tonight, and it's a surprise. Why don't you go take a dip in the creek? By the time you get back, I'll have supper on the table."

She raised an eyebrow at him. "Are you suggesting I need a bath, Mr. McBride? Or is this just another one of your attempts to get me naked and have your wicked way with me?"

He puffed out his chest, and his grin stretched into a lascivious smile. "You really think my ways are wicked?"

"Terribly wicked."

"Yeah, and that's why you like 'em."

"You've got that right."

With his laughter caressing her ears, she stacked the wood she'd just chopped, then went back inside to collect her towel, biodegradable soap and shampoo and fresh clothes. She had quickly learned to hate hauling water, but she couldn't bring herself to adopt the nineteenth-century tradition of limiting herself to a Saturday-night bath. She compromised with a fast dip in the cold creek and took her time combing out her hair and letting it dry in the last lingering rays of the sun.

Delicious smells met her at the cabin's front door. Stepping inside, she paused to absorb the scene Dillon had set for her. The jar of flowers still sat in the center of the table, but now a red-and-white-checked tablecloth covered the scarred wood. Real dishes and silverware graced their usual places across from each other. An opened bottle of red wine sat between a pair of long-stemmed glasses.

Clutching a metal spatula, he stood guard at the camp stove, looking lost in thought watching thick steaks and sliced potatoes sizzle in cast iron skillets. He jumped when she dropped her dirty clothes beside the panniers and crossed the room. Dillon might be a closet romantic, but this was all a bit much. Something smelled fishy here, and it wasn't the food.

"What's going on, Dillon?"

"Huh?" He looked over at her and smiled quickly. Too quickly. "Oh, uh, nothin', Blair."

She gestured at the table, then the wine bottle. "This wouldn't be your idea of a last-night celebration, would it?"

His guilty expression said it all. "Aw, shoot, I wasn't gonna tell you until tomorrow morning. How did you guess?"

Sighing in resignation, she crossed the room and stood beside him. "I suppose I simply realized something as wonderful as these past two weeks have been couldn't last."

"Yeah, it's been nice, all right." He turned over the potatoes and poked at the steaks. "But from the look of things at the ranch, I'd say the party's just about over, hon."

She wrapped her arms around him from behind and rested her cheek against his back. "So, what's going on?"

"You've got equipment rollin' in every day, and more and more folks are showin' up."

"Anyone I should know about?"

"Marsh called this afternoon and said he and your cousin Hope will arrive sometime tonight."

"Oh, dear."

Dillon glanced over his shoulder at her. "What's that supposed to mean?"

Wondering what her irrepressible cousin was into at the moment, Blair laughed and shook her head. "You'll have to meet Hope to understand. She's a little...different."

"Different how?"

Blair released Dillon and headed for the wine bottle. Hope could drive a fanatical prohibitionist to drink. "Well, she's a bit...flamboyant."

"Define *flamboyant* in plain English. Does she dress really weird, or what?"

"I suppose it depends on where you live. She's perfectly stylish in L.A. In Sunshine Gap—" Blair laughed, shook her head again, and poured herself a generous glass of wine "—well, most people here will think she dresses weird. She can be awfully entertaining, but she's usually quite harmless. Unless her hair is black, of course."

"What's wrong with black hair?"

Blair drank deeply from her wineglass. "It looks wonderful on you and your family, Dillon, but Hope colors her hair to match her moods. If it's black, I would assume she's extremely angry with someone and plotting revenge. Then I need to watch her very carefully.''

''Has she ever hurt anyone?''

''Oh, heavens, no, she would never physically hurt a living thing.'' Blair drained her glass. ''She's even a vegetarian. But she can be hell on property, and she has a knack for embarrassing people who upset her.''

Blair poured herself another glass of wine and filled one for Dillon. He took it, gave her a silent toast, then swallowed a hefty gulp.

''How long do you think she'll stay?'' he asked.

''With Hope, one never knows. She might stay until we're done shooting. Or she could leave by the end of the week.''

Dillon grinned. ''I'll try real hard not to tick her off.'' Then his expression sobered, and he said quietly, ''If you'd rather not tell her about...us...''

''She's not only my cousin, she's my best friend. Why wouldn't I tell her about us?''

He gave a shrug that looked entirely too nonchalant to be sincere. ''Well, you know, I just thought it might be a little awkward, is all. I mean, I'm probably not your usual type.''

Anger rose up inside Blair so fast she nearly choked on it, but she forced herself to speak in a calm, reasonably rational tone. ''Does this have anything to do with your scars, Dillon?''

''Yeah. So what?''

''So what? So, are you thinking I might be ashamed to have my cousin see us together?''

''You wouldn't be the first, Blair. Hell, why do you think my wife left me? And you know, your cousin and all those other folks are from Hollywood. I understand they put a lot of stock in how a person looks.''

''Wait a minute, Dillon. Back up. Did you just say your wife left you when you were hurt?''

''Oh, she waited until the bandages came off. But once

she got a look at the damage and figured out I'd never look the same again..." He shrugged, then raised his right hand, turning it as if to remind her of his missing thumb. "Well, then she told me it was bad enough havin' to let me touch her with this ugly thing, but she'd be damned if she'd spend the rest of her life lookin' at this god-awful face."

Unable to believe the sheer cruelty of what she'd heard, Blair stared at him for an agonizing, seemingly endless moment. Then fury shot through her again, propelling her across the room to stand directly in front of Dillon. Exchanging glare for glare with him, she yelled at him, repeatedly stabbing her index finger into his hard chest to punctuate her sentences.

"I am *not* like her, Dillon McBride. I have never *been* like her and I will never *be* like her. And so help me God, if you *ever* dare again even to *think* that I might be like her in any way, I'll...I'll... Well, I will just be so completely livid with you, I will tan your hide and nail it to the barn door. And then, I'll never speak to you again. I am not ashamed to be your lover, I'm *damned* proud of it. *Is* that clear?"

She had no idea how long he just stood there, looking deeply into her eyes, but she wanted to weep when he finally picked up the finger she had been poking him with and kissed it. Then the sides of his mouth curved into a slow, heartbreakingly sweet smile and he said in a ragged voice, "Yes, ma'am. It's real clear. And you'll never know how much I appreciate it."

"Oh, Dillon." Her voice wobbled. "I don't want to go back to the ranch, if everything's going to change between us."

Carefully setting down his wineglass and spatula, he turned off the burners on the camp stove, clasped her face between his palms and kissed her. "Now, darlin', you've got a movie to make. You really don't have any choice."

"But you'll leave me. I know you will, because you'll be uncomfortable with so many strangers around."

He scrunched up his nose as he thought about it. "Well, yeah, it'll be uncomfortable for me, but hell, I can handle it. I was really more worried over how you'd feel about the gossip that's liable to fly around if folks find out we're...together."

Blair huffed in disgust. "Honestly, after an extremely well-publicized divorce, do you think I'm not used to gossip? According to the tabloids, I've had sex with animals and aliens. One cowboy shouldn't cause any scandal."

"Animals and aliens, huh?" Dillon snorted with laughter. "So, uh, how do I compare with the aliens?"

"Oh, do shut up, McBride."

He picked her up and carried her over to one of the chairs at the table, nuzzling at the juncture of her neck and shoulder. "Come on, DuMaine, you can tell me. I'm bigger, right? You know, where it really counts?"

Giggling, she hunched her shoulder up to her ear. He sat down with her on his lap and nibbled at the other side of her neck. "And what do those alien guys look like? Are they green? Do they have special...parts?"

"Oh, stop," she begged, torn between laughter and a sob. "I mean it, Dillon. If it wouldn't offend your family, I really want you to stay with me when we go back to the ranch. Please? So I won't be scared in the night?"

He rested his forehead against hers and rubbed his left hand over her back in a soothing motion. "I'd like that, Blair. We'll have to be discreet around the kids, but you're the best thing that's happened to me in years. The very best. As long as you're here, we just won't let anything get in our way."

She searched his face, wanting desperately to believe him. He looked back at her with equal desperation, and she realized her doubts must have shown in her expression when he cursed under his breath, then pulled her close again and kissed her until she could barely breathe. She clung to his shoulders, as if somehow she could grasp and hold on to the happiness she had known here for such a brief time. With him.

It had been like a honeymoon, only better, and despite their brave words, she was still terribly afraid everything would change when the rest of the cast and crew arrived. His feverish kisses told her he shared her fear. They weren't ready for this. *She* wasn't ready. Why couldn't Hope and Marsh have waited? All she wanted was a few more days alone with Dillon.

The world tilted when he slid one arm behind her knees, scooped her up against his chest and carried her to the bed. Kissing her. Caressing her. And the love was there, an unspoken, shimmering thing between them.

With their mouths still fused, he lay down beside her. They tore at each other's clothes, needing to get closer, hungry for skin-to-skin contact, starving for the reassurance only a union of flesh could give them in this moment. And the love was there, convincing them both that it was real and alive and attainable.

She opened herself to him, welcomed him, held him fiercely, as if someone or something might enter their small haven and rip him from her arms. She rose to meet him, kiss for kiss, stroke for stroke, and they reached that elusive pinnacle of completion with gasps and groans and shouts, and then settled back with sighs and murmurs and shared smiles of satisfaction. And the love was there, uniting them in body and in spirit in a way nothing else ever could achieve.

It was so basic, almost primitive. A reaffirmation of everything they'd shared. They had not imagined this magical world with just the two of them. They could have it again, if they reached out to each other. Trusted each other. Loved each other enough.

She was tempted to tell him how she felt. So tempted, the words clustered on the tip of her tongue. She framed his face with her hands. He closed his eyes and turned his head, planting a kiss on her palm. It was a sweet, affectionate gesture, but when he severed the connection of their shared gaze and then rolled onto his side, all semblance of courage abandoned her.

She was prone to idealizing relationships, and she'd been wrong about men before. What if she was wrong about Dillon? What if he didn't love her at all? Maybe he didn't want anything from Hollywood, but what if all he wanted from her was sex?

He settled her head on his shoulder, wrapped his arm around her and pulled her snugly against his side, then rubbed his whiskery cheek against her hair with all the enjoyment of a big cat. She told all the scared, paranoid little voices inside her head to go away and leave her alone. What she and Dillon had shared over the past two weeks was more than sex. Way more.

No promises. No regrets. Dillon was starting to hate those words, but he figured they were a pretty good way to remind himself of the boundary between fantasy and reality.

Lying here in the cabin, in the middle of the night, with Blair cuddled up next to him all warm and naked and sleepy...well, he should get down on his knees and thank the good Lord for letting him have the past two weeks. He'd found a deeper, richer, more satisfying life in that fourteen days with Blair than he'd ever known in four years of marriage to Jill. It would be way too easy to want more—tons more—than she ever would be able to give him.

She was everything he could have asked for in a lover and in a friend. The thought of taking her back down the mountain in the morning and sharing her with the rest of the world made him feel possessive and stingy and all sorts of other emotions he had no business feeling. But he would do it—with a smile on his face—for her.

Somehow, he would deal with all those damned strangers, and he would love Blair each and every day she was here. And when the filming was done, he would let her go without a word of complaint.

No promises. No regrets. That was their agreement, and he would honor it. Even if it killed him.

Chapter Twelve

When they rode out of the foothills the next day, the first person Dillon saw was Hope DuMaine. Coming out of the biggest dang motor home he'd ever seen, she was a skinny little thing, dressed all in black, from her neck to her spit-shined, pointy-toed high-heeled boots. Must be Rodeo Drive's idea of western chic. She also wore more makeup than Grace and Alex would use in a year, and what was probably at least half of the entire Navajo nation's inventory of silver-and-turquoise jewelry.

With her short, spiky royal blue hair, a squash-blossom necklace that covered most of her chest, earrings dangling to her shoulders, bracelets on both wrists, a ring on every finger and long, shiny blue-painted talons, she was an amazing sight for Sunshine Gap, or any other town in Wyoming. Hell, she could've fooled him into thinking it was Halloween.

The instant she spotted Blair, she started hooting and yelling as if Blair had spent two years on Mars instead o two weeks in a cabin. "Blair! Blair, darling! It's me, Hope! Oh my gosh, girl, you look absolutely fabulous! Yeeee-haw!"

"So that's your cousin." Dillon shot Blair a pained look. "Tell me she didn't really say, 'Yee-haw.'"

"Yup, she sure did," Blair replied with an unperturbed smile. "Give her a chance, Dillon. She's actually quite sweet."

"Uh-huh. If you say so. Love that blue hair."

Blair's eyebrows drew together in that fierce universal scowl mothers use to warn children to behave. After turning it on Dillon for a moment, she nudged Molly into a trot. Figuring he might as well go along for the ride, Dillon signaled Sunny to follow.

"Yes! Yes, Blair! Ride 'em, cowgirl! Yeeee-haw!" Hope jumped up and down and waved so hard she looked in danger of falling off the motor home's steps.

Blair rode up to the rig, draped one forearm across the saddle horn and drawled, "Careful there, cousin. You'll spook the horses if you keep yellin' that loud."

Hope clasped both hands to her bosom and spoke to a companion only she could see. "Oh, my woooord, she's even got the drawl. Her parents, *the DuMaines*, are going to weep with envy when they catch this act."

Laughing, Blair dismounted. Dillon followed suit and took Molly's reins while the cousins embraced. Gut already clenching, he steeled himself for Hope's inevitable reaction when she saw his scars. Judging by her behavior so far, she'd probably be dramatic as hell about it. He'd just as soon get it over with while Blair was the only other person around to hear her screech.

Blair pulled out of the hug first. Hope turned to Dillon, looking up into his face with a smile. As he'd expected, her eyes widened and her mouth dropped open. To his shock, however, instead of pulling back, politely glancing away or trying to pretend she hadn't noticed anything un-usual, Hope stepped closer and raised her hand. Before he could jerk out of her reach, she gently traced the lines on his cheek with the honest curiosity of a child.

"Wow, dude," she said, her voice hushed, "you must have had one hellacious wipeout to get that hummer." Then she grinned at him. "Hi, I'm Hope. And you're Dillon."

Stunned speechless, Dillon gulped and nodded, which turned out to be the only encouragement Hope needed to continue a conversation. "Marsh told me you had some scars, but I didn't realize they were so awesome. How did you get them?"

"Uh, Hope," Blair said, placing one hand on her cousin's shoulder, "some people might consider that a rude question."

Hope's eyes widened again, and her mouth dropped open in exactly the same expression of surprise she'd had at the sight of Dillon's scars. "Really? Oh, I'm sorry, I didn't mean to be rude. I just find people so terribly interesting, don't you?"

Dillon cleared his throat and stepped back, but he couldn't dredge up any serious anger at this quirky little gal. She really did seem interested, and as near as he could tell, there wasn't any guile in those big gray eyes of hers, and no malice, either. "Yeah. I guess. Sometimes."

"So?" Hope said. "How did you get the scars?"

"Car wreck."

"Windshield?"

Dillon shook his head. "Fence. Barbed wire."

She grimaced. "Nasty. Were you alone?"

"No. My brother-in-law was there."

"You must mean Grace's husband?"

"Yeah. He died. From the wreck, I mean."

Hope reached out and squeezed his forearm in sympathy. "I'm so sorry. That must have been terribly sad for you."

Dillon wasn't sure *sad* was the word he would've chosen, but he found himself nodding at Hope anyhow. He just couldn't look into those utterly sincere eyes of hers and not respond. "It was a long time ago."

She squeezed his arm again, then smiled at him and gave Blair a one-armed hug. "I see you've been taking good care of our darling Blair. We are ever so much obliged."

Dillon gave a mental shake at the sudden change of topic, stuck his tongue firmly into his cheek and tipped his hat for her. If Blair's cousin wanted to do the cowboy thing, he didn't see any profit in disappointing her. "Just doin' my job, ma'am."

Hope rolled her eyes, swayed and grasped the handrail as if she suddenly felt faint. "Oh, you cowboys, you're so...my goodness, you're just so...cute, I swear—"

"Whoa, Hope. Down, girl." Laughing, Blair supported Hope's suddenly limp body with one arm. "Find your own cowboy. He's taken."

"Oooh, gossip?" Straightening, Hope raised her hands in front of her chest and wiggled her fingers like a manic typist, her blue nails glinting in the sunlight. "Do tell. And don't spare any details."

"And let you write about my private life in one of your racy books?" Blair demanded, imitating Hope's speech and mannerisms as accurately as she did Dillon's western drawl. "No, darling, I don't think so."

Hope froze with her hands in midair, then turned her head and gave Dillon a piercing, speculative look that made him feel like a side of beef. He met her gaze without flinching, and realized there was a lot more going on under that spiky spray of blue hair than most folks would ever suspect. The weird part was, he couldn't get a single clue from her expression as to her opinion of a romantic relationship between Blair and him.

Not that it mattered. They were both adults, and they didn't need anybody's permission to have an...affair. Damn, but he didn't like using that word to describe how he felt about Blair. She wasn't some floozy any saddle tramp could pick up in a bar. She was...

"I see." Hope glanced over at Blair, then looked back at Dillon. "We must become acquainted. Soon."

It was a command, not a request. Biting back a chuckle, Dillon tipped his hat to her again, then swung himself back into the saddle. "I'll look forward to it, ma'am." Blair reached for Molly's reins, but he wouldn't give them to her. "I'll take care of her. You gals have a nice visit."

He rode on over to the corral with the mare in tow and unloaded both horses. When he was halfway through the job, the back door of the main house banged open. Marsh sauntered out, spotted Dillon and waved.

Dillon returned the gesture and went back to work, smiling to himself at the memory of all the curses he'd called down on his little brother's head during the past few weeks. It was hard to believe, but Marsh had actually ended up doing him a favor when he brought Blair to the Flying M. Not that Dillon had any intention of admitting that to Marsh. At least not yet. The kid deserved to sweat a little.

"Hey, bro," Marsh called from the other side of the fence. "How're you doing?"

Dillon shrugged. "Can't complain."

"Where's Blair?"

Dillon hitched a thumb toward the motor home. "Over there. You ride all the way up here from California in that rig?"

"Yeah. It's nice inside. Just like a house."

"Well, it's big enough to be one." Dillon unbuckled Molly's cinch, dragged the saddle off her back and hauled it into the tack room. Marsh ducked between the fence rails and followed him.

"So, uh...how is she?" Marsh asked.

"How's who?" Dillon went back outside.

Marsh followed him again. "Blair. How is Blair?"

"Fine."

"How did you two, uh...get along?"

"Okay." Dillon lugged Sunny's saddle inside, with Marsh still tagging after him. Hating to see anyone waste that much motion, he handed Marsh the grain buckets before grabbing the currycomb and leading him back outside.

"So, uh...how did she do?" Marsh asked. "Learning to ride and do chores and all of that?"

"Not bad."

Marsh's muttered curse made Dillon laugh out loud. Marsh turned and glared at him, and the lines of strain in his younger brother's face almost made Dillon feel guilty about hassling him now. Almost, but not quite. He'd had some mighty bad moments since March, and his brother was responsible for every last one.

"Dammit, Dillon, that's not funny. I told you how important this is to me, and—"

Dillon clapped Marsh on the back, then gave his shoulder a squeeze and looked him right in the eye. "She did great. She can handle anything you've got in that script, no sweat. It's not a bad script, by the way."

Marsh's eyebrows shot up under the shock of hair that always tended to fall into his eyes. "You've actually *read* it?"

"Well, I *can* read, ya know. I even helped Blair study her lines a time or two."

"You *did?*"

"Yeah. Shut your mouth before you draw flies."

Marsh closed his mouth with an audible snap and studied Dillon for a long moment. Then, eyes narrowed, he slowly gave him one of those incredibly annoying grins only a younger sibling can produce. "You like her now, don'tcha, Dillon?"

Dillon shrugged one shoulder and went on grooming the horses. "She's okay. I guess. For an actress."

His deadpan expression didn't fool Marsh, damn his ornery hide. The words were hardly out of Dillon's mouth and his brother was jumping around, pointing and laughing, just the way he had when they were kids.

"Right. Try the other leg, bro. I took enough writing classes with Blair to know what a sweetheart she is, and I know you, so don't give me that line of bull about 'She's okay.'"

Refusing to answer, Dillon took off Molly's bridle, then Sunny's, and walked across the corral to open the pasture gate. Marsh waited until the horses trotted out, and helped Dillon put away the rest of the gear. Shoving both hands into his front pockets he ambled out of the barn beside Dillon.

"To tell you the truth," Marsh said, pausing to one side of the open doorway, "I was hoping maybe you and Blair would...get together while you were teaching her."

A streak of heat raced up Dillon's neck and into his face. Marsh noticed it, of course, but for once, he passed up a chance to tease. Instead, he clapped Dillon on the back and said quietly, "I'm glad. You'll be good for each other. You two have a lot in common."

Dillon snorted. "How do you figure that?"

Before Marsh could answer, they heard the screeching protest of the spigot around the side of the barn being turned on and water splattering into the dirt. Then their nephew, Riley, hollered, "Ow! Dammit , you low-down, stinkin' son of a b—"

"Riley, watch your language," Grace scolded, but there was more amusement than any real heat in her voice.

"Well, Mom, he stomped right on my dang foot."

"Well, Riley, get your dang foot out of his way."

"Yeah, Riley," Steven said. "Get your big old dang clodhopper foot outa the way!"

"Pipe down, squirt," Riley said.

"You better grab that rope, boy," a deeper, definitely male but completely unfamiliar voice said.

Dillon and Marsh looked at each other in surprise, then automatically headed for the side of the barn to find out who was hanging around their sister and nephews.

"Get him!" Grace hollered.

Next came the clang of a hoof making contact with a bucket, a splash, and a couple of thuds, followed by uproarious laughter and the frightened bellow of Riley's 4-H steer as he charged straight for Dillon and Marsh, his eyes rolling and his halter rope flapping in the breeze.

"Easy there, fella," Dillon said, hoping to calm the animal. "Nobody's gonna hurt you."

Red-faced, wild-eyed as the steer, and soaking wet, Riley skidded around the corner. Obviously more afraid of the boy behind him than he was of the man in front of him, the steer ran right over Dillon. So did Riley.

Marsh was laughing too hard to be of any help. Steven barreled around the corner, took one look at Dillon, and then Riley and the steer, who were rapidly disappearing down the driveway, and promptly cut loose with a surprisingly deep, booming laugh for a ten-year-old kid. Groaning, Dillon dragged himself to his knees, fished his hat out of the dirt, dusted it off and crammed it back on his head.

By the time he got his feet under him again, Grace and a tall, lanky cowboy Dillon had never seen before staggered into view, hooting like a couple of idiots and wiping at the globs of mud spattered all over their clothes. They were a little red-faced too, but not, Dillon suspected, from anger at the steer. They both came to an abrupt halt when they caught sight of him.

"What the hell's goin' on here, Grace?" Dillon asked.

Grace's chin rose. "Don't take that tone with me, brother dear. And for your information, we were just helpin' Riley give his steer a bath."

Marsh winked at Steven, whose eyes had bugged out like big marshmallows. "Uh-huh. Looks like you guys were loads of help."

"You, hush," Grace said, glaring at him.

"He just needs a little more halter work," the cowboy said. Stepping forward, he started to offer his hand to Dillon, looked at it, wiped more mud off on the side of his jeans, then offered it again. "Name's Wade Kirby. I'm the wrangler for the production company. Grace was kind enough to show me around."

"Dillon McBride." Dillon liked Kirby's firm handshake. The guy showed no reaction whatsoever to his scars, neither staring at them nor pretending they didn't exist, which was another point in his favor. Then Wade Kirby wasn't looking at him anymore; he was looking at Grace, and not in any platonic way, either.

Dillon intended to know one heck of a lot more about this character before he let him get within kissing distance of his little sister again. He couldn't imagine what had gotten into Grace, who hadn't even been interested in looking at a man since Johnny died. And where in the heck was Riley? The kid could've chased that steer to Montana and back by now.

"You folks sure have a beautiful spread," Kirby said, still looking at Grace.

"We like it," Marsh said, raising an eyebrow at Dillon.

Dillon gave him an almost imperceptible nod. Marsh grinned, then rubbed his belly. "Well, hey, Gracie, what's for supper?"

Grace grinned back at him and linked her arm through Kirby's. "I don't know what you're havin', but Wade's taking the boys and me to Cal's Place tonight. See ya later, guys. Come on, Steven. Let's get cleaned up."

Damn, Dillon thought, watching Grace, Kirby and Steven stroll off together. He'd been so focused on teaching Blair and spending every minute he could spare with her lately, he felt off balance. Besides the big, honkin' motor home parked at the eastern edge of the barnyard, there was a whole fleet of stock trailers lined up on the other side of the old toolshed, and he hadn't even noticed them before now.

"Oh, jeez," Marsh said, shaking his head in amazement. "Get a load of Riley."

And there the poor kid was, hauling on the halter rope, sweating and probably cussing the steer a blue streak, doing his damnedest to get the struggling, ornery critter back up the driveway. It was hardly a fair contest. Even soaking wet, Riley probably didn't weigh much over 125. The steer had to be close to a thousand pounds by now.

If Riley had been doing his job getting ready for the county fair, that steer should be a lot better halter-broke than this. Muttering under his breath, Dillon went to give him a hand. Couldn't he be gone for a few weeks without everything going to hell around this place? And what else was going on that he didn't even know about yet?

"Hey, Dillon, good to see ya. It's been so long since you've come to town, we've been takin' bets you were dead."

"No such luck, Sid," Dillon said, shaking the man's hand. "How's it goin'?"

While Sid gave Sunshine Gap's standard answer, which invariably involved the current price of beef, the weather, and what those idiots back in Washington, D.C., had been doing lately, Blair glanced around the restaurant. Grace's refusal to cook had resulted in a night out for the entire McBride clan and their guests. Since it was the only real restaurant in town, they automatically went to Cal's Place.

It was a busy, efficient establishment, pleasant in a rustic sort of way. But this definitely was not L.A. There were no vegetarian entrées on the menu, no oil paintings, soft music or green plants for atmosphere, and the only kind of water available came directly from the tap.

The air smelled of grilled meat, French fries and tobacco smoke. The jukebox blasted one country song after another, and occasional raucous shouts of laughter drifted through the doorway from the bar. Waitresses toted coffeepots from table to table, addressing the customers by name and dishing out advice and opinions that had nothing to do with the day's special.

Dillon nudged Blair's elbow to get her attention and introduced her to Sid. She smiled and shook the man's hand, ignoring his stares and exchanging polite chitchat with him until he reluctantly shuffled back to his own table. She managed to eat two bites before the next old friend approached Dillon.

"Well, I'll be damned if it ain't Dillon McBride. Where've ya been keepin' yourself, pard?"

"Out at the ranch," Dillon said. "How's it goin', Bill?"

When Bill started in on the usual spiel, Blair grinned at Hope and rolled her eyes. Of course, Hope snickered, and Blair felt a surge of affection for her cousin. This was her least favorite part of being a celebrity, but Hope could always help her keep any situation in perspective.

She was actually quite surprised at how well Dillon tolerated the constant scrutiny and continual interruptions. Then someone asked for his autograph, and she realized he must have had his own firsthand experience with stardom during his rodeo career.

A woman named Mabel replaced Bill, and an old man with a cane named George Pierson replaced Mabel. George insisted on meeting Hope, too, and eventually joined the McBrides' table at her invitation.

By the time their waitress brought the check, Blair felt as if she had met the entire adult population of Sunshine Gap. Word really did travel fast in a small town. Finally finished eating, she followed Dillon past clusters of friendly, interested faces to the cash register. A plump little white-haired woman wearing pearls and a pink shirtwaist dress June Cleaver might have worn back in the fifties took the check, *tsk*ed over the spelling and carefully added the total by hand.

Then she peered up at Dillon, her pale eyes blurry behind the thick lenses of her glasses. She frowned a little, as if she knew she should recognize him, but couldn't quite place him. Dillon grinned at her like a smitten schoolboy, then leaned down and kissed her soft, wrinkled cheek and said, "Good evening, Miz Hannah. How are you?"

Miz Hannah's mouth drew into a perfectly round O and she pressed one dainty, palsied hand over her pearls. "Dilly-boy? Is that you, Dillon McBride?"

Dillon's delighted laugh bounced off the back wall. He wrapped an arm around Blair and pulled her close beside him. "It sure is, ma'am, and I'd like you to meet a good friend of mine. Miz Hannah, may I present Miss Blair Du-Maine?"

Miz Hannah turned to Blair with a smile that transformed her face with a beauty born of character and dignity. "How do you do, Miss DuMaine? And where are you from?"

"I'm from Los Angeles, Miz Hannah," Blair said.

"How lovely." Miz Hannah paused for a second, tipping her head to one side, as if that helped her to concentrate. "Oh, my. Now wait just a moment, did you say Du*Maine?* You aren't by any chance related to Mr. Charles Du-Maine?"

Blair had to smile at the breathless, almost reverent note in Miz Hannah's voice. "He was my grandfather."

The woman's eyes closed in ecstasy and her hand trembled at her pearls again. "Mercy, mercy." She opened her eyes, leaned closer to Blair and lowered her voice to a deliciously conspiratorial whisper. "He was positively the most handsome and distinguished actor ever to grace the silver screen. My mother never approved, but I saw every film he ever made. Twice."

"I've always been proud of him," Blair replied.

"Miz Hannah was my second-grade teacher," Dillon said.

"I was everyone's second-grade teacher in Sunshine Gap, young man, including your daddy's and your mama's."

"Was Dillon a good student?" Blair asked.

"He was adorable," Miz Hannah said with a chuckle. "His printing was atrocious, and he had so much energy he could barely sit still, but he was the sweetest little boy I ever taught."

"I'm hurt, Miz Hannah," Marsh complained, crowding Dillon out of the way as he leaned down to kiss the old woman's cheek. "I thought I was your favorite."

"You were all my favorites in some way, Marshall, dear. Now *you* were a little stinker, but you always told the best stories."

Cal stepped behind the counter beside Miz Hannah and gave her a gentle hug. "Hey, you guys, quit maulin' my help. And where do you think you're goin'? I've already got a table set up for you in the bar."

Blair shot Dillon a doubtful glance. He'd already put up with an awful lot this evening. "Perhaps another time, Cal."

"Aw, come on, it's Friday night and it's not even ten o'clock yet. We've got a great band here, and since you've already met everybody, nobody'll bother you now. You can all just relax and have some fun. It may be hard for you to believe, but ol' Dillon here is one heck of a great dancer."

Blair shrugged and raised her eyebrows at Dillon, leaving the decision up to him. She would love to dance with him, but she refused to cause him any unnecessary discomfort. It was Miz Hannah who settled the matter.

"Oh, yes, Dilly-boy, please. You must stay and save me a waltz. I haven't waltzed since the last time you were here, and it's been much, much too long."

Dillon stiffened. "Well, now, Miz Hannah..."

Smiling with understanding and compassion, the little woman reached out and gently patted the fist he'd rested on the counter. "You have neglected your friends terribly, Dillon, dear. We haven't wanted to intrude, but we have missed you a great deal. It's time to come back."

No one spoke; Blair couldn't even bring herself to breathe until the rigid muscles in Dillon's back and shoulders slowly relaxed. He shuffled his feet and cleared his throat, then gave the old lady a resigned smile.

"All right, Miz Hannah, you win. Just this once, and just because it's you."

Cal wasted no time ushering them all into the bar and seating them at a group of small tables that had been shoved together to accommodate the whole family. Blair and Dillon sat with Marsh and Hope, while Grace and Jake entertained Wade Kirby. On the other side of Wade, Zack and Alex eagerly flipped through a stack of photographs that had arrived in the mail from the four McBride parents.

When Cal came back to take drink orders, Zack held up both hands and raised his voice to be heard over the music. "I'll be the designated driver tonight. The rest of you have fun."

Blair noticed a rapid relay of glances among the male McBrides that she didn't understand. She had an impression, however, that whatever it was all about was something quite serious, and had something to do with alcohol and driving. Which prompted her to glance at Dillon.

Other than what he'd told Hope today, Blair didn't know any details of the car accident. Was it possible he'd been driving under the influence and killed his brother-in-law? It was a horrible thought, but it might explain why he was so protective of Grace. And why he had become such a recluse.

While it was obvious his scars did attract enough attention to make anyone uncomfortable to be out in public, somehow she thought he could have learned to deal with it if he wanted to badly enough. He was too independent and stubborn to give up his whole life simply because of other people's reactions. And if it was only his scars that had made him withdraw, why hadn't he sought the aid of a plastic surgeon?

Modern medicine might not be able to repair all the damage done to his face, but with skin grafts and laser techniques, surely his scars could be made less prominent, perhaps barely noticeable. Her questions went unanswered. As the evening wore on and the drinks flowed, she was too swept up in the party-hearty atmosphere to worry about them.

To her surprise, Dillon joined in with the others. She'd thought keeping up with him was difficult enough at the ranch; on the dance floor, he was a demon. Using the exceptional sense of timing and balance that had made him a great bronc rider, he whirled and twirled her around the room through song after song, taxing her skills from hundreds of dance lessons to the limit.

When she begged for a rest, he simply grabbed the nearest available partner, and off he went again. Alex and Hope joined her at the table, leaning close to be heard over the music and laughter. Hope inclined her head toward Dillon as he escorted Miz Hannah onto the floor for a waltz.

"He's dancing like a man let out of prison," Hope said.

Alex nodded and smiled at Blair. "I think he has been. It's great to see him act this way again. It's like getting my old cousin Dillon back. Thank you for whatever you've done for him."

"I didn't do anything, Alex," Blair said. "He's the one who's been helping me. He's really a delightful man."

"Speaking of which…" Resting one elbow on the table, Hope raised her hand and twirled a tuft of hair around her index finger. "Alex, do tell me about your brother Jake."

"Jake?" Blair said, choking down an appalled laugh, automatically shaking her head at the familiar gleam in her cousin's eyes. "Oh, no, Hope. Don't even think about it."

Hope shot Blair a reproving frown. "Excuse me? Don't even think about what?"

"I know you, and I know what blue hair means. Forget it."

"Forget what?" Alex asked. "And what does blue hair mean?"

Before Blair could answer, Jake stepped out of a dim corner of the room, a long-necked beer bottle in one hand as he headed for their table. Eyes narrowed as if she were a lioness on the hunt, Hope rose gracefully from her chair, straightened her shoulders and sauntered over to intercept him. He smiled indulgently, leaned down to listen to her, then set his beer bottle on the table and gallantly guided her onto the dance floor.

Alex turned to Blair, her eyes wide with disbelief. "Hope and...*Jake?* Tell me she's not serious."

Blair sputtered with laughter. "I'm afraid so, Alex. Blue hair always means Hope is ready to fall in love again."

"But he's as conservative as they come, and at least ten years older than she is, and—"

"That's part of the attraction for her," Blair said. "She always chooses a man who is completely inappropriate, and believe me, she's not easily discouraged. I hope she doesn't drive poor Jake too crazy."

"Poor Jake can take care of himself," Alex said, suddenly grinning, as if the thought of anyone bugging her big brother held tremendous appeal. She picked up her gin and tonic and took a sip, idly watching the dancers shuffle by until one particular couple caught her eye. "Uh-oh. I was afraid of this."

Blair followed the direction of Alex's gaze and saw Marsh dancing with Sandy Bishop, the petite, auburn-haired woman Cal had introduced earlier as his fiancée. Though they moved well together, they didn't look as if they were enjoying the dance.

Pulling away from Marsh when the music stopped, Sandy left the floor without waiting for him to accompany her. Blair could have sworn she'd been ready to burst into tears. Still standing on the dance floor and staring after Sandy, Marsh didn't look much happier. It was so unlike the happy-go-lucky man Blair had always known, she had to wonder what was going on.

When she asked, Alex sadly shook her head. "Just some unfinished business, Blair. But it looks like maybe Marsh is finally waking up."

Blair would have pressed for more information, but suddenly Dillon was standing in front of her. Holding out his hand in invitation, he smiled at her, with a look in his eyes that drove all thoughts of Hope, Jake, Marsh, Alex and everyone else from her mind. They would have to handle their own relationships. Dillon was the one who mattered the most to her.

When his arms closed around her, Cal's Place became more than a smoky little tavern in the boondocks. It was a wonderfully romantic spot, far away from Hollywood, where she was free from her family and the press and all their impossible expectations. She could do or say or be anything she wanted, even if she just wanted to be plain old Blair, who shoveled manure, hadn't seen a hairdresser in two months and didn't bother to wear makeup.

Whatever secrets Dillon carried from his past couldn't be any worse than her own. It wouldn't have mattered if they were, because she was in love with him. From this moment on, she intended to leave the past behind and live only in the moment.

If the cost of knowing such happiness was a broken heart at some point in the future, she would gladly pay the price.

Chapter Thirteen

During the next two weeks, the Flying M took on the appearance of a small city besieged by an army of rental cars, motor homes and eighteen-wheel trucks hauling double trailers. An amazing number of workers arrived, sporting T-shirts, sweatshirts, jackets and baseball caps with the logos of nearly every movie made in the past ten years. They took an incredible amount of equipment out of the trailers and proceeded to set up huge tents and even more equipment. The compound kept growing and growing, like a mushroom on steroids.

Dillon made it a point to stay as far away from the whole mess as he could. Since Blair was tied up in meetings every day, he caught up on chores he'd neglected—dragging the hay meadows, repairing the irrigation headgates and cleaning the dirt and weeds out of the ditches. He'd slip into the house with just enough time to shower before supper and conveniently vanish again if Blair had more meetings in the evening.

The woman worked just as hard with these movie folks as she had with him, and he wondered how she could keep up this pace through sixty-plus days of filming. Doing what he could to help her out, he rubbed her neck and shoulders at bedtime, held her when she had nightmares and pretended he was too tired to make love when any fool could see that she was. There were too many other people around putting pressure on her; he'd be damned if he would add any more.

So he did the best he could to be happy with whatever time she could give him and, from a safe distance, watched all the production people running around like crazed ants, yakking at each other over black headsets, changing direction for no apparent reason. About the time he started congratulating himself on escaping all that chaos and trouble, it came looking for him.

With Memorial Day and the June 1 deadline to start shooting the movie on the immediate horizon, Dillon decided it was time to get his spring roundup done. Some of the Flying M's herd would end up "working" in the movie, but he wanted to get all of his cows and calves vaccinated, brand the calves who wouldn't be branded on film and get the nonacting cows moved onto their summer pasture in the mountains.

He quietly went about his business until Jake and Patrick Quillen, the director, cornered him in the barn one morning and asked him to take the head wrangler along for the day and help him pick out the stock to use for the film's herd. It seemed a reasonable request, and since Wade Kirby was still hanging around Grace and the boys, Dillon figured it would be a good way to get to know the guy better.

Turned out Kirby knew good horseflesh when he saw it, he was a good hand with the stock, and he even stepped in and helped Dillon explain to the transportation director why his people couldn't drive their big trucks across Dillon's best meadows.

During a break to water their horses one day, Wade indicated the group of calves Dillon planned to brand over the weekend. "You folks still do it the old-fashioned way and have a big branding party?" he asked.

Dillon nodded. "There's so many of us, we've always got plenty of help, and it's more fun than usin' a squeeze chute."

"You might want to invite Quillen and the stunt people, so they can see how it's really done."

"Guess we could. You want to come?"

"You bet." Kirby grinned. "Thought you'd never ask."

"I haven't invited you yet, Kirby," Dillon said. "And I really don't know if I should."

Kirby's eyebrows rose in surprise. "Why not?"

"You've been sniffin' around my sister, that's why not. Gracie doesn't have much experience with men."

"Excuse me, but she's got two kids. She can't be totally innocent."

Dillon waved off that observation. "She's more innocent than you might think. Far as I know, the only man she's ever slept with was her husband. He's been gone for six years now, and she hasn't dated since. Until you showed up."

"Is that a fact?" Kirby's chest puffed out, and a smile spread over his face.

"Yup. I haven't got a clue what she sees in you—"

Kirby's smile vanished. "Well, jeez, Dillon, thanks a hell of a lot."

"Aw, don't get bent outa shape," Dillon said. "It's obvious she likes you, and the boys do, too. I just want to know what your intentions are."

"My intentions?" Kirby laughed, but his face turned red. "Wow. There's a phrase you don't hear much these days."

"We don't worry too much about bein' politically correct when it comes to protectin' our women," Dillon said, without a trace of apology in his voice. "If all you want is a roll in the hay, Grace isn't the gal to mess with, if you get my drift."

Kirby met Dillon's gaze without flinching. "Yeah, I get your drift. To tell you the truth, I'm not ready to marry your sister just yet, but I'd never hurt her on purpose."

"Glad to hear that. Because if you do hurt her or those boys, you'll answer to me, and I'll only be the first one in line." Since the horses had finished drinking, Dillon swung into the saddle. "By the way, if you're still interested, you're welcome to come to the branding party."

Before Kirby could answer, two horses and riders appeared on the far side of the pasture. "Yoo-hoo! Dillon! Wait for us!" The voice was all it took for him to identify Blair's cousin Hope, bouncing along on a showy chestnut gelding named Jocko. The other, shorter rider, turned out to be Dillon's ten-year-old nephew, Steven.

"Hey, Uncle Dillon," he called. "Mom asked me to bring Miss Hope out to find you."

Dillon waved at the boy. "Well, you did a fine job, Steven." Looking at Hope, he bit back a snort of laughter at today's getup, a red-white-and-blue shirt with cutout triangles below the collar and down both sleeves, powder blue jeans so tight it was no wonder she kept standing up in the stirrups and a red pair of fancy-stitched boots with leather fringes all around the tops, laced up over her jeans to her knees. He sure would love to see the stores where she bought her duds.

"Hello, there," he said.

She gingerly settled herself into the saddle, took off her hat and fanned her face with it, letting her bright blue hair shine in the sunlight. "Hello, Dillon. Wade. Goodness, these western saddles are just so *big*, aren't they? I really think the English have a much better design."

"Maybe in England," Dillon said. "What can I do for you, Hope?"

"Blair needs you to come down to the house right away."

"Why?"

"I'll be happy to tell you what I know on the way, but

I really do think we should leave now. Blair was quite upset when she asked me to come and fetch you.''

"Does she need me, too?" Wade asked.

"She only mentioned Dillon."

"In that case, I'll stay here and finish this job, if you don't mind, Dillon."

"Go right ahead." Dillon reined Sunny around. "You comin', Steven?"

The boy shook his head. "Nah. I'd rather stay here and help Mr. Kirby."

Dillon shot Kirby a questioning glance to make sure he didn't mind having Steven's company. Kirby nodded and waved him away. Hope and Dillon set off side by side. For the first time since he'd met her, Hope was silent.

"You got any idea what's going on?" Dillon asked.

"Oh, it's simply an artistic difference, I'm sure." Hope wrinkled up her nose, then gave Dillon an impish smile. "Blair and Patrick were having an argument with her leading man. She did not look at all happy with Mr. Stanton, I promise you."

Dillon kept his grim smile to himself, but it didn't exactly hurt his feelings to hear Hope's news. Keith Stanton was considered one of Hollywood's most handsome actors, and he'd taken a real shine to Blair since arriving three days ago. Although Blair didn't appear to return his interest, the guy acted as if he couldn't believe any woman would resist his charm.

Needless to say, Dillon wasn't real fond of Stanton, and from the grin on Hope's face, she obviously knew the reason why. A moment later, she looked over and frowned thoughtfully at him.

"What?" Dillon asked.

"You're jealous of Blair, aren't you, Dillon?"

"I don't see how that's any of your business," he replied.

"Oh, but it is," Hope insisted. "Blair is the only relative

I have who ever cared a damn about me. And I'm the only one who ever really cared about her.''

"How can you say that?" Dillon demanded. "You both have parents, don't you?"

"Yes, but they're all so involved in their own careers, they've never had a clue about us or what was happening in our lives. We were actually raised by servants and boarding schools.''

"What's your point, Hope?"

She reined Jocko to a halt and waited until Dillon did the same with Sunny. "It's going to get extremely crazy while they're filming, and Blair is going to need every ounce of help she can get. I'm here right now to lend her my support. Are you willing to give her yours?"

"Of course," Dillon said. "Why wouldn't I?"

Hope shrugged. "It could well be that you're simply interested in sleeping with a movie star."

"Dammit, Hope—"

"She's already had a man who vowed to love her, but used her instead and broke her heart," Hope said, interrupting him. "I would like to believe you're different, because I know Blair cares deeply for you. But if you're not prepared to go the distance with her, then please leave her alone and let her make this movie in peace. She can't afford any unnecessary distractions, and she doesn't deserve any more pain than she's already had.''

Dillon met and held Hope's steely gaze, and suddenly felt intense sympathy for Wade Kirby. "I'll keep that in mind.''

"You do that. And remember, if you hurt her, I will not be happy with you." Hope turned Jocko back toward the barn, and they rode the rest of the way home in silence.

Torn between laughter at her not-so-subtle threat and anger that she thought it was necessary, Dillon followed. Dang that little blue-haired witch, just who did she think she was talking to? He was no Don Juan, and he'd cut off his other thumb before he'd willingly hurt Blair.

Dammit, he loved her. He was *in* love with her. And he wanted nothing more than to see her succeed and be happy, even if it meant he would ultimately lose her. Which it probably did.

That thought put such a sour taste in his mouth, when he saw Riley struggling with his steer again, his first reaction was less than diplomatic. Dismounting, he tied Sunny to the corral fence, stomped over to his nephew and started yelling.

"Come on, Riley, that steer is just a dumb animal. I know you can handle him better'n that. Why haven't you been workin' him like I told you to?"

"I *have*, Uncle Dillon," Riley said, his voice cracking the way it did more and more often lately. "He's just so dang stubborn—"

"Well, he wouldn't be, if you'd get out here and walk him when you're supposed to."

Riley's chin quivered as if his feelings were hurt, but he straightened his shoulders and glared at his uncle. "Oh, yeah? Well, *you* were supposed to help me, weren't you? And you haven't been around hardly at all."

"Don't try to blame this on me," Dillon said. "You need to get him out there and walk him, two miles, twice a day."

"Fine, we'll take care of it," Grace said.

Dillon turned and found his sister standing right behind him. "The steer is Riley's responsibility, Grace. Not yours."

"Yes, I know. And Riley is *my* responsibility, Dillon. Not yours. I'll handle this."

She looked into his eyes long and hard, and there was a determination in her expression he hadn't seen since she informed their parents that she'd rather marry Johnny Kramer than go to college. Damn, what was going on here? After the wreck, he'd rebuilt his whole life around her and Riley and Steven. Surely she didn't mean she didn't want him to help her with the boys.

She smiled a little, as if to soften her words. "Blair and

the others are in the kitchen, Dillon. Why don't you go on in and see what they need?''

''But—''

Grace shook her head. ''You're dealin' with too much other stuff right now. We can get one steer ready for the fair by ourselves.''

Shrugging as if her rejection hadn't stung, Dillon headed for the house. First Steven wanted to stay with Kirby. Now Grace and Riley. He didn't like feeling quite so dispensable. He sure as hell hoped he'd get a warmer reception from the Hollywood folks.

''I've tried everything to make it work, but we can't switch the shooting sequence, unless we replace Whitney Morgan.'' Patrick Quillen swept one hand over the shiny bald crown of his head in frustration. ''She won't be available for another month.''

Blair rubbed her left temple, where a headache threatened to start any moment. What had possessed her ever to think she might want to produce or direct? She turned to the location manager. ''But is that our only real obstacle? Can the dates be changed for the permits to use Old Trail Town in Cody?''

The location manager nodded. ''They're great people, and they're willing to accommodate us any way they can.''

''What if we wrote that part out of the script, Marsh?'' Patrick asked. ''I mean, think about it. Do we really need Belle Flannigan?''

Blair and Marsh both gaped at the director, aghast at his suggestion. ''Of course we do,'' Blair said. ''Belle makes the choice facing Elizabeth so clear—''

''I don't believe you said that, Patrick,'' Marsh said. ''You can't just rip out a character and not expect repercussions.''

Patrick shoved back his chair, carried his mug to the coffee maker and banged it on the counter. ''All right, all right, don't freak. I'm just trying to think outside the box. I understand how you feel, but what else can we do?''

"We can buy out Whitney Morgan's contract," Blair said.

"And replace her with whom?" Patrick demanded.

Marsh frowned at the casting director. "There must be *some*one available. What about a soap-opera actress? Surely one of them would—''

The kitchen door opened, and Dillon walked in. Blair took one look at his disgruntled face and wanted to hug him and kiss him and be up at the cabin with him again. Alone. When he met her gaze, his eyes brightened and he gave her a slow wink that made her toes curl.

"Thank you for getting here so fast," she said softly.

He nodded, then poured himself a cup of coffee and took the chair beside hers. "Well, don't all talk at once. What's up?''

"We have some problems," Patrick said. "Blair and Marsh think you can help us solve them."

"I'll do what I can," Dillon said. "What kind of problems are you talkin' about?''

"We need you to do some more coaching," Marsh said. "Keith can barely ride, and none of the stunt men can rope worth a damn.''

Blair leaned closer and laid her hand on Dillon's arm. "In fact, if you would act as a stunt double for Keith, you could—''

"Whoa." Emphatically shaking his head, Dillon pulled away from her. "Hold on there, DuMaine. I'm no actor.''

"You wouldn't really have to act," Marsh said. "Not the way you're thinking, Dillon.''

Sitting forward in his chair, Patrick braced both elbows on the table and held his hands out toward Dillon in a gesture that came close to pleading. "That's right. You wouldn't have any dialogue, and we'd always shoot you from a distance or from the side or the back, so the audience will think you're Keith. We need to have you do the

branding and the roping so we don't have to do take after
take until one of our people gets lucky.''

"You'd only be doing what you've been teaching me,
Dillon." Blair leaned closer to him again and gave his knee
an affectionate squeeze under the table. "We'll even make
sure Kirby has some extra palomino geldings for the Riley
McBride character, so you can ride Sunny in your scenes.''

"How long would it take?''

Patrick squinted at the storyboard. "Ten days, perhaps.
Two weeks at the most.''

Dillon grimaced, but before he could speak, Marsh
scraped back his chair and paced from one end of the big
kitchen to the other. "Honest to God, Dillon, I don't believe you. Do you have any idea how many guys would
kill for this opportunity? Go out there and talk to some of
those stuntmen, and—''

"Knock it off, Marsh," Dillon said. "I didn't say I
wouldn't do it. I was just tryin' to figure out how to cover
the ranch for that long. Summer's a busy time around
here.''

Relief swept over Blair in such a rush, it was all she
could do not to laugh out loud or weep. This had turned
into a ridiculously huge problem, and Dillon had been
avoiding everyone so completely, she hadn't dared to guess
whether or not he would be willing to help. Of course, if
they couldn't replace Whitney Morgan and shoot the town
scenes while Dillon worked with Keith, they would have
to postpone everything and lose God only knew how much
money anyway.

Marsh did laugh. "Well, hell, Dillon, we'll just call in
the family reserves. Zack and I can handle one hay-cutting,
and Alex and Grace and the kids could drive the herd up
to summer pasture. Cal and Jake can pitch in, too. Just give
us a list of jobs, and we'll do them.''

Alex. Blair's heart thumped at the sound of that name.
She blinked, then stared at Marsh. Alex would be perfect
to play Belle Flannigan. She already knew the lines from

their practices. She'd had some experience, and she was good. She was available. She was here. She would be thrilled at the opportunity.

Dillon would hate the idea.

"Just to make sure we're absolutely clear," Patrick said, "does that mean you'll do it, Dillon?"

Dillon gave Blair a crooked smile and drawled, "Yeah. Just tell me where and when and what you want me to do. I won't have to take all my clothes off, will I?"

"A nude roper," Marsh said, while the others cracked up. "Now there's a scary picture. Think of the saddle sores."

Standing, Patrick held up his hands for attention. "Let's take a break, people. We'll meet again at Dillon's house. Seven o'clock, tonight."

Patrick came around the table and shook Dillon's hand. "I don't know how to thank you."

"Don't thank me yet," Dillon said. "Blair was a good student. Could be my teaching style won't agree with Mr. Stanton."

"He's an actor," Patrick said. "Believe me, all you have to do is tell him he'll look better if he does things your way. You'll be amazed at how hard he'll work."

Blair moved up beside Dillon and took his arm. "Take me for a walk, Dillon. I need to speak with you in private."

Dillon looked down into Blair's sweet face and felt a familiar surge of warmth at the base of his breastbone. The rest of his body acted in a predictably male way, too, but that spot up under his heart always got to him a lot worse than anything going on below his belt buckle. She could ask him for dang near anything right now, and he wouldn't be able to refuse her.

He liked the way she didn't hesitate to touch him, even in front of her Hollywood friends. He enjoyed the possessive way she tucked her fingers into the crook of his elbow and curled them around his biceps. He loved the way he felt when he was with her—big, strong, masculine, admired.

In fact, when Blair was there, he didn't even mind meeting the new movie folks coming in too much. Oh, they'd give his face a curious look, but that was all it ever amounted to. Of course, it was impossible for him to judge his own looks objectively. His scars could have healed up better than he'd thought, or maybe he'd made too big of a deal about other people's reactions to them from the start.

He set off with Blair, their hips and shoulders brushing, aimlessly wandering away from the house and the campers and trailers, savoring the simple joy of being alone together. Though the silence wasn't really tense, it wasn't exactly peaceful, either. The farther they walked, the more he sensed Blair's anxiety building up, but he waited for her to find her own moment to tell him what it was all about.

They reached the north pasture's circle of cottonwood trees before she finally gestured toward a fallen log. Once he'd settled himself on a patch of bark and stretched out his legs, she sat beside him. Lacing her fingers together at waist level, she cleared her throat, looked up at him, glanced away again. Lord, but she was tense enough to pass out, if she wasn't careful.

"What's goin' on, Blair?" he asked.

"Dillon, I appreciate what you did back there at the house. It will save us a lot of time, and for us, time is money. With so many people on the payroll, and the rental fees on all of our equipment, we can't afford to waste a minute."

"I can see that," Dillon said. "I'll do my best for you."

"I know. It's not you I'm worried about...exactly."

"Then what *are* you worried about exactly? C'mon honey, stop that fidgeting and just tell me."

Briefly she explained about needing to change the production schedule in order to give Dillon time to work with Keith and the other stuntmen. "The main problem we have now is that Whitney Morgan is tied up for another month, and so far, our casting director hasn't been able to come up with anyone to replace her on such short notice.''

"Yeah," Dillon said. "That's a problem, all right."

"Well, there is someone right here in Sunshine Gap who could take Whitney's place, and I know she would do an excellent job."

Dillon frowned. "You mean Alex?"

Blair nodded. "She'd have to do a screen test, but I think she'd be perfect. It's a small role, but a good one, and it could conceivably lead to bigger roles for her in the future. She's really quite talented."

"So, why haven't you already asked her?"

"Because I promised you I would leave her alone, and I always keep my promises."

"What happens if I say no?"

"We'll keep looking until we find another actress or Keith is ready to work."

"And lose a lot of money."

"It happens." Blair shrugged, but her pinched features told him she was more worried than she was letting on. "We'll simply do what we can to minimize the loss."

It humbled him to realize she would put her production in jeopardy before she would renege on her promise to him, and suddenly Dillon couldn't handle the anxiety in her eyes another second. "Ask her."

"Are you sure you won't mind?"

Thinking about what had just happened with Grace, Dillon realized this situation with Alex wasn't a whole lot different. Maybe he'd been poking his nose in where it wasn't welcome. "Well, I might not like all of the results, but I'm beginning to see the truth of what you said before. Alex is a grown-up. It's her decision to make. Not mine."

"My goodness, Mr. McBride." Blair slid her arms around his neck and rubbed the tip of her nose against his. "You're positively evolving."

"Yeah." Dillon wrapped his arms around her hips and pulled her closer. "Scary, isn't it?"

"No," she murmured. "It's wonderful."

She kissed him. Then he kissed her. And it was wonderful to hold her again and to be held by her. He kissed his way up the side of her face and rubbed his cheek against her hair, inhaling the sweet scent of her.

"I've missed you, Dillon," she whispered.

"I've missed you, too, darlin'."

The bushes off to the left rustled, but Dillon didn't pay any attention to it. It was probably just a jackrabbit, or a bird. Or maybe even Curly. Needing to get closer, he lifted her off the log, turned her to face him and set her down again, straddling his lap.

She sighed against his lips, tossed his hat aside and plunged her hands into his hair while she kissed him again. Man, did she ever make him hot. There was probably steam billowing out of his ears and smoke puffing out of his pants.

He cupped her luscious breasts with his palms, swallowing her hungry little moans with a deep, openmouthed kiss that tasted like coffee. She popped the top three snaps on his shirt and gently raked her fingernails over his chest, making him shiver despite the warm air. Sliding his hands into her back pockets, he squeezed her firm backside, loving the way she wiggled closer, even though it made him groan with frustration.

Damn. He wanted to be naked and deep inside her. Not later on tonight, when all her meetings were finally over and she was exhausted. Now. He couldn't do that out here, of course. There were just too many people roaming around the ranch to guarantee their privacy. But he'd take whatever he could get.

The bushes rustled again. In some dim corner of his mind, Dillon knew it would have to be a mighty big jack or bird to make that much noise, but he was so involved in making out with Blair, he still didn't pay any attention.

Then a voice he'd never heard before said, "Hey McBride! Over here!"

Like an idiot, he looked up, and was instantly blinded

by the bright flash of a camera going off at close range. It went off again and again, from different angles, and the voice went right on talking.

"This is great. Tell me, Blair, how do you like cowboys in bed?"

"Oliver, you slimy little sneak. Stop that right now," she said, holding one hand in front of her face.

"What about you, Mr. McBride? It must be pretty exciting for a guy like you to sleep with a movie goddess. Any comments?"

"Who the hell is this guy?" Dillon demanded, setting her, none too gently, off his lap.

"Oliver Rankin. He's with the tabloids. You're about to become famous in every grocery store in America."

"Did you invite him here?"

"I wouldn't invite him to a gang war."

"Good."

Dillon rose and advanced on the photographer. "This is private property, mister. Get the hell outa here."

Rankin walked backward toward the fence, still snapping pictures. "Aw, come on, I'm just trying to make a living."

"Make it somewhere else or I'll have you arrested for trespassing."

Lowering his camera, Rankin snorted in disdain. "Oooh, I'm scared. Like this place is really crawling with cops."

"Nope, we've only got one cop." Dillon grabbed Rankin by the front of his shirt, yanked him up onto his tiptoes and hustled him toward the gate.

"Let go of me," Rankin sputtered. "I'll have you arrested for assault."

"Good luck," Dillon replied with a grim smile. "You know that one cop? His name's Zachary McBride. He's my first cousin."

"Oh, I get it. He won't enforce the law."

"Sure he will. But you're a little short on witnesses, and he's a hell of a lot more likely to believe me than you." Dillon tightened his grip on Rankin's shirt and lifted him

completely off the ground. "Now, do you want to walk
through that gate or fly over it?"

"I'll walk, I'll walk," Rankin squawked.

Dillon set him down and grabbed his camera before letting loose of his shirt.

"Give that back!" Rankin demanded. "You have no
right to—"

Dropping the camera into the dirt, Dillon shook his head
with feigned sadness. "Aw, gee whiz, I'm sure sorry about
that accident you had there—"

"You bastard!"

"That's no way to talk about my mama." Dillon booted
the camera into the gravel road beyond the fence. "Now
beat it, or I'll help you over the fence the same way."

Rankin scrambled through the gate, scooped his precious
camera into his arms and cradled it as if it were a wounded
child. "You'll pay for this, you stupid hick."

"Don't trespass again, Rankin. Stupid hicks tend to
shoot first and ask questions later."

Dillon watched the man stomp off down the road. Blair
walked over and slid her arm around Dillon's waist.

"I'm sorry, Dillon. He's a jerk, but there's not much I
can do to stop him. And when he shows up, the rest of
them follow within a few days. We'll increase our security,
but—"

"No problem, honey. Next time one of those guys comes
onto the Flying M, we'll sic the dogs on him." After giving
her a one-armed hug, Dillon took her hand and headed back
to the house. "Come on. Let's go tell Alex she's gonna be
a movie star."

Blair's forlorn expression brightened, as Dillon had
hoped it would. Sometimes her life sure was complicated.
Half of him wished he could always be a part of it. The
other half didn't know if he'd have the guts to try. Maybe
it was just as well he'd never have to make that decision.

Chapter Fourteen

"Let's do it, people," Cecil Dixon called, holding up his
hands in a prearranged signal. "Roll sound."

The sound mixer called back, "Rolling."

A production assistant held the clapboard in front of the
camera. "Scene twenty-two. Take one."

At the loud crack from the clapboard, Patrick Quillen
nodded, Cecil dropped both hands in a chopping motion
and yelled, "Aaand...*action!*"

Standing out of camera range between Hope and Marsh,
Blair held her breath while the first camera truck raced by.
Next came Dillon, bending low over Sunny's neck as they
galloped across the field. Playing rustlers, the rest of the
stunt people charged after him, shooting blanks from their
six-guns.

"He looks so real," Hope whispered.

"Oh, yeah," Marsh whispered simultaneously. "Damn,
but that brother of mine can ride."

Blair nodded her agreement, refusing to take her gaze

from Dillon even for a fraction of a second. He looked magnificent, just as he had in every other scene they shot with him. They were now three full days ahead of schedule—a miracle in this industry—and the crew loved working with him.

He reported on time, in the appropriate gear, and did what he was told without complaint. From the first take, he performed whatever job he'd been assigned with the ease and confidence of long practice. For all the notice he paid the cameras and the fascinated crowd watching him while he roped a steer, branded a calf or shod a horse, they might have been fence posts.

And when he was finished with the film crew for the day, he usually went right back to his regular ranch work, as if being in a major motion picture were no big deal. From Dillon's point of view, Blair supposed, it really wasn't much more than an interesting experience. He had nothing to prove, no one to impress in the hope of building a career as a stuntman, although he certainly could have done so had he wished.

Hope grabbed Blair's hand and squeezed it. "It's happening. That old Hollywood magic is happening. I can feel it, darling. *Against the Wind* is going to be a box-office smash."

Blair squeezed Hope's hand in return. "Are you positive we're not just dreaming how well everything's gone so far?"

Marsh laughed and ruffled Blair's hair. "Will you stop being so paranoid and superstitious? We've got the best script, the best cast and the best crew. We're going to win big with this one."

A lot of people agreed with Marsh's assessment of the film's progress. Patrick was ecstatic about the dailies, as was her coproducer, Ian Finch, who was still in California. With so much positive feedback, Blair found it difficult to remain merely cautiously optimistic, but it wouldn't do to let go of her doubts just yet. A little healthy fear was an excellent motivator to bring out the best performance from her.

"Cut!" Cecil yelled.

The crew relayed the order via headset and hand-held radio until it reached the riders. While they slowed the horses to a walk, then circled around and came back to their starting positions, Patrick, Cecil and Bert Grayson, the cinematographer, crowded around the monitor to watch the playback of the chase. Patrick and Cecil conferred for a few minutes, and then Cecil jogged out to give the riders their instructions for the next take. Bristling with nervous energy, Patrick paced over to Blair and the others.

"Well?" Marsh said. "How'd it look?"

"Wonderful." Patrick rubbed his hands together like a miser getting ready to count his piles of money. "We're going to do it again, just to make sure we've got enough coverage, but it looks fantastic. I keep waiting for a disaster, you know? But everybody's having so much fun out there and they're all working so well together I have to keep pinching myself to make sure I'm not dreaming."

Blair laughed to hear Patrick repeat the sentiment she had just voiced. "See, Marsh? I'm not the only one who's paranoid and superstitious."

After rolling his eyes in mock disgust at Marsh, Patrick took off his baseball cap, ran one hand over his sweaty bald head and put it back on. "A lot you know about the creative genius it takes to make a film, you…you…lowly writer."

Marsh clutched his chest with both hands, as if he'd suffered a mortal wound. "Don't *say* it like that, Patrick."

A food-service worker walked through the crew, passing out fruit and granola bars. Patrick, Marsh and Hope each accepted a snack. Blair shook her head. She would choke if she tried to eat anything now.

"All right, places, everybody," Cecil called. "Get ready."

Stuffing half a granola bar into his mouth, Patrick trotted

back to the monitor. Blair crossed her arms over her stomach and paced with the nervous energy Patrick had exhibited, while the camera operators finished resetting for the next take.

"Roll sound," Cecil called, going into his starting ritual.

"Rolling," the sound mixer called back.

"Scene twenty-two. Take two."

The production assistant banged the clapboard. Patrick nodded, and Cecil dropped his hands, yelling, "And...*action!*"

The scene unfolded again. While the time between takes invariably dragged like a long-winded political speech, once the call for action sounded, whole minutes whipped by like a hot sports car with a fearless teenager at the wheel. Blair held her breath, crossed her fingers, bounced up onto her tiptoes, watching Dillon's wild ride across the field with a giddy mixture of exhilaration and terror for his safety and Sunny's.

It was silly, of course. Their stunt coordinator had one of the best safety records in the industry. The crew had walked this field in a foot-by-foot grid, looking for gopher holes and rocks that might trip up one of the horses, and if anyone could handle a problem on horseback, Dillon could. This was literally his home turf. The other stunt people were in more danger than he was.

Her mind might accept all of those logical arguments, but her heart didn't believe any of them, as long as the man she loved was out there risking his neck for a few feet of film that might well end up on the cutting room floor. She wanted to bang Patrick and Cecil's heads together and yell, "Cut!" If anyone else on this set knew what she was thinking and feeling, they would call for a straitjacket. This film meant more to her than anything else in the world. Didn't it? Well, *didn't* it?

She should have been able to answer that question immediately, and with a resounding "Yes!" Realizing that she couldn't made her chest ache and her stomach hurt. It was all right to love Dillon, or even be *in* love with him, as long as she could keep it in perspective.

Falling in love was the most wonderful feeling in the world, but there was always a price to pay. It was self-destructive, if not insane, to allow herself to become so deeply caught up in a relationship that wouldn't last. She couldn't afford to lose herself and lose sight of her own goals because of a man again. Certainly not now.

Of course, Dillon was different from Ted; compared to him, her ex-husband was nothing but a selfish, spoiled little boy. But Dillon didn't want a commitment; he had only agreed to a mad, glorious affair. Though he already had done far more for her than she ever would have expected him to do if he was her husband, he had given no indication that he wanted to change the terms of their agreement.

"Cut!" Cecil yelled.

The horses circled back again. Patrick, Cecil and Bert crowded around the monitor. Blair's heart left her throat and settled back down where it belonged. She suddenly felt herself sway, and her vision wavered around the edges.

Hope took one look at Blair's face, placed a hand on the back of her head and forced it down between her knees. "Don't fight me. Breathe, dammit. You're as white as a ghost."

To Blair's chagrin, nearly everyone noticed her distress, and by the time Hope let her straighten up again, there was a circle of concerned faces hovering around her. "Relax," she said with a shaky laugh. "I'm fine, really."

"You didn't look fine, darling," Hope fussed, laying the back of her hand against Blair's forehead like a mother checking for a fever. "You were going to faint."

Blair batted Hope's hand away. "Well, I'm not going to faint now, darling. Like everyone else, I'm simply a little tired."

Cecil raised a doubtful eyebrow at her. "Are you sure? We need you to be healthy, Blair. Tomorrow's Sunday, so you'll have the whole day off, but Monday we'll be shooting the birth scenes. It will be a difficult week.''

"That's right," Patrick said. "What are you doing out here in this heat and all this dust, anyway? You're not in this scene. You should be resting."

"Patrick," Blair drawled in exasperation, "this is one of the most exciting scenes in the whole script. Everybody's here."

"Well, we're done, and the light's going, so we'll all go back to the house, okay?" Not waiting for an answer, he turned to the crew members and clapped his hands for attention. "That's a wrap. Great job, folks. Everything's fine. Let's move along. See you Monday."

When the crowd finally started drifting away, Dillon and the other riders arrived back at the starting point. Of course he heard about her being sick, and of course he came charging over to see how she was. She looked up into his worried face and gave him what she hoped was a reassuring smile.

"I'm okay, Dillon. Please, don't fuss at me."

He studied her intently for a moment, then put his arm around her shoulders and led her away from Marsh, Hope and the others. "Me? Fuss? Bronc riders never fuss, darlin'. Is there anything I can do for you?"

"Yes. Take me away from all of this."

"Where do you want to go?" He smoothed a flyaway strand of hair behind her ear.

"It doesn't matter. I just want to be alone with you."

"I like the sound of that," he said, with a slow, sexy smile that drove her temperature up at least five degrees. "How about the cabin? Think you can ride that far?"

She nodded eagerly. "I won't have to be back until suppertime tomorrow night."

"All right. I'll help Kirby take care of the stock and meet you back at the house."

He gave her a quick, hard kiss and walked back to Sunny with a definite swagger to each step. She watched him mount up with the others, then turned back to find Hope and Marsh watching her with identical smug grins on their faces. Looking toward heaven to ask for patience, she strolled over to join them.

"So, I guess things are getting pretty hot and heavy between you and Dillon, huh?" Marsh said.

Blair plastered a bland smile onto her mouth. "Mind your own business, Marsh. Why don't you go and find Sandy Bishop?"

"Ooooh, claws," Hope said. "She's testy. That's definitely a good sign, Marsh."

"Will you two please stop it?" Blair grumbled, climbing into the van that would transport them back to the main house.

"No." Since the driver hadn't arrived yet, Marsh continued teasing her. "I know when my big brother is in love. Don't I have a right to know if you're going to become my sister-in-law?"

Blair emphatically shook her head. "That's not going to happen."

"Excuse me?" Hope said. "It looks like love to me. Trust me, honey, I've been watching people fall in love for years, and I know all the symptoms."

"We're having a mad, glorious affair."

Marsh frowned, as if he didn't believe what he was hearing. "That doesn't sound like either one of you. Besides, affairs have been known to grow and develop—"

"Don't be ridiculous, Marsh," Hope scolded, lightly slapping his knee. "If our Blair had affairs, she simply would have slept with that jackass, Ted, instead of marrying him. She must be wildly in love with Dillon, and he's taking advantage of her at this vulnerable moment. The cad."

"Oh, please, Hope, be quiet," Blair said. "Dillon is not a cad. We have an agreement. No promises. No regrets."

"And whose brilliant idea was that?" Hope demanded.

"Mine."

Hope stared at her, then slowly shook her head. "I don't

believe it. I want you to look me in the eye and swear you don't love Dillon McBride.''

''I never said I didn't love him,'' Blair protested.

''Gee, this just keeps making more and more sense,'' Marsh muttered. ''She loves him, but she only wants an affair.''

''Agreements are always subject to renegotiation.'' Hope said. ''If you love him, why are you willing to settle for this...affair?''

The driver arrived before she could formulate a suitable answer. Hope's last question lingered in Blair's mind, taunting her while she packed her gear, saddled Molly and rode up the mountain trail ahead of Dillon. By the time they arrived in the clearing, the sun had slid behind the mountains, leaving only a soft twilight to filter through the trees.

After days of frenzied work on the set and endless production meetings every evening, the solitude of Elizabeth's little cabin was heaven. The simple chores of hauling water, cooking a meal in the fireplace and rolling out the double sleeping bag drove home the realization that they were once again absolutely alone. There were no phones here. No pagers, headsets or radios. No means of interruption short of an earthquake or a forest fire.

When the dishes were done, Dillon produced a bottle of wine, spread an extra blanket on the floor in front of the fire and sat on it, using the platform bed for a backrest. After pulling Blair down to sit between his legs, he massaged the tension from her shoulder muscles. Practically boneless from his ministrations, she sprawled back against him.

He heaved a sigh that positively reeked of contentment, then stroked and played with her hair. She felt hypnotized by the flames, the wine, his solid warmth and strength behind her. A sense of intimacy surrounded them, an intimacy that had nothing to do with sex and everything to do with the joining of souls. Sex undoubtedly would come later, but for now, it was enough to touch and enjoy the quiet together.

The moment was so precious, so poignant, she was loath to risk losing it. But if she didn't speak from her heart now, they might never have another moment like this one. If ever there was a time to convince Dillon to renegotiate their agreement, this had to be it. They were alone and relaxed; their barriers were down. If only she wasn't such a coward.

Dillon twined a lock of Blair's hair around his right index finger and held it up to the firelight. It gleamed like his mother's polished brass candlesticks, and it was soft and silky as a rabbit's fur. He could have played with it for hours, except that Blair had just sighed for the third time in less than five minutes, and he could feel the muscles in her shoulders knotting up again.

"What's botherin' you, darlin'?" he asked, kneading her left shoulder.

She tipped her head back against his chest and studied him, her eyes big and so serious, a tingle of uneasiness skittered around the edges of his mind. "I want to tell you something, but I don't know how you'll react."

"The only way we're gonna find out is for you to come right out and say it," he said.

"All right." She sat up and turned around to face him, her legs crossed Indian-style. Then she took his left hand between her palms, inhaled a deep breath and looked straight into his eyes in a way that made his gut tighten. "I love you."

If he'd been standing, her words would have rocked him back on his heels. But then, a lot of people tossed the word *love* around like chicken feed. It didn't necessarily mean the same thing to Blair that it did to him.

"Yeah..." he said, "I'm, uh, real fond of you, too, hon."

Smiling slightly, she shook her head. "I don't just mean fond, Dillon. I'm *in* love with you. I want to renegotiate our agreement."

He hated to look stupid, but, man, she was going way too fast for him here. "Agreement?"

"You know—no promises? No regrets?"

"You want regrets? Blair, honey, you're confusin' the hell out of me."

She came up onto her knees and cupped her palms around his cheeks. "Just listen for a minute, okay? Of course I don't want regrets. But I know that if I simply walk away from you when we're finished shooting here, I'll regret it for the rest of my life. And I think you will, too. We're good together, Dillon. Extremely good. Don't you think so?"

He still couldn't quite believe she was heading where it looked like she might be going, but he nodded anyway. "Yeah. What're you drivin' at, exactly?"

She took another one of those deep breaths and smoothed his hair back at the sides, as if she thought that might make him understand her better. "I don't want to settle for an affair. When we're done shooting, I want you to come back to L.A. with me."

"And do what?"

"Well, *live* with me at first. And then, if we're as compatible as we've been here, maybe we could...get married?"

Words failed him. He knew he was staring at her, probably with his mouth hanging wide open, but he couldn't help it. From the first time he made love to her, he'd wanted to hold on to her so bad, his bones ached with it.

But he'd never dreamed she could ever feel the same way. About him? Oh, God, he didn't deserve her. Not someone as fine and beautiful and wonderful as Blair.

A cold, greasy sweat suddenly broke out all over his body. His stomach roiled with nausea. His lungs refused to inflate, and he had an almost irresistible urge to get up and run and keep on running until he dropped.

To his shame, and yet his utter relief, she lowered her hands and pulled back from him, and he finally could draw a shallow breath. Her eyes looked even bigger now, and they were filled with hurt—no tears, but that was worse, somehow—and he didn't know what to do or say to make things right. But he had to do *something*. He couldn't just leave her like that—feeling so...terrible.

"Blair, wait."

Holding her hands up in front of her chest, she scooted back, shaking her head all the while. "No, Dillon, it's all right. You obviously don't feel the same way, and that's fine. You can't force something like this."

He grabbed her elbows, halting her retreat. "I love you."

Her eyebrows shot up, and she sniffed in obvious disbelief. "You don't have to do this, Dillon. I can handle rejection. Please, don't worry about it."

"I'm not worryin' about it, and I'm not lyin', either. You just...shocked me, is all. I can't go to L. A. with you, but don't you dare for one second believe I don't love you."

Her expression softened, and she stopped trying to pull away from him. "Oh, Dillon, do you really love me?"

"Yes, darlin', I do. So much it scares the hell out of me."

"Then there must be *some* way we can be together."

"No, honey, I don't want to give you any false hopes. We were right all along when we decided it would never work between us on a permanent basis. Our lives are just too different."

"So? There is such a thing as compromise." She jumped to her feet and started pacing and waving her arms around. "Other actors have ranches. I mean, remember what you said about Hollywood North? We could live up here most of the time. Or we could buy a ranch in California or Nevada or Arizona—and I don't work twelve months of the year, you know."

Her enthusiasm was infectious, and he couldn't help smiling at her. The instant she saw the smile, she pounced, coming back to the blanket, taking his hands in hers again, pleading with her eyes in a way that made him want to give her the world and the moon and all the stars, too.

"You're weakening, I can tell." Grinning wickedly, she crawled in between his legs again and looped her arms around his neck. "Now all I have to do is kiss you into submission."

"Whoa. Down, girl. Wait a minute," he said, laughing as he tried to fend her off. "Nothing is settled, woman."

She rested her forehead against his. "But it will be. Now that we know we love each other, nothing can stop us."

"That's a little naive, darlin'. You know it as well as I do. I have responsibilities to my family, and I just don't see how I'd ever be anything more than a liability to you."

"A liability?" She reared back and sat on her heels, scowling at him. "Everyone on the set loves you. You've done so much for this picture—"

"Yeah, for *this* one, because I happen to have some useful skills. But what about the next one, when you make another cop film, or a comedy, or somethin' like that? Your co-workers might not be so glad to have my ugly face around, and I'd go nuts just sittin' there watchin' other people work. Frankly, it's boring as hell, and in case you haven't noticed, I'm not real good at coolin' my heels."

"That's all small stuff. Trust me, we can figure this out as we go along." She climbed onto his lap, facing him, and put her arms around his neck again. "Will you at least think about it, Dillon? Please?"

How could he refuse? Being with Blair for the rest of his life was only what he wanted most in the whole world, anyway. And maybe…just maybe it could work out somehow. "All right, I'll think about it. But I still can't promise—"

"You don't have to. Once you get used to the idea, you'll see I'm right. I know you will. And besides, if we have some babies…well, we'll both be pretty busy."

She kissed him then, and wiggled her little tush against his groin, which pretty well short-circuited the few functioning brain cells he had left. He slid both hands into her soft hair and plunged his tongue deep into her sweet mouth and prayed she was right about everything. He still had more doubts than he wanted to admit, but he needed this woman so much he figured it would kill him if he ever had to give her up for good.

Wrapping his arms around her, he pushed himself to his feet, turned around and gently deposited her in the middle of the bed. She watched him hungrily while he sat beside her and removed first her boots and then his own. Grasping the front of his shirt, she popped open the snaps in one ripping motion. He performed the same service for her, and their hands and mouths were everywhere, searching out bare skin and pleasure points.

If there was an edge of desperation to their lovemaking, it was only because it meant so much more now that their feelings were out in the open. Every touch became a pledge, every kiss a reminder of all they had shared with each other. He wanted to make this so good for her that she would never regret giving him the gift of her love.

He could live for a thousand years and never be able to express with words how beautiful she was to him. He couldn't paint, either, and he sure couldn't carry a tune, much less write her a love song. The only thing he *could* do was give her pleasure, and that he intended to do, in spades.

Blair looked into Dillon's face and found him studying her body with an expression of wonder in his eyes. He touched her with a gentle reverence completely at odds with his callused, work-roughened hands. He made her feel precious, fragile, cherished.

She reached up and traced his eyebrows, the slope of his nose, his dear mouth. He captured her fingertip between his lips and bathed it with his tongue. She practically purred in response. He smiled and did it again.

Lying here naked with him on the big bed, with the fire

keeping them warm and a whole night ahead of them, was like being caught in the middle of a big, lush movie soundtrack. She could almost hear the strings, hundreds of them, bringing in a sweet, sweeping melody that built and built, swelling the heart with emotion, sending the blood racing, sensitizing nerve endings. He *did* love her. He had to love her to take such pleasure from giving her pleasure.

Oh, he still had doubts. She could hardly blame him. But this time was different. She knew it was.

No one else had ever brought her so much joy with only a look, a touch, a smile. When he made love to her, their so-called differences dissolved; they were simply two people who loved each other, and nothing else mattered. If he wasn't entirely convinced they could make it, she had enough faith for both of them.

She couldn't—*wouldn't*—imagine her life without his slow smiles, his dry humor, his passionate kisses.

When they had found their completion together, she dozed in his arms. Sometime later his body gave a single, hard jerk, and when she looked into his face, her heart contracted at his expression. His gaze was trained on some distant point she couldn't see, and in his eyes was a stark horror that made her chest ache.

"Dillon?" she whispered. "What is it?"

"Huh?" He blinked, shook his head slightly, glanced at her and gave her forehead a soft kiss. "Did I wake you up, darlin'? Sorry about that."

"What were you thinking about?"

"Oh, uh, nothin'. Nothin' import—"

She laid one finger across his lips. "It looked awfully important. We've been so...honest with each other tonight. Please, tell me the truth."

Frowning, he looked into her eyes for a long moment before slowly nodding. "I guess I had a dream about the, uh..." He paused and cleared his throat, but when he spoke again, his voice still sounded husky. "The accident."

"The accident...where you hurt your face?"

His lips twisted in a mockery of a smile. "My face, and most of the bones I hadn't already broken ridin' broncs."

"Tell me about it."

He pulled away from her. "That was years ago. Ancient history. You don't want to hear about it."

"Yes, I do. Tell me what happened."

He studied her, and when she studied him right back with an expectant expression, he gave an exasperated grunt. Breaking eye contact, he stared up at the ceiling while he recited the facts in a monotone he might have used to describe the accident to the police.

"I was tryin' to stop Grace's husband Johnny from drivin' drunk. He lost control of his pickup and rolled it a couple of times. We were both thrown out. Johnny broke his neck and died. I landed in some bushes and lived."

"I thought you told Hope you cut your face on a barbed-wire fence."

He swallowed, then slowly nodded. "The bushes had grown up around the fence, but I still hit it hard enough to rip the hell out of my face."

She flinched at the mental picture his words produced. His head whipped around, and he glared at her. "Don't even think about feelin' sorry for me, DuMaine."

"Don't even think about telling me what to feel, McBride."

"I don't need your damn pity."

"Pity? It's only natural to be sad when someone you care about suffers an injury, but that's not pity. If it bothers you so much, I could find a plastic surgeon for—"

"I saw one."

"And he couldn't help you?"

"He probably could have fixed me up some, but it wasn't real high on my list of priorities right then."

"Why not?"

"He was talkin' about five or six operations, and I was sick and tired of hospitals and surgery by then. They had to take out my spleen and do some orthopedic work on my left arm and leg. The hospital here is so small, I would've had to go to Salt Lake or Denver, and I didn't want to be so far away from Grace. She was really devastated by Johnny's death.''

Blair sensed there was more to Grace's part of the story than he was telling her, but she decided not to question him about it. She respected and admired Dillon's protectiveness toward his sister, and she didn't want to pry.

''What about now?'' she asked instead. ''They can do some amazing things—''

''It's too late now.''

''But, Dillon—''

He cut her off with a decisive shake of his head. ''I've learned to live with it.''

''But you haven't been *living* with it, Dillon. You've been hiding from it.''

''Blair—''

''No, it's my turn. You had a whole other life in rodeo, and dreams you never fulfilled.''

''Grace and the boys needed me.''

''For a while, I'm sure they did. And I know she's appreciated everything you've done, but you're not the only family she has here. Jake and Zack and Cal are all perfectly capable of helping her and acting as role models for the boys. When do you get to have your own life again?''

Dillon remained silent for a moment, then shrugged one shoulder. ''I don't know what else I'd do, now. Rodeo's a young man's sport. I'm too old to go back to it, even if I wanted to.''

''So, you'll find something else to do. I've been watching you very closely, and you're not like all of the other ranchers around here, Dillon.''

''Oh, yeah?''

''Yeah. You can always find something more to talk about than the weather, the price of beef and what those idiots back in Washington are doing.''

He burst out laughing at that. "Oh, you're a cruel woman, DuMaine. Funny, but cruel."

"I only meant that if ranching was all you ever wanted out of life, why did you leave the Flying M? And why did you get married and build that big gorgeous house? You wanted a family, Dillon. Well, I want one, too, and I want to have it with you."

"I promised I'd think about it, and I will." He tucked a strand of hair behind her ear, then kissed the tip of her nose. "But you need to do some serious thinkin', too. I really don't know how much a plastic surgeon could improve my looks at this point. You might have to live with my face just the way it is now."

"You're the one who's so sensitive about it, not me. And I don't need to think about anything. You're the man I want, and nothing's going to change that."

He raised a doubtful eyebrow at her. She looked right back at him, striving to communicate how certain she already was of her feelings. Stubborn man. Well, there were other ways of communicating.

Chapter Fifteen

For Dillon, the next few weeks were like riding an endless emotional roller coaster. When he could get a few hours alone with Blair, his hopes would soar and he'd be convinced they would live happily ever after. When she was too tied up with work to be with him, which was most of the time, doubts bombarded him from all sides, and he would plunge into depression. It was a hundred times worse than being a teenager.

Where once he had avoided the set, he now found himself hanging around it, along with just about everyone else on the ranch. Though the scenes weren't shot in the same sequence in which they would appear in the finished movie, he knew the story well enough to understand the action, and even he could tell something special was happening. With every crack of the clapboard, Blair brought his great-grandmother to life, portraying her with all the gritty determination, passion, enthusiasm, heartbreak and joy Elizabeth had recorded in her diaries.

He was amazed at her skill as an actress, proud of whatever help he'd been able to give her in getting ready to perform this role, convinced she was well on her way to becoming a "real" DuMaine. The closer the end of the filming came, the more ambivalent he felt about marrying her. She was so incredibly talented, acting would always be a big part of her life.

What did he really have to offer her? He wasn't polished or sophisticated; the last time he wore a tux had been to his own wedding. He didn't know beans about the movie industry. He was no hotshot businessman, and had never been more than moderately successful at anything but riding broncs and raising cows. He was far from a pauper, but he'd never earn the kind of money he knew she would soon be able to demand.

Of course, he loved her more than life itself, and maybe that was all that really mattered. But he just didn't know for sure. One thing he did know, though, was that if he ever got married again, he wanted it to last forever. Losing Jill had been hard enough; losing Blair would probably kill him.

He could picture living with her in his own house on the Flying M, no sweat; they were practically living together in the guest house now, and it was wonderful. It could only get better when all this equipment and all these people went away and left them in peace. And if they had a few kids underfoot...it'd be about as close to heaven as he'd ever hope to get.

But he couldn't even begin to visualize the times when he'd have to leave the ranch and live in Los Angeles or somewhere else while she made another film. Whenever he tried to imagine it, he broke out in a cold sweat and he had work hard to stave off a full-fledged panic attack. He was having more frequent nightmares about the accident, too.

As if that weren't bad enough, he was jealous as hell because Patrick Quillen had saved the movie's love scenes for last. Now the set was closed to everyone but essential crew members. It drove Dillon nuts to think about Blair pretending to make love with Keith Stanton all day, even if it was very professional and totally unromantic. Like Stanton wouldn't notice he was lying in bed with Blair, and both of them half-naked. Yeah, right.

Finally, in near desperation, Dillon drove into town one afternoon to get away from it all. He parked in front of Cal's Place and had the misfortune to meet Oliver Rankin coming out of the bar. He didn't like the way the tabloid photographer smirked at him one bit, but decided to let it pass rather than get into a hassle with the jerk.

Cal stood in his usual spot behind the bar, checking supplies and getting ready for the evening crowd, but his normally jovial mood was decidedly missing. Dillon slid onto one of the bar stools and ordered a beer. Cal produced a napkin, a bottle and a glass, then rested one elbow on the bar and studied Dillon's face.

"You look damn near as bad as I feel," he said.

"Thank's a lot," Dillon said. "What's goin' on with you?"

Cal glanced into the dim corners of the room, as if to make sure they were alone. "I miss Sandy, all right?"

"Why? Did she go somewhere?"

Cal's expression turned incredulous. "You don't know?"

"Know what?"

"She gave me back my ring. The engagement's off."

"Oh," Dillon said mildly. "Guess I've had my mind on other things. Sorry to hear that, Cal."

"Yeah!" Cal took Dillon's money and slammed the cash-register drawer shut. "And it's your stupid brother's fault. She's been upset and confused ever since he came back."

"Come on, Cal, you knew that was gonna happen. Those two have loved each other since the third grade. You didn't really think Marsh would just let you have her, did you?"

"Well, I hoped."

"You know you're not in love with Sandy."

"So? She's not in love with me, either, but it's not like we've got hundreds of other folks to choose from. She's the best single gal here in town."

"Doesn't sound like the best grounds for a marriage to me."

"Aw, I suppose not." Cal turned away, poured himself a cup of coffee and set it on the bar. "So, what's your problem? Tell your friendly neighborhood barkeep all about it."

Though he chuckled, Dillon soon found himself doing exactly that. Cal wasn't a successful bartender for nothing, and he usually had a lot of common sense when it came to fixing other people's troubles. "I don't know what to do, Cal. I love Blair, but I don't know if I can go with her."

"Maybe you wouldn't have to," Cal suggested. "Lots of couples live apart at least some of the time these days."

"If your wife looked like Blair, would you want her runnin' around loose?" Dillon asked.

Grinning, Cal shook his head. "No, I guess not. But I still don't understand what's holding you back. If your scars don't bother Blair, does it matter what anybody else thinks?"

"Maybe not." Dillon sipped his beer, then shrugged. "But what about the ranch?"

"You've been carryin' more than your share of the load there for a long time. The rest of us can fill in when you're gone, or we'll hire somebody if we have to."

"What about Grace and the boys?"

"I wondered how long it'd take you to get there."

"What's that supposed to mean?"

"You've been carryin' more than your share of the load here, too. You weren't the only one responsible for what happened to Johnny."

"I was the only one fool enough to jump into that pickup with him. I'd say that makes me pretty damn responsible."

"You were tryin' to stop him, Dillon. For God's sake—"

Dillon banged his beer glass onto the bar and stood. "Don't start, Cal. We've been over this so many times, I know every line you're gonna say."

"Yeah, well, maybe if you'd listen just once, you might learn something." Cal came out from behind the bar and poked his index finger at Dillon's chest, "So, here's a new idea for you. Even if you *were* the only one responsible for Johnny's death, there's not a judge in this country who would've sentenced you to a longer punishment than you've already given yourself. And that's not including any time off for good behavior."

Shaking his head, Dillon walked out of the tavern. Cal followed him to the door and yelled after him. "It's time you forgave yourself and got back out in the world and let the rest of us take our turns lookin' out for Grace and the boys. Dammit, Dillon, you deserve to be happy. Think about it!"

Dillon backed his pickup out of the parking space and roared off toward the ranch. Seemed like everybody wanted him to think about *some*thing. If he'd wanted to do that much thinking, he'd be a preacher or a teacher, not a rancher.

By the time he hit the gravel road, however, his temper had cooled and he felt a pressure growing in his chest fit to choke him. He pulled over to the shoulder, stopped and switched off the ignition. Maybe Cal did have a point.

He wasn't the one who'd been drinking, and he sure hadn't forced Johnny to drink or cheat on his wife. He hadn't hurt Johnny on purpose, and he'd sure paid one hell of a price—a career, a wife, and his face—for what amounted to an impulsive, somewhat stupid action. Besides, even if Grace knew the whole truth about Johnny's death, she'd probably be the first to forgive him.

And didn't that just sound like one huge pile of rationalization, so that he could do what he really wanted to do?

Setting his hat on the seat beside him, Dillon leaned his head against the back window and shut his burning eyes. A picture of Johnny's terrified face immediately formed in his mind, and he could hear his slurred pleas echoing down the years.

It didn't mean nothin', Dillon, you've gotta believe that. You can't hurt me, or Grace'll know what I did. That'll just hurt her, and my boys. You wouldn't hurt your own sister, wouldya? Please, don't tell Grace. Promise me.

The memories ended there, because Johnny's life had ended there. So had Dillon's. Cursing under his breath, he shoved his hat back on his head, turned on the ignition and slammed the truck into gear. He had some serious thinking to do, and he'd best get on with it. And he needed to see his sister.

He found her on the back porch with the boys, waving goodbye to Wade Kirby. Since they'd filmed all the scenes using his horses, the wrangler had run out of excuses to stay on at the Flying M. Damned if Grace, Riley and Steven didn't all look as dejected as a litter of pups left at home on the first day of school.

Hmm. Maybe he shouldn't have been so rough on ol' Kirby. If Grace got married again... Hell, what was he thinking? Any man worth his salt ought to be able to stand up to a woman's male relatives, if he loved her enough to get serious about her. Obviously, Kirby wasn't the right man for Grace, but that didn't mean the right man couldn't be found.

She looked up and caught him staring at her, crossed her eyes and stuck her tongue out at him, then flounced into the house, letting the screen door bang shut behind her. The boys let out a startled yelp of laughter at their mother's odd behavior. Dillon promised to check on her and sent them off to do their chores.

He walked into the kitchen, and saw her facing the sink, arms crossed tightly over her middle, head bowed. The pressure came back to his chest in a hurry. Sassy, stubborn, bossy, irritating as a splinter in the butt—he'd rather see Grace act any way but defeated. He crossed the room and stood behind her.

"Want me to go after Kirby for you?"

She uttered a strangled laugh, then wiped her cheeks with the backs of her hand. "It's probably that kind of an idiotic attitude from all of you guys that sent him packin'."

"I'll just go after him and bring him back if you want. Cross my heart, I won't lay a finger on him."

After wiping her cheeks again, she turned to face him, a tight, shaky smile on her mouth. "Don't bother. It wasn't that serious."

"Did you want it to be, sis?"

"I don't know."

She sniffled and tried for another smile, but then her face crumpled, tears gushed from her eyes and she threw herself into his arms. He held her close, patting her back and remembering a hundred other agonizing times when his sister had cried and cried and there'd been nothing he could do to ease her pain.

"I'm sorry," she said, gulping. "I just didn't realize how lonely I was till Wade came along. You know?"

"I sure do, hon."

She pulled back and looked into his eyes for the longest time. "Yeah, I guess you do. Jeez, Dillon, we're a pair, aren't we? It feels like we've been frozen in time ever since the wreck, puttin' one foot in front of the other to get by, but not really goin' anywhere."

"Where did you want to go?"

"It wasn't a place, Dillon. I love this ranch and Sunshine Gap. I just never figured I'd have to grow old alone."

"Who said you have to? If you'd get out there a little, you'd have more guys underfoot than you'd know what to do with."

"That wouldn't take much." She turned away from him, crossed her arms over her breasts and fastened her gaze on the mountains beyond the windows. "Half the time, I hardly even feel like a woman anymore."

"Aw, hell, you're still a young, beautiful woman, Grace. Ol' Kirby sure noticed that right off."

"Well, he's gone now." She sniffed, cleared her throat and started sorting through the stuff that seemed magically to pile up on the countertop every day. Then she glanced at Dillon and sighed. "Hey, don't look at me like that. I'm all done feelin' sorry for myself, now. I had a wonderful marriage. I've got two great kids and a family who loves me. All in all, I know I've had a pretty darn good life."

"But you're not happy."

"So? Neither are you. Besides, you can't make me happy, Dillon. I've gotta do that myself. I'm a big girl, now."

"Ha! Tell Mom that." Dillon chucked her under the chin with his forefinger. "You've been my baby sister since the day she brought you home, laid you in my lap and told me to protect you from Marsh and all the other little renegades in the family."

She grinned at him, and this time her smile stayed steady. "Yeah, yeah, I've heard about it a million times. Could you get it through your thick skull that I'm thirty-one years old now?"

"No way. You don't look a day over thirty and a half."

"Oh, get outa here, you big lug." She gave him a playful shove toward the back door. "I've got to figure out what to fix for supper."

He walked to the back door, hesitated, then turned back to her for a moment. "Sure you're all right, Gracie?"

"I will be. Go take care of your own life."

"What do you mean by that?"

"You know darn well what I mean. You're in love with Blair. Do something about it."

"You and the boys wouldn't mind getting rid of me, huh?"

"We wouldn't want you to go away forever, but you

don't have to baby-sit us. To be honest, I've enjoyed having them depend on me sometimes, instead of always goin' to you.''

"I never meant to interfere, sis.''

"You didn't do a thing I didn't let you do. I'm just askin' you to back off a little now and let me finish growin' up.''

Her brave smile followed him out of the house and across the barnyard to the pasture. He always thought better on horseback. He had a lot to sort out, and not much time to do it in. Kirby wasn't the only one who'd left the Flying M; the trailer city had already dwindled to half its original size. If the filming went well, they might even wrap it up today.

It was time to decide.

"Cut,'' Patrick called from the sidelines. "Blair, may I speak with you for a moment, please? Everyone else, take ten.'' Hearing the impatience in the director's voice, Blair quickly slipped into her robe and took the chair he indicated while the others filed out. "I'm sorry, Patrick. I'll get that line right on the next take, I promise.''

Patrick sat down beside her, frowning while he studied her face. "It's not just the line, Blair. You're not making eye contact, and your body language is all wrong. Is it Keith? If he's doing something that makes you uncomfortable—''

"No, Patrick. Honestly, Keith has been absolutely professional. He's trying hard to put me at ease.''

"Then what's wrong? You've had a stunning performance up to this point, and I don't see any reason you shouldn't be able to carry it through to the very end.''

"I know.'' She raised both hands, palms up, to show how helpless she felt. "It shouldn't be this difficult, but I'm not sure what the problem is.''

"Is it Dillon? Is he having trouble coping?''

Blair nodded. "A little.''

"More than a little?''

"Well, yes. It bothers him a lot."

"Do you want me to talk to him?"

Blair gave him a wry smile and shook her head. "No, but thanks for offering. I'll be fine, Patrick. Let's just get this finished, okay?"

Patrick rolled his eyes at her. "I'm doing the best I can. Why don't you take five and see if you can find Elizabeth again?"

With that, he got up and left her alone. Blair looked around the fake interior of the cabin. If one ignored the cameras, lights and cables, it was amazing how close to the real thing the set decorator and had been able to come. Perhaps that was the problem—it looked so much like the real cabin, she kept expecting and wanting to see Dillon's face, instead of Keith's.

The wretched man. Yes, she knew he was suffering jealous pangs because of the love scene they were shooting. It was rather sweet of him to be so...protective. Some people naturally had more problems with that than others. She suspected, however, that the real source of his discomfort involved the decision he needed to make. While she believed marriage was an important matter that deserved serious thought, she sincerely wished Dillon would hurry the heck up.

If he didn't agree to marry her soon, she undoubtedly would go quite insane. They both would. The uncertainty of their future together hung in the air like the stench of a cheap cigar, robbing them of sleep, making them snap at each other over ridiculous things and spoiling what little time they were able to spend together.

Disgusted with her own lack of professionalism, she jumped to her feet, muttering, "Enough is enough."

Patrick was right. She needed to look inside herself and find Elizabeth again. Elizabeth wouldn't have put up with Dillon's dillydallying. She wasn't asking him to give up his whole life, but she wouldn't give up her whole life, either. They would both need to adjust and make compromises. If she wasn't important enough to him for that, she needed to know about it.

But first, she intended to finish this movie in a way that would have made Elizabeth proud. She would stop worrying about Dillon and start putting all that wonderful passion he had taught her to feel to good use. And when she saw Dillon again, they were going to talk this out, once and for all.

Chapter Sixteen

Dillon rode back to the corral just after sunset. After three hours in the saddle, he hadn't come to any final conclusion, but he knew he had to do something different with his life. Like Grace, he was tired of being lonely. Unlike Grace, he was no longer willing to keep on putting one foot in front of the other just to get by.

It wasn't as if his marrying Blair would hurt Grace any more than she'd already been hurt. And if he showed his little sister he could build a new, better life now, maybe she'd follow his example and find some happiness for herself. That might just be a rationalization, but most folks couldn't survive without a few to keep them sane. Why should he be any different?

A cheer went up from the catering tent. Dillon noticed it was all lit up, and there were lots of folks heading that way. He called out to a couple of production assistants hurrying by.

"What's goin' on?"

"We just wrapped," one of them called back. "Come to the tent. It's time to party."

Eager to see Blair and talk things over with her, he stripped off Sunny's tack, rubbed him down and turned him into the pasture in record time. He put the oat bucket away and quickly washed his face and hands at the side of the barn, then realized he'd forgotten to get himself a towel. Shaking the water from his face and wiping his hands on his jeans, he heard male voices coming from around the corner.

"Oh, gross! Can you believe that?"

A newspaper rustled. A second voice answered. "No way, man. Look at that face. How can she even stand to touch him?"

Dillon froze. Surely they weren't talking about—

"You've got me," the first voice said. "The guys on the cameras said she practically set the sheets on fire with Stanton today. Maybe she's just been using the cowboy to get herself into the character."

Their laughter cut through Dillon's soul like a chain saw through a pine tree.

"Maybe he's hung like a horse. Or maybe he knows some weird cowboy technique we've never heard of."

"Oh, she probably feels sorry for him. She's really a nice lady, you know? She could just be giving him a thrill."

"Or get this—maybe she's really in love with him."

They both laughed uproariously. A new voice joined in. "What's happenin'?"

"Get a look at these pictures," the first voice said. The newspaper rustled again. "No way those were faked."

"Ugh city, man! She deserves an Oscar for not throwing up. Is she blind or what?"

"That's what we've been trying to figure out. Do you think she loves him?"

"Not even. Lots of babes like the idea of a cowboy. You know, this story is really romantic and everything. She could have just gotten swept away by it all."

"Oh, right. I bet she sees ol' Mr. Dillon as an insurance policy."

"Huh? That sounds pretty cynical, even for you."

"Think about it. If this picture bombs like the last three she was in, she's history in Hollywood. But there's no shame in leaving the business to marry a rich rancher. His face just adds pathos to the whole thing. Makes her seem…noble, you know?"

Dillon charged around the side of the barn and found three young men looking at the front page of an all-too-familiar tabloid. They automatically stepped back when they saw him, their mouths dropping open in shock, their eyes widening with fear. Dillon grabbed the newspaper and, without saying a word, carried it into the barn.

At first it felt as if the bottom of his stomach had dropped right onto the floor. Then it took a slow, nauseating roll and all the air whooshed out of his lungs. No wonder those guys had laughed. And no wonder Rankin had smirked at him. He wished he'd stomped that little son of a bitch's camera instead of just kicking it.

Rankin had caught him and Blair dead to rights. Jeez, what a clinch. They were kissing like they couldn't get enough and grabbing each other's behinds, leaving no doubt for anyone with half a brain that they'd been doing some serious carrying-on.

The first picture showed the ruined side of his face, his scars standing out like lines on a road map. The second one highlighted his right hand, making his missing thumb painfully obvious. Blair looked so damn beautiful, it seemed obscene, even to him, that she would let anyone so disfigured touch her, much less kiss her. The headline read: Beauty and the Beast.

He wished he'd never been born. He wished he'd died in the wreck with Johnny. He wished he could die right now. And if he felt this humiliated, how would Blair feel when she saw this rag?

Oh, Lord. Blair *was* a nice lady, a kind and compassionate lady. She would never admit to feeling embarrassed, even if she was completely mortified. And this was only the first time the tabloids had noticed him. If she married him, she'd have to face this over and over again.

His stomach did another slow, nauseating turn, and his skin felt cold and slick with sweat. The barn walls closed in on him, cutting off his air supply. His mind raced on.

Every time Blair was in the news, some sleazy creep of Rankin's ilk would trot out pictures just like these to remind everyone that she was the actress who'd married a freak. People would always laugh at her, at him, at the thought of them making love together. He couldn't let her do that to herself or to her career.

Crumpling up the newspaper, he stuffed it behind a sack of feed and went to find her. The catering tent suddenly fell quiet as he approached it. He hesitated outside the rear doorway and decided to stay there until he could figure out what was going on. Blair and Keith Stanton stood up front with Patrick Quillen, and all of them were holding champagne glasses.

Stanton raised his glass and smiled at Blair. "To our lovely, talented star, who has made working on this project a pleasure for all of us. We love you, Blair, and when this film is released, so will the rest of the world. Ladies and gentlemen, a toast to our own Blair DuMaine."

While everyone echoed the toast, Stanton leaned down and kissed Blair's lips, lingering with obvious enjoyment to the crew's delight. Their whoops and catcalls hit Dillon like physical blows, hammering into his brain the jolting comparison between the pictures he'd just seen of himself kissing Blair and this whole, handsome man kissing her.

Unable to watch any more, he bolted. One thought ran through his mind again and again. Blair deserved someone like Keith Stanton. At the very least, she deserved someone a hell of a lot better than him.

Giddy with excitement and relief, Blair accepted a second glass of champagne from Patrick and sat back to watch the rest of the cast and crew celebrate. There would be more work to do before *Against the Wind* was released—editing, additional dialogue recording, adding the soundtrack—but for this crew, it was the end of their job together. By tomorrow, most of them would be packing up and going home, or moving on to the next job.

The catering people must have cleaned out their seemingly endless supply of snacks for the party. Patrick had added his usual generous contribution of alcohol. Someone else had produced a portable CD player, filling the tent with music to accompany the loud talk and laughter.

Smiling and chatting, Blair did her best to participate, but all she really wanted was to be alone with Dillon. Where was he? He must have heard about the party, or rather *heard* the party, by now. She could not have done this movie without him. She had told him all about the tradition of celebrating when the last scene was finished. Surely he would want to be here and share this moment with her.

Exhausted and mentally wrung out, she waited and waited for him. She ate food she didn't want, drank more than she should have, and even danced a little to fill the time. But Dillon didn't arrive.

Along with Patrick and Keith, she toasted the crew and accepted their toasts, applause and good wishes for a blockbuster opening in return. She signed autographs. She spoke via telephone with her co-producer, Ian Finch, who was thrilled they had finished on time and within the budget. But Dillon didn't arrive.

The food and drink dwindled. People drifted away, all except the last few, who were too polite to leave one of the stars alone at the wrap party. But Dillon still didn't arrive, and finally she had to accept that he wasn't going to show up at all. Not tonight, or any other night.

Dillon had made his decision about marrying her. His answer was no.

* * *

It was late, probably close to midnight, when Dillon heard Blair's voice outside the guest house. He'd been sitting in the darkened living room for hours, waiting for her. He'd never acted like such a miserable coward before, but he just hadn't been able to force himself to step over the threshold at the catering tent.

The door creaked open, and a wave of sweet night air touched his hot skin. Blair stepped inside, said good-night to someone through the screen, then shut the door behind her and clicked on a light switch. A forty-year-old floor lamp came on, blinding Dillon with its sudden brightness.

He heard her gasp and knew she had seen him. Silence followed, thick and heavy. When his eyes adjusted to the glare, he saw her standing in the entryway, staring at him with such an air of disappointment, he wanted to vanish in a puff of smoke like some cartoon character.

"Hello, Dillon." Her voice was husky with weariness, but you'd never know it to look at her. She held her head high and her shoulders back, and her eyes glinted with temper. "I'm surprised to see you here. Is there something I can do for you?"

"Don't, Blair."

"Don't what? Don't be angry?" She smacked her tote bag onto an end table, crossed the room in four fast strides and glared at him from the other side of the coffee table. "Too late. I'm so furious with you, I don't think it's a good idea for us to talk right now. Why don't you go back to the house tonight, and I'll try to be rational enough to speak to you in the morning?"

He wasn't going anywhere. Somehow, he had to make her understand. "I'm not much for parties."

"Try again. You wouldn't even have needed to change your clothes. I wasn't the only one who was disappointed you didn't show up. If you didn't want to be there for me, you could have at least stopped in to say goodbye to everyone."

"It wasn't that I didn't want to be there for you—"

"I know why you didn't come, Dillon."

The thought of her seeing those pictures made his guts hurt. "You do?"

"You've decided you don't want to marry me. There, I said it. It's out in the open, and I'm fine—see? Now go away."

"It's not that I don't want to marry you, Blair. I *can't*."

She started to pace, hands gesturing every which way, as if she had to expel some energy or explode. "Oh, really? You've already got a wife tucked away somewhere you haven't told me about?"

"Of course not."

"I can't think of any other reason you *can't* marry me. You're certainly not impotent—not that that would necessarily be a wedding-stopper for me. I'm not aware of any warrants out for your arrest, or any jail sentences hanging over your head."

"Dammit, Blair—"

"Dammit, Dillon, don't try to tell me what to do or how to feel when the man I love with all my heart won't come to my wrap party and refuses to marry me." She stopped pacing and propped her fists on her hips. "What's wrong with me, anyway? Is it my age? Should I get breast implants? Have my thighs and butt liposuctioned? A tummy tuck? A nose job? A face-lift?"

"Stop! It's not how you look. It's how *I* look."

"Well, I suppose, if you really want them, we could get *you* some breast implants, but your butt's already pretty skinny."

"That's not funny," he muttered, snorting to cover a chuckle in spite of himself.

"Then why are you laughing?"

"I'm not laughing, dammit."

"Neither am I." She started pacing again. Damned if she didn't look like a big cat in a small cage. "This whole subject is utterly ridiculous, and we've already been over it. What's really the problem?''

''I guess you haven't seen Rankin's rag today.''

''Yes, I saw it. But I'm not complaining about how you look, and I'm the bride, so my opinion's the only one that counts.''

''Don't tell me those pictures didn't bother you.''

''Of course they bothered me. No one likes having their privacy invaded, but it happens to come with the territory I work and live in. We'll simply have to be more careful, and you'll have to learn to expose a photographer's film instead of kicking his camera. It's hardly the end of the world as we know it.''

''Easy for you to say. You're not the one they're callin' the beast.''

''Oh, puh-lease. You can't allow Oliver Rankin to get to you like this. He's just one slimy little bastard—''

''And there are dozens more where he came from. I've seen what these guys do to people like you, Blair. If I married you, this would never end. They'd be after you like—''

''No matter what I do or don't do, they're going to be after me anyway,'' she said. ''They've *always* been after me. If I don't give them something to write about, they simply invent something. I'd rather have them write about you than animals and aliens.''

''Will you take this seriously?''

''No! You're taking this entirely too seriously for both of us.'' She paused and held her hands out to him, palms up. ''I love you, Dillon. You love me. We can be happy together. I don't care what other people think.''

''Maybe I do. You should marry somebody who looks like Stanton.''

''Been there, done that. And guess what? Ted thought he could build his acting career with my family's contacts. I'm not the least bit impressed with a pretty face, Dillon.''

''Well, pardon me all to hell if it bothers me to know

other people are laughing at the thought of us being together because of my damned face and wondering why you don't throw up when I touch you because of my damned hand.''

Something in his voice must have penetrated her anger. She paused, looked deeply into his eyes, then sank into the rocking chair adjacent to the sofa and tucked one foot under herself. ''What happened, Dillon?''

He told her about the three young crew members he'd overheard, and when he'd finished, she sadly shook her head. ''I'm sorry you were hurt, but they're the ones who are pathetic, not you. Everything they said is just so stupid, I—''

''I know that with my head,'' Dillon interrupted. ''It's my gut that hasn't quite figured it out yet.''

''Well, there *is* another solution. You probably can't do anything about your thumb, but if your face really bothers you that much, you could always have reconstructive surgery.''

''No. I already told you that.''

''Why not?''

''It's too late.''

''I doubt it. You could at least check it out.''

''No, I can't.''

''If it's a question of money—''

''Hell, no. That's never been the issue.''

''Then what *is* the issue? If you're going to break my heart, I think I deserve to know the real reason you're so abominably stubborn about not having surgery.''

''It wouldn't make any difference, Blair. Even if I had the surgery, I still couldn't leave the ranch.''

''Dillon, we talked about this before, and—''

''It's because of Grace and the boys.''

''I'm afraid I don't understand.''

''I know you don't. Grace doesn't know the whole truth, either. Not really.''

''What are you saying?''

"It's my fault my sister is a widow. It's my fault Riley and Steven don't have a father. It's my fault Johnny Kramer is dead."

Blair frowned in confusion. "You said you were trying to stop him from driving when he was drunk."

"That much is true. It's just not...everything."

"Tell me, Dillon."

He sat forward, legs apart, and laced his fingers together between his knees. "I was home from the circuit for a quick visit. Jake and Zack and Cal and I were playin' poker in the back room at Cal's Place one night. I wasn't drinkin', because I was takin' pain medicine for a separated shoulder at the time. The other guys'd had a few beers, but nobody was really blasted or anything. We were just shootin' the breeze and havin' fun."

"What happened next?"

"When we went out to go home, Zack noticed Johnny's truck parked around the corner at the other bar we had back then. We decided to see what he was up to. We caught him havin' sex with another guy's wife."

"Oh, dear."

"Yeah, no kiddin'." Dillon sighed and rubbed the back of his neck. "We didn't really mean to just stand there and watch, but we were all so surprised.... Anyway, he looked up and saw the four of us. The gal scrambled off his lap and slid out the passenger door and left it hangin' wide open. It was my sister he was cheatin' on, so I yanked open Johnny's door and pulled him out by the front of his shirt. He was drunk, but he wasn't so far gone he didn't know what he was doin'."

"What did you do to him?"

"Nothin', really. Oh, I cussed him out good. But I guess he must've figured all four of us were gonna work him over. That sort of thing's been known to happen around here."

"But you didn't."

Dillon shook his head. "Johnny didn't give us the

chance. After ₁ cussed him, he jumped back into his pickup and fired up the engine. I ran around and jumped in on the other side, 'cause I knew he wasn't in any shape to drive. He took off like a bat outa hell, beggin' me not to hurt him and not to tell Grace what he'd done.''

"Oh, Dillon."

"I tried to calm him down, but it was like he couldn't even hear me. He kept drivin' faster and faster, and all I could do was hang on for dear life. Then he missed a curve and rolled the truck. He died and I didn't, and I'm responsible.''

Blair nodded, then said quietly, "A lot of people wouldn't see it quite that way, but it doesn't surprise me that you do.''

"I just thought you should know that about me.''

"That's why you wouldn't have the surgery on your face, isn't it? To punish yourself.''

Dillon shrugged. "I don't know. Yeah, maybe. And, see, that makes me responsible to take care of his wife and kids. That's why I gave up rodeo, really. And maybe that's partly why my wife left me. She really enjoyed travelin' around on the circuit with me. Anyway, she liked the idea of bein' married to a rodeo star more than to a plain old everyday rancher.''

"You could take care of Grace and the boys without being here every single day, Dillon. There are always telephones and airplanes.''

"It's not the same as bein' right there when somebody needs you.''

"Believe it or not, that's something I do understand," Blair said, smiling sadly. "You said that Grace doesn't understand all of this?''

"She doesn't know Johnny was cheatin' on her. If he'd lived, I suppose we would've had to tell her. But she was already hurtin' so much when he died, there didn't seem to be any point in hurtin' her more. She always did love that guy.''

"Do you think that's really fair to her?"

Dillon glanced at Blair in surprise. "Sure. Why wouldn't it be?"

"She deserves to know the truth about her own life. When she talks about Johnny, she makes him sound like such a saint, how could any other man ever take his place? She certainly didn't give poor Wade much of a chance."

"She gave him more of a chance than she's given anyone else since Johnny died. Do you think that's why she's never dated?"

"It's possible she's still clinging to the memory of a man who was no more than an illusion. Think about it, Dillon. She may be stuck in a past that never existed."

"So you think we should tell her?"

"That's something you'll have to decide. Personally, I've always found the truth to be less painful in the long run than a lie. The lie always makes one feel like such a fool."

"I'll talk it over with Jake," Dillon said.

A moment of silence followed, stretching his nerves to the breaking point. God, he didn't want to leave her tonight, but after everything he'd told her, would she even let him touch her again? Just one last time? And then she uncurled herself from the rocking chair and stood, holding out her hand to him.

"Come to bed," she said softly. "I need you to hold me."

He looked up into her eyes and saw such an expression of love and acceptance, it nearly brought him to his knees. In fact, he wasn't too sure his legs would work at all until she came closer, took his hand in hers and tugged him to his feet. He accompanied her to the bedroom, barely able to believe this was really happening.

Feeling slow and awkward, he submitted to her murmured instructions and gentle guiding hands. She undressed them both with a minimum of fuss and crawled into bed beside him. She was the one who held him, and every kiss, every touch, she gave him became a healing balm to his wounded spirit.

It was like having an angel stroke him from head to toe with her wings, leaving him renewed and whole again. A soft, warm light filled the aching hole that had lodged up under his heart when he came to after the accident and found out Johnny was gone. The light dispelled the darkness, and it felt as if he'd been blind and his vision magically was now restored.

Suddenly, for the first time in six years, he could see himself and his life clearly; it was not a pretty sight. He'd withdrawn into himself, clutching at his own pain and guilt and self-pity. He'd holed up, cranky as an old wolverine, snarling and snapping to keep his family and his friends away from him.

He'd even pushed Jill away. She hadn't tried very hard to stay, and when she turned on him, she'd gone for his jugular. But he had definitely rejected her first.

And yet, here was Blair, the most beautiful woman he'd ever known, lying in bed with him. She knew his most damning secrets, but she was making love to him with her hands, her mouth, her whole body, holding him as if it would kill her to let him go, when it was really the other way around. He might be the lowest form of slime on earth, but he wasn't strong enough or noble enough just to let her walk out of his life forever.

There had to be some way they could be together.

Desperate to make Dillon feel how much she loved and needed him, Blair straddled his waist and planted feverish kisses along the heaviest line of scar tissue on his cheek. He turned his head, aligning his lips with hers. Sighing his name, she slid her hands into his hair and held him still while she plundered his mouth.

She tasted the salt of tears, but wasn't sure if they were her own or his. Perhaps they were both weeping, at the thought of making love for the last time. Well, she wouldn't have it; she hadn't given herself to this man lightly, and she would not go away without so much as a whimper and allow him to suffer alone with his overactive conscience.

From his mouth, she kissed her way across his scratchy chin, down the front of his Adam's apple and over his knobby collarbone. He reached for her, but she firmly pushed his hands back onto the bed and held them there while she nibbled her way down the center of his chest. If she couldn't get him to see reason with her words, she simply would have to use other methods, and he would have to endure the consequences.

He could try to send her away, but he was not going to forget her. He groaned when she dipped her tongue into his navel. He writhed when she stroked his arousal with her fingers. He came up off the bed when she took him into her mouth and loved every delicious inch of him.

If only she could love him enough, touch him deeply enough, heal him enough to make him see himself the way she saw him—as the warm, loving, intelligent, talented man he really was. She gave him everything she had to give, hoping and praying it would somehow be enough to shake him out of his prison of self-punishment and free him to find his way back to a life in the sunshine. A life with her. A life with the children she wanted to give him.

She'd never wanted to have children with Ted. But Dillon was so different; he had such integrity and such maturity. She *knew* she could depend on him to be a good father and share the responsibilities of raising a child. The thought of carrying his baby and sharing the birth experience with him was an incredible turn-on.

She rubbed her breasts against his groin, his belly, his chest, and offered them to his mouth. She stroked and petted and gently used her fingernails on his skin, making him groan and laugh and sigh. She straddled his hips again, laced her fingers with his and took him inside her, riding him to a delirious completion.

Then she collapsed on top of him, boneless as a blanket

feeling their hearts pounding in a shared, frantic rhythm. She didn't realize she was crying again until he caressed her back with long, sweeping strokes, from her hair to her thighs, gently shushing her. It would kill her to walk away from him now.

"Don't, darlin'," he murmured. "Don't cry."

"I can't help it." She pushed up on one elbow and looked down into his eyes. "I love you, Dillon. You've given me a glimpse of heaven, and now you expect me just to leave it. Well, I don't want to be alone anymore, dammit. And I don't want to leave you."

He reached up and wiped away her tears with his fingertips, but more replaced them. "Aw, sweetheart, it's okay. We'll figure somethin' out."

"What do you have in mind?"

"I don't know yet, but I don't want to be alone anymore, either. It's time to start thinkin' about solutions instead of problems."

She collapsed on top of him again, and rubbed her cheek against his chest while a huge yawn overcame her. "Okay. Tomorrow. We're both too tired now."

A chuckle rumbled beneath her ear, and his warm, strong arms folded around her. "All right, darlin'. Go to sleep. Everything's gonna be all right."

Like any foolish woman in love, she believed him.

Chapter Seventeen

"**Y**ou want me to *what?*" Blair demanded, coming half-way out of her chair the next evening. The ranch had been in chaos all day, with the crew leaving. She and Dillon had retreated to the guest house after supper, desperate for an opportunity to speak privately again.

"You heard me." Dillon leaned across the dinette table in the kitchen and gently pressed on her shoulder until she sat down again. "Don't fly off the handle until you hear me out."

"I don't need to hear anything to recognize a man breaking his word. Last night you said—"

"That everything's gonna be all right," he finished for her, in a voice she instantly despised. How could he sound so calm and firm when he was breaking her heart? "And I still believe it will be."

"Oh, yes, of course, we should be able to build a wonderful relationship when we're separated by a thousand miles for God knows how long. And I'm not even supposed to call you on the telephone? Is that what they call cowboy logic?''

''No need to be sarcastic, DuMaine. I've been thinkin' about it all day, and I'm convinced this is the right thing for both of us. You know it, too, and that's why you're gettin' all steamed up at me. Because you don't want to do it.''

''You're damn right I don't want to do it. Why, it's…it's…''

''The right thing to do,'' he repeated in that same calm, horrible voice. ''Last night you told me you don't want to be alone anymore. All I'm askin' you to do now, is figure out what you really *do* want.''

Folding his arms over his chest, he tipped his chair onto its hind legs, which, in her opinion, made him look maddeningly arrogant. How could he be so damnably sure of himself, when she felt scared to death? He obviously didn't care about her as she did about him. Otherwise, he never would have suggested that they separate until *Against the Wind* was released.

He lowered the front legs of his chair to the floor, leaned across the table and grasped her right hand between both of his, refusing to let it go when she tugged at it.

''I'm not doin' this to be mean, Blair,'' he said. ''I'm gonna hate it every bit as much as you are. Probably more.''

''Then why do it?''

''Because this has all happened so fast. You're the one who said set romances rarely work out. How are we gonna know that's not all we've got here if we don't go back to our own lives for a while and get some perspective? Before we can build any kind of a life together, we both need to know who we are and what we really want.''

''Oh, please, I'm the Californian. I'm supposed to be the one who says things like that. We're not teenagers, Dillon.''

''Well, then, tell me somethin', darlin'. A while back,

you said to me you had to prove you were a real DuMaine. Are you a real DuMaine or not?''

''Of course I am.'' He simply sat there, holding her hand and looking at her, and looking at her and looking at her, until she started to squirm and added, ''I think.''

''When you can answer that question without any hesitation or doubt, it'll be time for us to talk again.'' With a sad smile, he patted her hand, then released it.

''But, Dillon, you're talking about *months* of postproduction,'' she protested. ''At least five. Perhaps as many as eight.''

''I understand that, but I want the whole enchilada here—marriage, kids and forever. What's eight months, compared to the rest of our lives?''

''That's not fair.''

''Sure it is. You're gonna be so dang busy gettin' that movie finished, you'll hardly even miss me.''

''Yes, I will, and I'll hate it. I still don't understand why you're insisting on this.''

''Blair, our chances for a successful marriage aren't great to begin with. Our backgrounds are totally different, we haven't known each other very long, and we've spent so much time just workin' together or gettin' into each other's pants, we haven't really thought this all through. We haven't even met each other's parents yet.''

''Mine certainly won't be a problem,'' she muttered. ''I rarely see them.''

He went on as if she hadn't spoken, firmly laying out more of his blasted reasons. ''With the career you've got, we're bound to have long separations sometimes, so we're gonna have to learn to cope with it sooner or later.''

''I vote for later.''

''We've got two divorces between the two of us, and pardon me all to hell if I don't want to go through that again.''

''I certainly don't, either. No one enjoys a divorce.''

''Exactly. So, let's take our time with this decision.

You've had a lot of pressure on you ever since you started this project, and I think you should see it through to the end without any unnecessary distractions.''

"You wouldn't be a distraction, Dillon."

"That's exactly what I'd be. I wouldn't know anyone but you, and I wouldn't know my way around. And you won't have time to teach me how to survive in L.A. until you've finished your movie. I'd probably whine and fuss and turn into a royal pain in the rear end."

"As if you're not being one now," she grumbled. Then she sighed and raked both hands through her hair. "Assuming I agree to this plan of yours, what will you be doing while I'm finishing my movie?"

"I need to do some cleanup in my own life. I want to be sure of what I want, too. I've got some important things to think about."

"Such as?"

"Well, such as how I'm gonna make a living if we get married. I don't want to be a kept man, you know."

"Honestly, Dillon—"

"No, I mean that. Maybe we could live up here most of the time, and I'd keep on ranching, but I'd never want to lay around like a bum."

"I doubt there's any real danger of that."

He shrugged, then grinned. "Yeah, that's not really my style. Somehow, I always find plenty to keep me busy. Shoot, I'm gonna be so dang rich from all this money you're payin' me, I'll probably finish my house once the cows are shipped."

She hated him for winning this argument. She hated him for acting so pleasant and optimistic while she simply wanted to pout and rage at the unfairness of it all. And she hated him for being so relentlessly...*rational,* when it would have been much more romantic to be swept off her feet.

And yet, in a bizarre sort of way, she found it reassuring that he wanted her feet firmly planted on the ground, so to speak, if and when they decided to marry. Somewhere inside herself, she knew it was Dillon's integrity and maturity—the same two qualities she had admired so much in him last night—that were prompting him to do this.

Everything he'd said *did* make sense. She did *not* want to endure another divorce. And she *did* have a tremendous amount of work left to do before she could command her own time again. But what they had found together was so precious—what if it vanished while they were apart?

As if he could read her thoughts, he leaned closer and looked straight into her eyes. "If what we're feelin' now is the real thing, it'll last six months or ten months or whatever it takes. If it's not, we'll have saved ourselves a whole lot of grief. Let's find out."

"All right," she whispered, defiantly holding his gaze, as she'd done every other time he issued such a direct challenge. "Let's find out. But I hope you miss me like hell and suffer a whole lot."

The heartless wretch laughed at her. "You can count on that, sweetheart. I wouldn't doubt it for a minute."

Those words repeated themselves over and over in Dillon's mind while Blair wound up her business and packed her belongings into Hope's motor home in preparation for the trip back to California. It was a good thing he honestly believed he was doing the right thing, because it took every bit of self-discipline he possessed to let her leave without him.

For one thing, Blair was so damned sad about the separation, she nearly broke his heart every time she looked at him. For another, Hope kept scowling at him like he was abandoning Blair or something, which made him feel guilty as all get out. And for another, he was scared spitless that once she got back to Hollywood, she'd figure out it really had only been a set romance and she didn't love him after all.

Oh, yeah, he most definitely was going to miss her like

hell and suffer a whole lot. He was already suffering. Sometimes being noble stunk worse than a bunch of damned sheep.

When the time finally came to say goodbye, he had a lump in his throat the size of a fist. Marsh had decided to stay in Sunshine Gap for a while, and he walked out to the motor home with Hope while Dillon pulled Blair over to the side of the house for one last scorching kiss. He poured every bit of feeling he had into that kiss, trying to memorize her taste and her smell, how soft her hair felt against his skin and how perfectly she fit against him.

He finally pulled back when Hope gave the horn an impatient honk, then rested his forehead against Blair's. "I'll be waitin' right here, darlin'. Don't hesitate to call if you need me."

"Okay." She gave him a wobbly smile. Then she went up on her tiptoes, kissed his scarred cheek, and ran to the motor home. Of course, Curly had to chase after her and beg for her attention, and she cried harder over saying goodbye to him than she had with Dillon.

Hope revved the engine while Blair got settled. Dillon came across the lawn to stand with Marsh. They both returned Hope's jaunty wave, backing up when the big coach belched out a cloud of diesel smoke. When it pulled out, the lump in Dillon's throat grew to the size of a cantaloupe and took on hard, jagged edges.

Curly ran down the drive after the motor home, bawling his fool head off. Dillon had to get a halter and drag the damn calf home again. God, he must have been crazy to send two women off traveling alone in that thing. Hope was probably a terrible driver. What if they broke down somewhere out in the boondocks?

And how in the hell did he think he could stand living without Blair for six days, much less six whole months? What if he never saw her again? Where was all this panic coming from? He had faith in Blair and faith in their love for each other, right? Well, *right?*

Marsh turned back toward the house, glanced at Dillon's face and paused, facing him. "You sure you know what you're doing, bro?"

Clearing his throat, Dillon shook his head. "Hell, no. Why? You think I just made the biggest mistake of my life?"

"You're asking *me?* The guy who's totally screwed up his own love life?" Marsh gave a bitter laugh. "I've got no room to give anyone advice in matters of the heart."

"Aw, you'll get it all straightened out with Sandy and make me an uncle before it's time to brand again," Dillon said. "You can name your first boy after me."

Marsh grinned. "I guess we'll see." He paused and let his expression turn serious. "And for whatever it's worth, I really don't think you've made a mistake here. Blair needs to finish this picture before she does anything else. Once she's done moping, she'll be glad you made her wait to make any big decisions."

"That's how I see it," Dillon said. "I just hope she doesn't forget all about me in the process."

"Forget *you?*" Laughing again, Marsh punched Dillon's arm. "No way, pal. She wouldn't forget you in a hundred years."

Dillon prayed Marsh was right about that, day after day and week after week. He figured this had to be damn near as nerve-racking as waiting for a baby to get born. Marsh heard from Hope occasionally, and kindly passed any word of Blair on to Dillon, but Dillon never heard a word directly from Blair.

Who'd have thought an actress would take everything so dang literally? If she'd called him on the phone once or twice, he wouldn't have hung up on her. And after everything he'd said about not putting any pressure on her, he sure as hell couldn't call her himself. He'd been trying to look out for her interests as much as his own.

When he thought the waiting would drive him totally over the edge, he worked the ranch until he could drop into bed and nearly pass out from exhaustion every night. Putting up hay, scattering the bulls among the cows, checking the cows in their summer pasture, and continually riding fence, kept his hands and body plenty busy, but none of those tasks occupied his mind enough to make him stop missing Blair.

It might have helped if Curly hadn't taken to following him around the way he used to follow Blair. The calf was big enough now, Dillon could have put him in with the rest of the herd, but he was so tame, it just didn't seem right. Everybody got a kick out of Curly's antics, anyway.

Determined to follow through on his plan to clean up his act while Blair was gone, Dillon forced himself to get out into the community more and worked at renewing old friendships. When he had to go to Cody one day to pick up some vaccines, he stopped by a place that sold videos and found a couple of Blair's old films. Of course, he played them over and over. It was comforting to see her and hear her voice again, even if she did say the same things every time and kiss other guys.

In August, Riley took a third place with his steer at the county fair and cheerfully sold the stubborn cuss at the auction afterward. Dillon took both boys to one of the nightly rodeos in Cody. He enjoyed mingling with the guys behind the chutes for a few minutes after the show, but he felt no real sense of loss about his old career. The thought of risking a major injury for an eight-second ride on some rank bronc just didn't hold much appeal for him anymore.

September came, and the boys went back to school. Marsh returned to Hollywood—without Sandy, much to his disappointment. Dillon and Jake put up the last cutting of hay and repaired all of the fences around the stack yards to keep the cows, the elk and the moose out of it for the winter. They brought the herd back down from summer pasture before hunting season started and weaned the calves.

Dillon wore out his videotapes of Blair's old movies and

drove back to Cody to buy some more. Dang woman still didn't call him, but according to Marsh, she was workin' real hard. Dillon ordered a hot tub. Californians were supposed to like those things a lot.

In October it was time to vaccinate the herd again, test the cows for pregnancy and cull out the ones who were dry or too old to produce another healthy calf next year. The semis arrived to take the animals they wanted to sell to the livestock market, and the belch of diesel smoke reminded Dillon of the day Blair and Hope had left. He moved Curly to a permanent pasture behind his own house and cleaned out a spot in his trophy case for Blair's Oscar.

The first heavy snow of the season fell on November 2, starting the ritual of hauling feed and making sure the herd had access to water. Once those jobs were done for the day, Dillon had more free time. He filled as much of it as he could with working on his house, trying to guess what Blair would like. By Thanksgiving he had the master suite ready for occupation and had finished one of the other upstairs bedrooms—the one he thought would make the best nursery.

However, he wasn't so busy that he didn't notice one of the local ranchers showing a lot of interest in Grace. Logan Tyler was a widower and on the bashful side, but he was a nice guy. According to Alex, he'd had a mighty crush on Grace in the seventh grade. Grace had liked him back for a while, but something had happened between them and Grace had ended the relationship and never given a reason for it.

Whenever Logan tried to approach her at church or the grocery store or at a school function, Grace did a vanishing act a magician would have envied. Wanting *some*body in his family to have a happy love life, Dillon decided to give poor Logan a hand and invited him to dinner one Saturday night in early December. The evening couldn't have been a worse disaster.

Grace was obviously shocked and upset by his interference. Riley and Steven took an instant dislike to the situation and acted like a couple of polecats. Logan retreated into a tortured silence and left early.

Dillon gave up any illusions about being a talented matchmaker, and would have forgotten the whole thing if his little sister hadn't practically taken his head off. There was just something about the way she reacted to what he'd done that aroused his curiosity. He gave her a couple of days to cool off, then strolled into the main house after feeding one morning and found her in the kitchen, up to her wrists in bread dough.

Grabbing a fresh cinnamon roll, he poured a mug of coffee and plunked himself onto one of the stools at the breakfast bar beside her work counter. "You want to tell me what that fit you pitched the other night was all about?"

She shot him a filthy look and kneaded the dough so hard, he was almost surprised it didn't shriek with pain. "Nope."

"Aw, come on, Gracie, I was only tryin' to help."

"By inviting that...jerk to dinner?"

"He seems like a nice enough guy to me. What'd he ever do to you?"

"None of your business."

Dillon braced one elbow on the counter. "Whatever it was, it must have happened a long time ago. Why are you still holdin' such a grudge?"

"Because I don't like Logan Tyler. Now, don't go away mad, Dillon. Just go away."

"I can't do that, sis. Not until I get some answers."

She glared at him. He glared back. She looked away first, snorting with what sounded like exasperation. Dillon smiled.

"All right," she said. "Logan was jealous of Johnny from the day he moved to town. And he said some nasty things to me about him, even after Johnny and I were going steady."

"What kind of things?" Dillon asked.

"Oh, you know…like Johnny wasn't always honest, and he was a user, and he was foolin' around with other girls. That kind of stuff. None of it was true, of course. Logan was just trying to make trouble between Johnny and me. Johnny was the most wonderful husband any woman could have asked for."

Dillon's heart contracted, and he knew an important moment of truth had come for him and for his little sister. He sure wished Blair was here to give him a hand. She'd know how to say this the best way. But maybe there really wasn't any best way.

Taking a deep breath for courage, he got up and poured Grace a mug of coffee, grabbed her hand and dragged her away from her bread dough and said, "Sit down with me, Grace. I've got something important to tell you."

Chapter Eighteen

The screening room lights dimmed. Conversations ended in midword. Music poured from hidden speakers. The screen glowed with the name of the production company and then burst into a colorful panoramic shot of northwestern Wyoming's rugged, snowcapped mountains.

Waiting for the first viewing of the final edited print of *Against the Wind* had been the most exquisite form of torture for Blair. Now, at last, the moment of truth had arrived. Unable to tolerate even an accidental touch from anyone, she huddled—heels pulled up next to her bottom on the seat, knees hugged to her chest—three rows behind Patrick, Ian, Marsh, Hope, Keith Stanton, Cecil Dixon and the other cast and crew members who'd been invited to the event.

If only Dillon were here to hold her hand, she might be able to survive this without throwing up. Damn the wretched man for making her do all this alone. A clammy film of perspiration broke out at her hairline. Her chest hurt.

Her jaws ached. She could feel each thump of her heart at the base of her throat.

Oh, God, please, please, *please,* let it be good.

And then a young woman appeared on the screen, stumbling along behind a wagon carrying her father's pine coffin to the cemetery. Wonder of wonders, the young woman wasn't Blair DuMaine. She was Elizabeth Clark, and the year was 1880.

Her story unfolded with a rare, simple magic. Blair tasted the dust and felt the wind tearing at Elizabeth's hair and clothes, experienced her grief and fear at being left alone in the world, agonized with her over the decision to marry her father's prospecting partner, Bear Swanson. She was so sweet, so determined, so courageous. Blair loved her.

The photography was gorgeous. The editing seamless. The acting understated, yet powerful. The soundtrack rich and full, effortlessly supporting the moods and actions developing on the screen. The combination banished any lingering disbelief, transporting the viewer into Elizabeth's world.

The knot in Blair's stomach eased. Her fists uncurled. Her throat and chest relaxed, allowing her to take full, deep breaths for the first time in what felt like weeks.

Seeing Alex in her saloon-girl outfit made Blair smile and the rest of the audience chuckle. The first time Dillon rode Sunny into view, her heart raced with joy. Of course, the audience would think it was Keith Stanton playing Riley McBride, but Blair would have known Dillon's posture on a horse anytime, anywhere. Busy and frantic as she'd been ever since she left Wyoming, she had missed him to the depths of her soul.

And there he was, literally larger than life. Every gorgeous, strong, stubborn bit of him. A tear trickled down her cheek. She wiped it away with the back of her sleeve and sniffled out loud. If the others didn't like her making noise, they could wait for the next showing.

A close-up of Keith took her back into the story, helping

her to regain control of her emotions. Of course, every time Dillon returned to the screen, her tears flowed again. It was a wild, exhilarating two hours. When the credits stopped running and the studio projectionist shut down his equipment, there was a moment of absolute breathless silence, as if everyone were waiting for someone else to pronounce judgment on their work.

Hope bounced to her feet, held her hands up beside her head and shook her fire-engine red hair, which had grown out to frame her face like dandelion fluff. "Hot damn," she drawled, "don't you guys know a hit when you see one?"

Laughter bounced off the walls. Applause erupted. The audience members got up and congratulated each other on a job magnificently done, if they did say so themselves.

Blair wiped her eyes, fished a tissue out of her pocket and blew her nose. Straightening her shoulders, she plowed her way through the group, smiling, handing out compliments and accepting them in return, all the while making steady progress toward the exit. To hell with waiting for distribution.

She knew who she was and what she wanted, all right. If Dillon knew what was good for him, he would have figured out his own feelings by now, as well. If he hadn't, she would simply *tell* him what they were. As far as she was concerned, Mr. Dillon McBride had just run out of time.

Her office was only a short sprint down the hallway from the screening room. She skidded through the doorway yelling, "Yee-haw!" much to the amusement of her sedate, middle-aged secretary. Nicole hung up the telephone with a broad smile and opened her mouth to speak. Blair held up both hands to cut her off.

"It was faaabulous, Nicole. Book me a flight to Cody, Wyoming. I know it's the holidays. Any seat's fine. More than twelve hours, charter a plane."

She hurried into her own office, cleaned off her desk and

retrieved her purse and coat, calling instructions to Nicole through the open door. "I'm going home to pack. Leave a message on my machine about the arrangements. Oh, and don't forget I'll need a rental car."

Nicole got up and walked around in front of her desk as Blair emerged into the reception area. "Blair, dear, there's—"

Blair smiled and stepped past the secretary. "No time to talk. Have a wonderful Christmas. Refer all problems to Ian. You don't know where I went, and you have no idea when I'll be back, okay?"

"No. Please, stop one second."

Nicole scurried on high heels to get ahead of her again. She planted herself in the doorway, arms and legs spread out, blocking Blair's path. Such behavior was so unusual for the normally dignified woman, Blair finally halted her headlong rush and fell silent, raising her eyebrows in query.

"You have a visitor," Nicole said, inclining her head toward the waiting area, tucked into a far corner of the room.

Slowly pivoting on the balls of her feet, Blair saw a big, dark-haired man unfold himself from one of the overstuffed chairs provided for visitors. A glimmer of suspicion started a warm glow in the pit of Blair's stomach. Oh, God, could it be? Oh, yes, yes, yes! What a marvelous gift!

He wore a western-cut suit with a white shirt and shiny black boots. Carrying a beige Stetson, he walked toward her, wearing the most sheepish, lopsided, wonderful grin she'd ever seen. "Hello, darlin'."

Clutching her coat and purse to her chest, Blair gaped at Dillon for a long moment. Her first impulse was to charge across the room and throw herself into his arms. She forced herself to resist it, deciding a moment such as this deserved more than an impulsive reaction.

Buying a little time, she shook her head and drawled, "Well, I'll be damned if it ain't Dillon McBride. What brings you to town?"

Dillon's grin widened. "Marsh told me this was gonna be a big day for you," he said, taking a step closer. "I wanted to be here and share the celebration."

"Or give consolation?"

He shrugged, then stepped closer again. "Whatever. Truth is, I couldn't wait another minute to see you. Do you still hate me, darlin'?"

"I never hated you." She took a step toward him. "Did you miss me like hell and suffer a whole lot?"

"Oh, yeah." He came closer again. "All day, every day. More than you'll ever want to know."

Blair glanced at her fascinated secretary. "Nicole, please have my car sent around immediately."

"Of course." Nicole scurried back to her desk and picked up the phone.

The instant the older woman moved safely out of the way, Blair flung her coat and purse on the floor and launched herself at Dillon's chest. His arms closed around her with the most exquisite sensations of warmth and strength, hugging her so tightly her feet dangled above the floor while he rocked her back and forth.

She buried her face in the crook of his neck, breathing in the scent that had haunted her dreams and her memories. Yes, yes, it really was him, the man she had ached for night after night. After all these weeks and months of separation and uncertainty, at long last, she was home.

Dillon gulped and rubbed the side of his face against Blair's silky hair, inhaling the scent of her perfume and soap as if it were life-giving oxygen. Holding her again was like having an amputated limb magically restored. He'd dreamed of this so many times, he could hardly believe she was real.

Even with Marsh's call, it had taken every ounce of courage he owned to show up here without an invitation. Whatever happened, it was worth the whole miserable trip just to hold her for a moment. Hell, he'd willingly move to this ridiculous city that considered glitter on the streets a Christmas decoration if it meant he could be her lover again.

Too soon, she was pulling away, putting her coat on over her sweater and slacks as if it were cold outside, when the sun was shining and it had to be sixty degrees, hustling him out to a long black limo, complete with a uniformed driver who took his suitcase and snapped to attention like he was somebody real important. Feeling as disoriented as if he'd landed in Oz, Dillon glanced from Blair to the scenery beyond the tinted windows and back to Blair.

She seemed perfectly content to sit close beside him and hold his hand. Not that he minded it, but he sort of felt like they should be talking or...something. Maybe she was worried about privacy, having a driver and all, even though the window behind the front seat was closed.

Still, after ten minutes of watching big archways with silver stars and tinsel hanging over the street, store windows sprayed with fake snow and fancy hotels with decorated entrances and roofs going by, he couldn't take any more silence. He tugged at his tie. Damn thing was tryin' to strangle him, for sure.

"Did I hear you say you were headin' for Cody?"

She smiled at him. "Uh-huh."

"And you were gonna rent a car?"

"Uh-huh."

"And you were gonna drive to..."

She laid her right hand on his knee. "Sunshine Gap, of course. I was coming to see you, darling, so relax now. We'll be home in thirty minutes."

Dillon shifted around on the soft leather seat, resisting a fierce urge to jiggle his foot. Relax? Oh, right. No problem. It was only the longest thirty minutes since Genesis.

About the time he was ready to start fidgeting like a kid at a piano recital, the limo turned into a gated driveway. Blair whisked him inside before he got much more than a glimpse of the exterior of her house; other than to say that it was big and had a Spanish look to it, he couldn't have described it. The foyer was airy and spacious, with a curving staircase leading to the second floor, the banister decorated with white Christmas garlands.

After hanging their coats in a closet, Blair turned and held out one hand to him in invitation. He accompanied her into an elegant great room with muted oil paintings on the walls, a white baby grand in one corner and a Christmas tree decorated in white and silver bows, bulbs and lights beside a gas fireplace. The carpet, sofa and chairs were all done up in white, too.

He'd never seen this much white outside of a blizzard. Maybe he'd better go back to the front door and check his boots. He was just about to do that when Blair hit a switch and a whole wall of white drapes opened, revealing a bank of floor-to-ceiling windows. Dillon crossed the room and looked out, admiring the stunning view of lights blinking on all over the valley below.

Blair came up behind him and wrapped her arms around his middle, and his uneasiness faded. He'd known all along that she wouldn't live in a ranch house; no need to let the reality of their different life-styles throw him. If she could make the adjustments she'd made to live in his world, he could make a few to live in hers.

If that was what she really wanted.

And there it was, the question that had tormented him since the morning she drove away from him in Hope's motor home. Had it been just a mad, glorious affair, after all? Or did she want him forever?

Before he could lose his nerve, he turned to face her. She returned his gaze without flinching, but her expression looked every bit as anxious as he felt. Because she wasn't sure of him? Or because she didn't know how to let him down easy?

"Let's talk," he said.

She took his hand and led him to a long white sofa. They sat angled toward each other, but not touching. The two inches between them might as well have been two miles, for all the clues he could read in her eyes. He'd climbed onto some damned vicious horses in his day and never felt this much fear.

Finally, Blair let out a nervous little laugh. "Wow. Alone at last, and I have no idea what to say to you."

"Just tell me what's in your heart, Blair. The truth, the whole truth, and nothin' but the truth. Why were you comin' to see me?"

"Because other than a publicity tour, I'm finally finished with *Against the Wind.*"

"The movie turned out all right, then?"

Blair's whole face lit up, and her hands waved around in dramatic gestures. "Oh, Dillon, it is absolutely *faaabulous.* I can't wait for you to see it. It's simply...perfect."

She laughed, then hugged herself. He wouldn't have been surprised to see her get up and do a gleeful jig, but she just hugged herself again. "That must sound horribly conceited, but I don't know how else to describe it. It was such a great script to start with, and the picture is even more wonderful than I imagined it would be."

"That's great, darlin'. I've already cleared a space in the trophy case for your Oscar."

"That's sweet of you." She leaned over and kissed his scarred cheek. "But you know, I'm honestly not worried about that anymore. I mean, it would be nice to win one of course, but I don't need one to know *Against the Wind* is good. Some people—those with no taste whatsoever—might not like it, but it's the best picture anyone could have made."

"Now, that's what I like to hear," he said. "Confidence."

"Damn right." She wrinkled her nose at him, and her smile turned smug. "And I am a DuMaine, Dillon. A *real* one."

"Even without that little gold statue?"

"It's not the statue that makes one a DuMaine." She touched her index finger to her own breastbone. "It's in here. In the love of acting, and being willing to stretch and grow and try new things.''

"You did a lot of that last spring. I never saw such a gutsy little woman before in my whole life.''

Blair laughed out loud. Then, in a second, her expression became solemn. "I know what I want, Dillon. I want you. Please, tell me you came here because you still want me, too.''

The tension he'd been carrying around relaxed so fast, he felt dizzy. He slumped back against the sofa and closed his eyes while relief flooded over his whole being. Of course, Blair was hovering over him in a heartbeat.

"Dillon? Dillon, are you all right? Oh, my God, he's fainted.''

Dillon opened one eye. "I'm fine, darlin'.''

Then he reached up, grabbed her wrist and pulled her onto his lap. He looked into her eyes and saw the same raw hunger burning in her eyes that had been burning a hole through his gut for weeks. He had no idea who moved first, and it didn't matter worth a damn. The only thing that mattered was holding Blair in his arms, kissing her, loving her. When he finally let her up for air, she stayed on his lap, snuggled against his chest.

"I've missed you every single day we've been apart,'' he said. "Anytime I saw something new or weird or interesting, I wanted to share it with you. Anytime I heard a good joke, I wanted to laugh with you. And anytime I felt discouraged, I wanted you to be there to hold me and harass me into trying again. You've become a part of me, Dillon. I'm not happy without you.''

"I've felt the same way.''

She tipped her head back and looked up into his eyes. "I do love you, Dillon, so very much. But I don't believe I could be happy without acting. There are times when an artistic career causes great disruption and demands sacrifices from everyone in the family. You've seen what it's

like on a set. Could you live with that once a year? O
tolerate my being gone if you couldn't come with me?''

Her eyes looked huge in her face, and her skin looke
so pale, he realized she must be exhausted and running o
the adrenaline produced by a momentous day. He rubbe
his hand over her back and planted a kiss on her hair.

"I love you, Blair. The only thing I can't tolerate is no
having you in my life at all. I'll do anything I need to d
to make this work. That includes getting surgery on m
face."

"You know that doesn't matter to me," she said. "It'
completely your decision."

He nodded. "And I'm okay with it, either way, now.
just wanted to let you know I'm not rulin' it out. I've bee
a lot more relaxed about the whole thing since I took you
advice and told Grace the truth about Johnny."

"How did she take it?"

"About like you'd expect. She's havin' a hard time, bu
I think she'll be better off in the long run. I sure feel bette
about myself without that secret to haul around all th
time."

"I'm so glad, Dillon."

"Yeah, me, too." He hugged her closer. "So, uh, yo
still think you might want to marry me, DuMaine?"

Her smile was brighter than all the lights on her Chris
mas tree. "Yes, McBride, I do want to marry you."

He dug into the right inside pocket of his suit coat, e
countered a sharp edge and remembered he'd switche
what he wanted to the other side. Feeling incredibl
clumsy, he shot her a nervous grin, poked the first tw
fingers of his right hand into the left inside pocket and cam
up with the small velvet-covered box.

"This belonged to my grandmother, Jenny McBride.
He flipped open the lid and showed her the ring inside. '
always thought it was kind of nice, but we can always g
buy somethin' else, if you don't like it."

"Oh, Dillon, it's more than nice. It's gorgeous. What is that stone in the center? It looks a bit like a ruby, but—"

"It's a Montana garnet. Elizabeth's first husband, Bear Swanson, found it when he was prospecting west of Alder Gulch, and had it made into a ring for his wife. It's been reset with those little diamonds since then. I don't suppose it's worth all that much moneywise, but it has some sentimental value, I guess."

"You guess? Dillon, it's unique. It's wonderful." She held out her left hand and sighed softly when he slid it in place. She admired the ring on her finger for a moment, then wrapped her arms around his neck and covered his face with enthusiastic kisses. "You're wonderful. I love you, I love you, I love you."

Laughing, he slid sideways until the back of his head rested against the arm of the sofa, bringing her to rest on top of him. "Don't hold back, now, darlin'. Tell me how you really feel."

She planted an elbow on his chest and raised an eyebrow when his pocket made a crackling noise. "What was that?"

"That" was his last, desperate secret weapon to convince her to marry him. Since it wasn't really needed, he didn't see any reason she had to know about it just yet. Dang woman had him wrapped around her pinkie tight enough as it was.

"Oh, uh, nothin' important, honey," he said, struggling for a straight face. "Probably just my boardin' pass."

Now both eyebrows went up. Aw, hell, she was on to him, for sure. He'd never be able to lie to her about anything, except maybe surprises, and he wasn't even doing too well on that account right now.

"Oh, really?" she said, already pulling up his suit coat and digging into the pocket.

It took her two seconds to find the photograph. She yanked it out, studied it, then uttered a soft chuckle and smiled down at him. "Aw, Dillon, you old softy. Curly certainly has grown, hasn't he? And he's not even a bull like Samson, so he must be a…pet.''

Feeling distinctly foolish, he sat up and straightened his suit coat. ''Let's don't make a big deal out of this, okay?''

''Oh, let's do. It'll be so much more fun. Where do you keep him, Dillon? In your backyard? Next to the pool?''

His neck and ears felt awful dang hot. ''Now, look, everybody else in the world is teasin' me about that stupid—''

She cut him off with a kiss that made him forget all the abuse he'd taken. ''I'm sorry. Your saving Curly is the nicest thing anyone's ever done for me. I adore you for it.''

''It's okay, darlin'.'' Grinning, he combed his fingers through her hair. ''I knew I'd never be able to ship him that day you and Hope left. Ol' Curly chased after that motor home, bawlin' just like I wanted to. Seemed like he was the only one who understood how much I missed you, 'cause he missed you that much, too.''

Tears puddled up in her eyes. Dillon slid one arm behind her knees, lifted her high against his chest and stood. He kissed her with all the love and longing he felt for her, walking slowly back toward the staircase he'd seen in the foyer.

He hadn't noticed any servants in Blair's house, but he wouldn't have bet his saddle there weren't any hanging around. He was going to make love to this woman now, and he wanted to do it right—on a real bed, behind a locked door. There must be bedrooms at the top of those stairs.

Blair sighed and rested her head against his shoulder. ''I never would have believed you'd turn out to be such a romantic. This is just like that wonderful scene in *Gone with the Wind*. You know, where Rhett carries Scarlett up the stairs?''

Dillon laughed. ''Yeah, I know the one. Tell me, are there any other movie scenes you want to act out with me?''

''You mean…love scenes?''

''Yeah.'' He paused at the top of the stairs and looked

straight into her eyes. "I figure a great actress like you must have a rich fantasy life. I wouldn't want to disappoint you."

She caressed the side of his face with her free hand. "I'll never be disappointed, as long as you love me with your whole heart."

"Oh, I do, darlin', and I always will." He walked down the hallway, then turned into the room she indicated and set her on the bed. "But have you ever thought about makin' it in the back seat of a limo? I saw a movie where these people did that once, and I've always thought the idea had real possibilities."

Her giggles warmed him better than a fire on a freezing winter's night. Her arms pulled him down beside her. Her kisses healed the aching, empty spots her long absence had left in his soul. Their marriage was bound to have rough spots now and again, but that was okay with him. This woman was worth any amount of trouble she was liable to cause him.

After all, she was a *real* DuMaine. She wasn't a bad ranch hand, either. If she ever really learned to rope...

* * * * *

Don't miss URBAN COWBOY, the next installment of Myrna Temte's exciting new series, **HEARTS OF WYOMING**—*coming to you only from Silhouette Special Edition!*

Take 4 bestselling love stories FREE

Plus get a FREE surprise gift!

Daniel MacGregor is at it again...

New York Times bestselling author

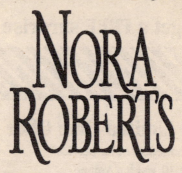

NORA ROBERTS

introduces us to a new generation of MacGregors
as the lovable patriarch of the illustrious MacGregor
clan plays matchmaker again, this time to his three
gorgeous granddaughters in

THE MacGREGOR BRIDES

From Silhouette Books

Don't miss this brand-new continuation of Nora Roberts's
enormously popular *MacGregor* miniseries.

Available November 1997 at your favorite retail outlet.

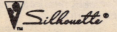

The Stars of Mithra

**Three gems,
three beauties,
three passions...
the adventure of a lifetime**

SILHOUETTE·INTIMATE·MOMENTS®
brings you a thrilling new series by
New York Times bestselling author

Nora Roberts

**Three mystical blue diamonds place three close
friends in jeopardy...and lead them to romance.**

In October
HIDDEN STAR (IM#811)
Bailey James can't remember a thing, but she knows
she's in big trouble. And she desperately needs private
investigator Cade Parris to help her live long enough to
find out just what kind.

In December
CAPTIVE STAR (IM#823)
Cynical bounty hunter Jack Dakota and spitfire
M. J. O'Leary are handcuffed together and on the run
from a pair of hired killers. And Jack wants to know
why—but M.J.'s not talking.

In February
SECRET STAR (IM#835)
Lieutenant Seth Buchanan's murder investigation takes
a strange turn when Grace Fontaine turns up alive. But
as the mystery unfolds, he soon discovers the notorious
heiress is the biggest mystery of all.

Available at your favorite retail outlet.

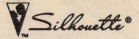